GHOST MOVIES

with contributions from

Robert Bloch
John Carpenter
James Herbert
Shirley Jackson
M R James
Eric Keown
Gerald Kersh
Nigel Kneale
Dorothy Macardle
Daphne Du Maurier
Michael McDowell
J B Priestly
Thorne Smith

Further Collections in this series from Peter Haining

GHOST MOVIES
Famous Supernatural Films

Collected and edited by
Peter Haining

with contributions from

Robert Bloch
John Carpenter
James Herbert
Shirley Jackson
M R James
Eric Keown
Gerald Kersh
Nigel Kneale
Dorothy Macardle
Daphne Du Maurier
Michael McDowell
J B Priestly
Thorne Smith

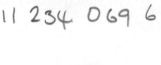

This first world edition published in Great Britain 1995 by
SEVERN HOUSE PUBLISHERS LTD of
9–15 High Street, Sutton, Surrey SM1 1DF.
First published the USA 1995 by
SEVERN HOUSE PUBLISHERS INC., of
595 Madison Avenue, New York, NY 10022.

British Library Cataloguing in Publication Data

Herbert, James and others
  Ghost Movies
  I. Title
  823.0873308 [FS]

  ISBN 0-7278-4853-4

Typeset by Palimpsest Book Production Limited,
Polmont, Stirlingshire
Printed and bound in Great Britain by
T J Press (Padstow) Ltd, Padstow, Cornwall.

PROGRAMME

Note: This is a list of film titles. The original works on which these films were based may have had different titles from those listed above.

CREDITS

The Editor and publishers are grateful to the following authors and agents for permission to reprint copyright stories in this collection: Heinemann Ltd for 'Night Sequence' by J.B. Priestley and 'The Extraordinarily Horrible Dummy' by Gerald Kersh; Punch Publications for 'Sir Tristram Goes West' by Eric Keown; Methuen & Co for 'A Smokey Lady in Knickers' by Thorne Smith; The Harrigan Press for 'Samhain' by Dorothy Macardle; Michael Joseph for 'The Bus' by Shirley Jackson; Fleetway Publications for 'The Trespassers' by Nigel Kneale; A.M. Heath Literary Agency for 'Lucy Comes To Stay' by Robert Bloch; Victor Gollancz Ltd for 'Don't Look Now' by Daphne du Maurier; Montcalm Publishing Corporation for 'Harlequin' by John Carpenter and 'Halley's Passing' by Michael McDowell; and David Higham Associates for 'Hallowe'en's Child' by James Herbert. While every care has been taken in securing copyright permissions for this collection, in case of any accidental infringement interested parties are asked to contact the Editor in care of the publishers.

PROLOGUE

Things That Go Bump on the Screen

One of the most curious ghost movies of which a print still exists is *A Place of One's Own* filmed exactly fifty years ago in the final months of the Second World War. It was curious not just because the ghost was presented as a real figure rather than a misty apparition who appeared and disappeared at will, but because the picture was actually filmed *in a haunted house*.

Authenticity is an element that film makers have often tried to duplicate on the screen, but *A Place of One's Own* represents one of the rare excursions where the producer, R.J. Minney, and his team decided to risk supernatural intervention. The exteriors were shot at an old house at Esher in Surrey which was reputed to be haunted by the ghost of a white lady who walked in the spacious grounds on certain moonlit nights.

Filming began in the Spring of 1945 and for three days (and nights) the picture went ahead without any problems. But on the fourth night the production was suddenly brought to a shuddering halt – not from a ghostly manifestation, but something far more substantial and a lot more deadly. A German flying bomb, part of Hitler's last ditch efforts to win the war, suddenly plunged out of the night sky and exploded in the garden. Fortunately, none of the film crew were working nearby, and apart from leaving a large crater in the garden, the bomb only blew in the front doors of the house. In the first hours of the following day, the props people were quickly on the location to build replicas and within a few hours the filming – like life in the rest of Britain at that time – was soon underway once again.

The plot of *A Place of One's Own* concerned a middle-aged couple who had moved into the elegant house despite warnings that it was haunted. Accompanying them was a young companion who soon found herself being influenced by the spirit of another young woman who had died mysteriously in the house some years earlier. It required the intervention of another ghost, the dead girl's father, to restore the young companion to her former self and also return the house to its usual tranquility.

Sadly, *A Place of One's Own* is rarely seen today, yet it reprents an interesting landmark in the genre of ghost movies. Its authenticity also owes much to the fact the three principal creators were all journalists: producer R.J. Minney was the editor of *Everybody's Weekly*; scriptwriter Brock Williams was a newspaper reporter from the West Country; while the director Bernard Knowles had begun his career as a photographer on the *Detroit News*. All three were making their film debuts and their background undoubtedly contributed to the film's feeling of realism.

It was apparently Knowles' idea that no trick photography should be used when filming the veteran actor Ernest Thesiger as the ghost intervening in the life of the beautiful but susceptible companion, played by Margaret Lockwood. Under his direction, Thesiger appeared as real, but spoke in a soft accent and used mysterious words to give the impression of being someone unusual and otherworldly. As the actor himself later explained, "I looked at distant objects without focus whenever I spoke and put a faraway tone in my voice – those are the secrets of being a ghost!"

There have, in fact, been many secrets tried by directors

and actors in attempting to portray the supernatural on the screen. From the stop-camera techniques of the pioneer French film maker George Melies in his brief silent picture *The Haunted Chateau* filmed in 1897 – and almost certainly the first film in the genre – to the pyrotechnics employed by Steven Spielberg in his 1982 production, *Poltergeist*, ghost stories have all had to make the unseen and the unbelievable somehow real for audiences all over the world armed with varying degrees of scepticism and belief. While Melics only had his imagination and his camera shutter to work with, the special effects men of a century later have a truly amazing array of technical and scientific wizardry at their command. Still, though, the greatest films of this kind are almost invariably those in which the mind of the viewer is given the necessary stimulation to make the impossible seem possible.

In the fifty years since ghost movies really became an established genre in the cinema there have been many different kinds of supernatural pictures. Some of the very best of these have been based on works by leading writers of fiction – and it is a representative cross-section of these which I have selected for my evening's entertainment in the pages of this book. Some bear titles that will be immediately familiar to the reader, others may be less well known. All, I can assure you, make as interesting reading as the films they inspired or are associated with.

The lights, then, are about to go down on the world where things go bump not in the night but on the screen.

PETER HAINING

HAUNTED

(CIC, 1995)
Starring: Aidan Quinn, Sir John Gielgud
& Anthony Andrews
Directed by Lewis Gilbert
Story 'Hallowe'en's Child' by James Herbert

James Herbert (1943–) has been called the English master of horror, and certainly on this side of the Atlantic he ranks in popularity with Stephen King – whose work he greatly admires. Amongst his seventeen varied and stylistically brilliant novels which have together sold around 40 million copies worldwide and made him a millionaire, Jim has also written three of the best supernatural novels published in recent years: *The Survivor* (1976), *Haunted* (1988) and his latest, *The Ghosts of Sleath* (1994). His interest in horror goes back to his harsh childhood in Bethnal Green – Jack the Ripper territory, he says with a smile – mixed with his intimate knowledge of the darker side of life as he grew up surrounded by poverty and crime. In fact, Jim delights in telling the story of a man known as Mad Mick who his parents used to pay to take him to the cinema. "He was a nice, gentle man as far as I was concerned," he recalls, "but I later discovered he chopped up a man with an axe and went to prison." Although the young James Herbert was already something of a writer and storyteller at school, his ambition was to be an artist and after attending the Hornsey College of Art, he went into advertising and became art director of an ad. agency before the success of his first book –

The Rats (1974) based on his childhood memories of a rat-infested cellar – set him on the path to literary and financial success. His early books which were all set against recogniseable contemporary backgrounds and often featured people thrust into situations of disaster, earned him comparison with Nigel Kneale – though today his work is acknowledged as uniquely his own and often singled out for praise for being unafraid to tackle controversial as well as horrific subjects.

Curiously, it is James Herbert's three ghostly novels that have attracted the most attention from film makers. *Survivor*, with its vivid mystical elements, was filmed in Australia in 1980 by Hemdale, directed by David Hemmings and starring Robert Powell, Jenny Agutter and Joseph Cotten. This year it has been the turn of *Haunted*, with Aidan Quinn as the investigator of a haunted house called Edbrook in which he has to face the blood-chilling enigma of his own past before he can solve the building's terrible secret; while there is already film interest in *The Ghosts of Sleath* about an apparently idyllic village which harbours a number of dark secrets. (Another of Jim's earlier books, the easy-going fantasy *Fluke* has also just been filmed in Hollywood with Matthew Modine, Nancy Travis and Eric Stolz, directed by Carlo Curlei.) "Hallowe'en's Child" is a rare James Herbert short story and was written in 1988 for publication on that most haunted night of the year, 31st October. It is a doubly fascinating story because, as Jim told me, "It is embroidered from my own experience – for my youngest daughter, Casey, was born on the evening of 31st October." Bear that in mind as you read this unique chilling story by the man who has done so much for both ghost fiction and films . . .

If I hadn't been in such a rush then it probably would never have happened.

And if I hadn't been so tired.

Maybe if I hadn't been so scared.

Yes, that above all. So scared for Anne. Our first baby meant seven months (once we knew for sure) of scariness for both of us. Eleven years of hoping – the last few of those we spent in despair – then those torturous/ecstatic months after we were informed yes, something was there and all we now had to do was be patient. Twenty weeks into Anne's pregnancy and the amniocentesis results told us to expect a girl. Everything appeared to be fine, but we took no chances, none at all. Anne had already given up her secretarial job the moment we knew the egg really had embraced the seed, but now she went underdrive – that is, she cut out all unnecessary effort. Totally. She invalidised herself. You see, Anne was 38, an uneasy time for some women, and even worse for those who've never given birth before. 'Barren' is an appropriate word – 'desolation' might be even better. I'm not sure that men, even the most sensitive, truly appreciate the condition. Those of us who have been as desperate for offspring as our wives or lovers might catch a glimmer, but there's no way we can experience the real trauma.

The labour pains started around eight o'clock on a Sunday evening. We were prepared; we'd been prepared the whole of that month of October. Anne was perfectly calm and I did my best to appear that way too (she offered no criticism of my two abortive attempts at ringing the doctor – my index finger was wayward). When I got through, Dr Golding asked me the usual questions (usual for *him*, that is; it was all new to me) about time lapses between pains, where the actual pain was coming from, Anne's general condition, etc. He was kind, as if he cared as much about me as he did my wife. But then, I was the one paying for his services for, selfishly, although perhaps understandably given the circumstances, I'd decided our baby would be born privately rather than nationally, if you get my meaning. Besides, the National Health Service had enough to cope with, so if I could ease their burden in some small way by taking my custom elsewhere, well that was fine by me and I'm sure by them also.

The doctor informed me he would alert the hospital but that it was too early for panic stations just yet. I was to ring him again when the contraction pains regularised.

That happened around midnight, maybe just a little after. This time Dr Golding told me to get moving.

It was about 12 miles to the hospital, a long drive through country lanes and villages, but Anne, unlike me, was serene throughout the journey. Uncomfortable, true, but every time I glanced her way, she was smiling (I tried *not* to look at her during the spasms). The hospital itself was small and cosy, a country establishment that had a few private rooms for those who were willing and able to pay. The night sister herself took 'charge, leaving me alone while they got Anne settled in. When I next saw my wife she was sitting up in bed looking plump and content, although her smile was a little strained by now.

I stayed for an hour before they told me to go home and get some sleep. Nothing was going to happen for a while and when they were sure things were about to break – literally – they would phone Dr Golding first and then me.

Fine, I said. But it wasn't. I was scared. It was our first time and I for one had all the pessimism that comes with maturity. I agreed to leave though; Sister gave me the impression that choice was not really involved.

Nothing at all happened that day. I rang the office and let them know my week's leave had just begun. My business partner informed me of his favourite brand of cigar. I moped around the house for most of the morning, watching the telephone, vacuuming, watching the telephone, loading the washing machine, watching the telephone, dusting and . . . you know.

I went back to the hospital twice, once in the afternoon and then again in the early evening. Anne was still the blissful Buddha, the swelling she cradled in her arms showing no imminent signs of collapse. Dr Golding looked in on my second visit and uttered reassuring words. However, just before he ducked out the door he mentioned something about 'inducement' if nothing had happened by tomorrow. It was Anne who patted *my* hand and told me not to worry.

*

I returned home and cooked a meal, leaving most of it uneaten on the plate. I was over-anxious, to be sure, but after waiting 11 years for this event, who could blame me? The phone call came at quarter to ten that night.

Things were beginning to move, Dr Golding informed me. My daughter had suddenly become curious about the outside world. If I got to the hospital soon enough, I'd be there to greet her when she arrived.

The night was chilly, but I didn't bother with an overcoat. I grabbed my jacket, scooped up the car keys and was inside the car without taking a breath.

It wouldn't start. The bugger wouldn't bloody well start.

I smacked the wheel, but that had no effect. I stomped the accelerator, and the engine rasped drily.

Then I swore at my own stupidity. The night *was* chilly. The car needed some choke.

It roared fruitily enough when I corrected my mistake I had to brake hard as another vehicle rushed past my drive.

Take it easy, I scolded. Getting myself killed wouldn't have pleased anybody, least of all me. I eased the car out gently and gathered speed once I was on the highway. A truck coming towards me flashed its beams and I quickly switched on my own headlights.

As I left the quiet streets of the town and headed across country, I saw there was a low-lying mist settling over the fields. The moon was bright though, its cold glow bringing a spookiness to the landscape.

They were cute, these little kids togged up in their witches and monster outfits, several bearing homemade lanterns and broomsticks. I could hear their giggling and excited chatter as they 'trick or treated' their way along the high street and tried to scare the hell out of each other.

October 31. My daughter was going to be born on Hallows' Eve. Hallowe'en. I was neither pleased nor dismayed at the idea. I just wanted her there.

A kid jumped to the kerbside and leered crazily at me as I passed, his green face lit by a flashlight beneath his chin. My mind was too preoccupied to retaliate with a leer of my own.

My foot stamped on the brake pedal as the headlights picked out more of the stunted ghouls on the crossing ahead. The car rocked and the kids laughed. They crowded around the side window and tapped on the glass. "Trick or treat, trick or treat."

Tempted to drive on, I nevertheless dug into a pocket for loose change; maybe the fact that two of the masqueraders had remained on the crossing and were leaning on my car bonnet, luminous plastic fangs caught by the moonlight, had something to do with my decision. Better to pay up rather than waste time arguing my case. Winding down the window I dropped coins into the greedy hands that thrust in.

Out into the cold night again, the mist enveloping the car as though it had been waiting for me to leave the village refuge. I shivered, reached forward, turned up the heater. Still a ways to go yet. Hold on, Anne, don't start without me.

Now I saw the lights of a hamlet ahead, just a street with a few houses on either side and nothing else. I didn't slow the car; in fact, I increased speed, for the mist had little substance beneath the sodium lights.

Darkness dropped heavily once again, the car's headlights bouncing back at me from the rolling grey blanket (which seemed even thicker now). I slowed down, dipped the beams.

Dear God, let it lift. Please let me get to Anne.

And you know, the mist actually seemed to lift; or at least, a hole in the whiteness opened up before me. Taking full advantage, I accelerated; unfortunately, the relief was only temporary. The swirling clouds came back at me with a vengeance.

I braked, tightening my grip on the wheel, keeping the vehicle in a straight line. I heard the thump – *felt* it – and shouted something, Lord knows what.

Rubber scraped tarmac as the car screeched to a halt. I sat frozen, the engine stalled; a sickness swelled inside me.

I'd hit something. No, the thump had a softness to it. I'd hit *someone*. For the second time that night, this time with a cold dread dragging at me, I beseeched God. Let it be an animal, I said. Please, an animal. But I'd seen a small black bundle hurl over the side of the bonnet an instant after the impact. Its apparent size suggested I'd hit a child.

I think I was mumbling a prayer as I lurched from the car.

There wasn't too much to see out there, although the mist didn't seem quite as dense in the open. Only in the light beams was there real substance; beyond them the low fog was more tenuous, less compact. I searched around the car, stumbling over the grass verge on the left, moving in a crouched position, fearful of what I might find.

I called out, but there was no reply. And there was nothing lying close to the vehicle. For one wild – almost feverish – moment, I considered jumping back into the car and driving on. There was nobody there, I told myself. I hadn't run into anything; the haste, the anxiety, had got the better of me. Maybe a bird, a large crow perhaps, had flown up in front of me. I returned to the car.

But a sudden rush of guilt (and reality) prevented me from climbing in.

And a faint scratchy moan caused me to look back along the road.

I moaned myself. The mist had drifted enough for me to glimpse a dark shape crawling along the road.

My steps were slow at first, as though apprehensive of what they would lead me to; compassion however soon hurried me forward. As I approached the moving figure, my worst fears were realised: I *had* hit a child.

He or she appeared to be clothed in a long black cloak or gown – not the first such costume I'd seen that night. Except that whereas most of those other children had elected for pointed hats, this one had favoured a cowl, one that covered his or her head completely. Why was the kid out here alone? What the hell were the parents thinking of to allow their child to be unaccompanied at this late hour? These thoughts were probably no more than a feeble attempt to shift the blame for the accident from myself.

I reached the crawling figure and bent low to touch its shoulder, the tenderness and pity I felt all but consuming me. I became weak; my outstretched hand trembled.

"You'll be all right," I said softly and with no confidence in my heart. "I'll get you to a hospital."

I knelt, reaching around to turn the child over, my face close to the hood.

Something sharp raked across my eyes. The figure had twisted suddenly, lashing out in panic (I thought then) or in pain. Blinded for the moment, I sensed the child scrambling away; its cries were sharp little sounds, not unlike the yelps of a wounded animal.

"Stop!" I called. "I want to help you."

All I heard was a scurrying.

The sting left my eyes, although a wetness still blurred my vision. I managed to discern a dark shape shuffling away from me, though, heading back towards the car.

"Stop! I'm not going to hurt you," I shouted and took off after the cloaked figure. He or she leaned against the bodywork for support, staggering onwards, one leg dragging behind. With surprising speed, considering the injuries the child must have sustained, it was beyond the car and moving into the beams of the headlights. I gave chase, afraid for the poor little wretch, afraid that it might come to more harm because of its hysteria.

I quickly caught up and yelled: "Wait!" A tiny scream curious in its fierceness was the reply. I snatched at the cloak, grasped cloth and held firm. But fear or confusion had lent the child unreasonable strength, for it was I who was tumbled onto my knees in the roadway. As I fell my other hand clutched the figure so that it was forced down with me. The child squirmed in my grip as we rolled over and I had to hold fast to prevent damage to either of us.

And then I turned the child over to face me.

It was a few seconds before I staggered away to fall heavily onto my elbow. A few seconds of staring into the most grotesque, the most evil, face I'd ever seen in my life.

The cowl had dropped away as she – yes, it was a woman, at least I *think* it was woman – raised her head from the road to stare with filmy yellow eyes into mine, her ravaged and rotting countenance caught in the full glare of my car's headlights. But it wasn't just the shock of seeing the sharp, hawked nose, swollen near its tip with a huge hardened wart from which a single white hair sprouted, the cheeks with hollows so deep they seemed like holes, the thick grey eyebrows that joined across her forehead, the cruel, lipless mouth from which a black tongue protruded, that made me throw myself away.

Oh no, it was when that pointed black tongue slicked from sight and she spat a missile of green slime into my face, that did that.

Shocked, bubbly liquid dripping from my chin, I stared across the tarred surface at her. She sat up, thin grey strands of hair stiff against her shoulders. Her dwarfish legs were splayed, the long gown she wore beneath he cloak risen above bony knees.

Something moving beneath the hem of her skirt captured my attention. It slid from cover as if uncurling. A grey-pink tip appeared. It slithered further into view, growing thicker. It was ringed with horny and hairy scales.

Probably, if I hadn't already been in such an extreme state of tension, I might have behaved more calmly. As it was, that scaly tail weaving between her legs tipped the balance between rational reaction and blind panic. Her gnarled and ravaged features, the scratchy, high-pitched laughter, the sheer aura of *malevolence* around her, didn't help; but no, it was definitely that horny swaying thing that sent me tearing back to the car.

I'd left the door open and I bundled in, the cackling chasing through the mist after me.

And suddenly she, it, the *thing*, was on the bonnet, peering through the windscreen at me. The grotesque creature mouthed something, something that I didn't hear but which *looked* foul. She grinned toothlessly, that black tongue flicking out to lick the glass. My brain told me this was all impossible; my emotions were not prepared to listen.

Then she began to scratch the windscreen with clawed fingers, her long, curling nails screeching against the glass. The scratch marks she left were clearly visible.

I think I screamed. Certainly the car's brakes did as I jammed my foot on the pedal.

The midget monster disappeared from view, propelled by the abrupt halt. Immediately, in a reflex action, I stepped on the accelerator again. The brief bump I felt was sickening: I was *sure* I heard the crunching of crushed bones.

My inclination was to drive on, to leave the nightmare behind. But basically, and as far as any of us are, I'm a normal human being: I have a conscience. I also possess – at least I did then – some soundness of mind. I'd hurt someone, someone unlike you or me, but a person, dwarfish and deformed though she was (my mind was already refusing to acknowledge what I'd seen with my own eyes – the tail, the black tongue, the fingernails tearing through glass). I stopped.

The low mist had thinned considerably, possibly due to the rush of air the speeding car had created. The body was easy to find. It lay in the road, unmoving, one part – the chest – strangely deflated. A further coldness ran through me when I realised that it was my car's tyres that had flattened her little body.

There was no need to look closer to conclude she was dead; yet closer I did look. Her eyes were half-open, just a crescent of watery yellowness showing on either side of her hooked nose.

But as I watched, her eyelids slid fully open, an almost languid movement, and her pupils seemed to float to the surface from deep within the eyeballs.

Her voice was no more than a peculiar croaking:
Hallow's Eve, Hallow's Eve
Beware hobgoblins on Hallow's Eve.

Those taloned claws grabbed my clothing and pulled me down onto her. We rolled and rolled in the road, this way and that, with me yelling and her screeching, and when I felt those fingernails digging into my chest, reaching for my heart, I knew I was in mortal danger.

Despite the terrible injury, the thing was strong; but I was bigger and more afraid. I managed to rise over her, my hands clasped tight around her scrawny neck. I could feel bones breaking beneath my fingers.

She smiled blackly up at me.

"Can't kill me, can't kill me," she chanted.

Her pointed tongue shot from her toothless mouth like a long, striking snake. She scratched (the tongue was *rough*) the tip of my nose.

"Beware hobgoblins," she warned when the tongue had slithered back.

My only excuse is that total, mind-shocking hysteria took over. I cracked her head against the shiny surface of the road. And then again.

"Can't kill me," she taunted.

The last crack had a mushy softness to it, like delicate porcelain filled with sugar shattering inwards.

With a rasping sigh, she finally lay still. Then she said: *"We don't die."*

I scooped up the limp form, my intention, I think, to lay it on the grass verge, or perhaps even in the back seat of the car; but I became overwhelmingly repulsed by what I held in my arms when I heard her say: *"You'll be sorry. You and the baby."*

I threw the little monster over the hedge beyond the verge and was startled to hear a splash. There must have been a water-filled ditch or a pond on the other side. I listened to the gurgling that came through the leafy hedge, not letting my breath go until the bubbly sound had ceased. Dread upon dread. She, it – the *thing* – said *"the baby"*. What the hell had she meant?

I fled the scene and scrambled back into my car. What had she meant? Dear God, what had she meant? Surely . . . I blanked the terrifying thoughts from my mind. I had to get to the hospital, that was the important thing.

By the time I reached the hospital, the long cracks in the windscreen had healed over, by the time I drew the car to a halt near the maternity unit, the marks had disappeared altogether. I spared no time to wonder.

Anne's private room was empty. I hurried through the main ward, searching for a nurse, a doctor, anyone who could give me a hint as to my wife's whereabouts. Those women still awake in the ward, some of them suckling newborn infants, looked up, startled at my unkept appearance (I'd been rolling around in the road, remember, I suppose I was looking pretty wild-eyed too). A nurse came striding towards me.

Fortunately she recognised me. "Your wife went up to the delivery room 20 minutes ago," she said, her voice low. "Now calm yourself, everything's fine." I brushed by her, heading for the stairs beyond the far doors. The waiting room was empty, the door to the delivery room closed. Resisting the urge to rush through, I rapped on the wood.

Someone on the other side murmured something, then I heard approaching footsteps.

"Just in time," the midwife said as she peered out at me. "Come inside and hold your wife's hand. My goodness, I think she might need to comfort you."

*

Dr Golding smiled at me, then frowned. "Sit yourself down," he said. Anne looked drained, but she managed a smile. She clasped my hand and I winced when I squeezed hard as a spasm hit her. Her eyes had a dreamy look that even the pain could not cut through.

"Wonderful," I heard the doctor say. "That's wonderful. Your daughter's well on her way. One last push, I'm sure that'll do the trick. You're doing marvellously."

"You'll be sorry. You and the baby."

The voice was in my mind, not in the room.

Anne gasped, but it was not from childbirth pains; she swung her face towards me questioningly and I realised it was *I* who had clutched *her* hand too tight.

". . . *You and the baby* . . ."

"Excellent," said the doctor.

It couldn't have happened, I told myself. Stress, exhaustion, the culmination of months of anxiety, praying that finally a child would be ours, that nothing would go wrong, nothing would spoil our ultimate dream . . . I'd imagined everything that had happened during the rushed journey to hospital.

And the ugly, gutteral voice in my head at last withered away. "Welcome," said Dr Golding.

For my daughter had slid smoothly and effortlessly, it seemed, after so many hours of labour, from her mother's body into the ready hands of the doctor.

The room dipped and banked around me; my head felt feather-light.

"Good God, catch him," I heard someone say.

Firm hands gripped my waist and I blinked my eyes to find the midwife's face staring down at me.

"It's not the first time the proud father has fainted on us," Dr Golding said cheerily. "You take yourself outside for a moment while we tidy things up."

"The baby . . . ?" I said.

"A perfect little girl," said the midwife.

I rose, just a bit unsteady, and bent to kiss Anne's lips. "You're both perfect," I whispered to her.

I went to the door and turned to catch sight of my child swaddled in white in the arms of the midwife before I stepped outside. With relief I sank into a stiff-backed chair in the waiting room. Thank God, I said silently to myself. Thank God . . .

But I heard a muffled shout from back there in the delivery room. I was frozen, body and senses, as I listened. "It's impossible." It was the doctor's voice. "There can't be another . . ."

The woman's shriek drove me to my feet. The delivery room door opened before I could reach it. The midwife's face appeared whiter than the uniform she wore. A hand shot to her mouth as her chest seemed to heave. She pushed past me.

I prevented the door from swinging closed with a raised arm. I entered the room. Anne, our baby held tight to her breasts, was staring from the bed to the doctor, a look of abject horror frozen on her face.

Dr Golding had his back to me. He, too, was strangely immobile. And he, too, held something.

I knew it was another baby, my daughter's twin.

I heard a tiny, scratchy cry.

And as I watched, a small, scaly tail curled up around the doctor's elbow.

THE OLD DARK HOUSE

(Universal, 1932)
Starring: Boris Karloff, Melvyn Douglas &
Gloria Stuart
Directed by James Whale
Story 'Night Sequence' by J.B. Priestley

The Old Dark House, which was made during the height of Hollywood's first boom in horror pictures in the Thirties and was directed by James Whale, the man who had been a key figure in this trend by making *Frankenstein*, also earned its own slice of fame as the first major ghost movie in the Sound era. Indeed, it was the success of Karloff as the shambling creature in the film version of Mary Shelley's classic novel that made Universal look quickly for a suitable follow-up vehicle for him and give him the leading role as Morgan the scarred and lecherous butler in the weird old house beset by nightmare sights and sounds that may or may not be supernatural. Once again Karloff's make-up was by Jack Pierce who had created the enduring image of Frankenstein's monster, and such was the power of his performance and the overall quality of the acting under James Whale's direction that some critics believe *The Old Dark House* is one of the finest productions in that first group of Universal chillers. Whale, a former theatrical set designer in London before coming to Hollywood, was an ideal person to film the story based on a novel, *Benighted*, by his fellow countryman J.B. Priestley. Although the set he had to use was sparse and economical, it was nonetheless capable of generating a wonderful sense of brooding menace. Ron Goulart, a great admirer of the 'old dark house' tradition of movies has called the film, "a prime example of how to scare an audience without resorting to monsters . . . it's the people, the shadowy halls, the gloomy rooms, and the oppressive weather that work on you."

Author John Boynton Priestley (1894–1984), the Yorkshire-born novelist and playwright, had a life-long interest in the unusual and the supernatural which can be seen in his novels like *Benighted* (1929) and *The Magicians* (1954); his plays including *Dangerous Corner* (1932) and *Time and the Conways* (1937) which dealt with space-time themes; and his numerous short stories such as 'The Grey Ones', 'The Strange Girl' and 'Night Sequence'. *The Old Dark House* movie strayed very little from Priestley's original novel in the recounting of what happens to an argumentative young couple whose car breaks down in a terrible rainstorm, forcing them to seek shelter in an isolated old mansion. The theme was also one that inspired Priestley more than once as the story which follows will demonstrate. For here again a quarrelling husband and wife are forced to seek shelter in an old house after their car becomes trapped in a ditch. It is a story in which Priestley again introduces his fascination with space-time and, aside from acting as a reminder of the classic 1932 movie, is surely ideal for adaptation for a modern TV series of the supernatural . . .

. . . And then – this was the pay-off – he reversed so hard that they went into a ditch. It was a shallow ditch and they were in no danger. But the car would not budge, and the rear end of it, with all their luggage at the back, was well under water. With some difficulty, for the car was at a sharp angle and outside it was nothing but rain and darkness, they climbed out and scrambled on to the road.

"And now what?" Betty was shrill, not having recovered yet from her fright.

"Don't be a bloody fool. Why ask me?" Luke was angrier than ever. "You know all about it, don't you?"

They glared at one another through the dark and the curtain of rain between them. Idiotic, of course, but there you are. "If you hadn't got into such a foul temper when I told you that was the wrong turn," she cried, not far from tears, "you wouldn't have backed into that ditch."

"No doubt. But who wanted to come this way? What was the point? Just tell me that." He had been wet for some time, because the old canvas hood was far from being waterproof; but now the rain was running icily down his back. "No use blaming me now. Got a cigarette?"

"No, of course I haven't got a cigarette. Didn't I ask you to stop at that pub for some cigarettes – and you wouldn't?"

"Oh – for God's sake!" He stamped about in a meaningless fashion, only to realise that his shoes were full of water. He could feel it oozing between his toes. "We've had nothing to eat, nothing to drink. We're miles from anywhere. And now we can't even raise a cigarette between us."

"And whose fault is that?" she demanded.

"What the hell does it matter whose fault it is? Don't go on and on like an idiot." He could hear his voice reaching a high wobbling note, as it often did, to his disgust, when he was agitated. Why couldn't he be really tough and stay in the bass register? Why had he to be here with Betty? Why did she want to come this way? Why had he to miss the turn, reverse so savagely, land them in the ditch? Why – why – why?

"We're only wasting time. The question is – what do we do now?"

"Well, that's what I was asking when you told me not to be a bloody fool – thank you very much." Betty really was crying now; it seemed even sillier than usual, seeing there was so much water about. She moved a little closer. "Can't you do anything about the car? Is it hopeless?"

"Of course it's hopeless."

"What about our bags?"

There was a time when it had made him feel proud and happy to be regarded by Betty as a kind of magician; now her helpless questioning only fed his disgust. "They're in the middle of that ditch and as far as I'm concerned that's where they're staying. If you want to try undoing those straps under water go on – try it. But I warn you that everything will be soaked. So forget 'em."

"Okay." She was the continuity girl now, not the appealing wife. "If we've had it, we've had it. Come on."

"Come on where?" he shouted angrily. The downpour was worse than ever, more like a cloudburst than ordinary autumn rain.

Betty stopped being the quiet capable continuity girl. "How do I know and what does it matter where? But we can't stand here all night, getting wetter and wetter, just screaming at each other like lunatics. We can find some sort of shelter, can't we?"

Luke admitted that they could try. It did not matter which way they went, for, as he had already announced, they were miles from anywhere. He was not sure what county they were in. Northampton, Bucks, Bedford? At the crossroads nearby, where she said he had taken the wrong turn, she moved to the right and he followed without protest. They went squelching along, through rain darkly drumming away; trudging and muttering like a pair of outcasts. Sometimes their shoulders bumped, but they left it at that, without any arm-taking or hand-holding, though they were young and had been married only three years and were not at the moment having affairs with anybody else. They might have been any two employees of the New Era Actuality Film Company, which did indeed still employ them, Luke as a director, Betty on scripts and continuity, after it had first brought them together. Stumbling on, cold now as well as wet, with his head well down, Luke thought of the job from which they were returning, the usual Documentary Short, this time on a big new cement works near Nottingham. A few nice shots, mostly long shots of the exteriors, but basically a corny job. He knew it, the unit boys knew it, and very soon the cement people and the public, if any, would know it.

"I see a light," Betty announced.

He came out of his sour reverie. "Where?" But then he saw it too. Well off the road, and rather dim. "Doesn't look promising."

"Neither does this filthy dark road," she snapped. "And I've had enough of it. At least they can tell us where we are – and let us use the 'phone if they have one."

"We might find something better round the corner." But he said this without conviction, just to raise an objection.

"Oh – don't be stupid. I'm half-drowned. There's some sort of drive there, I think."

While they were hesitating, the night turned into a black cascade, soaking them in a cold fury. Without another word, they turned in the drive at an irregular trot and splashed their way, head down and half-blinded, towards the light. Luke arrived first between the two pillars, snapped on his lighter in the shelter there, and was thumping away at the massive old knocker when Betty joined him. They stood there shivering, still silent.

There was nothing remarkable, as they agreed afterwards, about the woman who opened the door: she was dumpy and elderly, dressed in black. They began explaining themselves and their plight and were still at it when they found themselves indoors and the woman, who had not spoken, was turning a key in the door, locking out the night and not them. She held a lamp up towards their faces, gave them another long look, muttered something they could not catch, and then, putting down the lamp, hurriedly left the hall, closing the door behind her. It was a square hall, not very large, sparsely furnished, with no suggestion of comfort and good cheer about it. Indeed, it was rather like an entrance to a museum.

"I hope she understood what we said," Betty muttered, wriggling a little in her discomfort. "And has gone to ask somebody what to do about us. My God – I feel like a drowned rat."

"You look like one," said Luke, without a smile.

"And what do you imagine you look like?" She was furious with him, turned away, and tried to do something with her hair, which might have been wet, dark string. The dripping old raincoat, streaked purple sweater and tweed skirt, muddy stockings, completed the picture. Luke stared at her with distaste.

"As a matter of fact you've been looking tatty all the week," he told her. "I wanted to mention it before, but hadn't time."

"You'd plenty of time to put down double gins with Bert and Mack. And you ought to see yourself. You haven't even bothered shaving today, though you've had oceans of time. Oh – I know the idea. Trying to look like the overworked director – the Hollywood touch."

"Oh – for Chrissake—"

"That's right," she said, still not looking at him. "Let's have the dialogue now. And start shouting. That's all we need to be turned out." She shook herself. "And I never felt so wet, cold and damned miserable in my life."

"Go on, then, cry. Perhaps they'll let you stay and only turn me out." This was worse than usual; but he hated himself for suddenly hating her, then found himself hating her more for making him hate himself.

She faced him, looking so bedraggled that she was almost grotesque, but very young. "I'm not going to cry. If I once started, I think I'd never stop. And it's not just this – now. It's everything. The way you went on up there with the unit. Even the work you did – lousy—"

"Oh – it was lousy, was it?"

"Yes, it was – lousy, lousy, lousy – and you know it. Then the way you'll behave when we get back. As if it wasn't bad enough, trying to exist in that crummy little flat you had to take over from Sonia and Peter—"

"*Your* friends—"

"They aren't anybody's friends. We haven't got any friends," she continued wildly. "We haven't got anything. You're thirty-two and I'm twenty-seven – and already we've had it. Why – why? Is it you? Is it me? Is it everything? I thought it was going to be all different – and it was at first—"

He nearly told her that a girl ought to pipe down when she's looking like something the cat brought in. "You can't say I didn't warn you. Right from the start. I told you I couldn't see myself marrying anybody. Though I thought it couldn't be much worse for you than living with old Charlie Tilford, which is what you were doing, more or less, at the time. That can't have been very glamorous. He was old enough to have been your father – and then some."

"That matters less than you think," she retorted. "And Charlie was always kind."

"He was always plastered—"

"All right, he was plastered. And he was old." She pushed back her wet fringe, to glare at him. "But he was kind – he was sweet. We weren't always shouting at each other – like this."

"I'm not shouting," he told her. "You're doing the shouting. And if you want to go back to old Charlie, you know what to do. That is, if you can persuade our little Mavis to move out." He produced a laugh of sorts but did not enjoy it.

Her mouth seemed to fall open and her eyes widened, as if to reveal some sudden desolation. Then she shook her head slowly, still wearing this tragic mask. It was not an act, and Luke found it very disturbing, as if Betty was turning into somebody else. What happened next was even more disturbing, for she began to swear at him, using the worst language she could ever have overheard in the studio, and she did it without heat and violence, almost like an obscene talking doll.

"You're talking like a foul-mouthed little slut," he announced when she had finished.

"Perhaps that's what I am." Her tone was more normal now.

"I wouldn't be surprised."

"If I am, then it's your fault," she said. "You've turned me into one, Luke."

"If it had been anything good, you'd have claimed the credit yourself. But because it isn't," he continued, with a heavy sneer, "then it's my fault. I've noticed that before about women." Which was untrue but sounded well, he thought.

He did not deceive her. She was in fact hard to bamboozle in this sort of mood. "You've never noticed anything about women except the shape of their legs. So don't pretend." She wriggled impatiently. "God – these clothes! I'll have pneumonia in a minute. If you'd any sense you'd know that if you had turned me into anything we could both be proud of, I'd have given you all the credit, adored you for it. That's what a girl wants to do. Like Sonia with Peter."

"They're a bright example." He made it another heavy sneer, though actually he knew what she meant.

"All right, you don't like them. And I don't much. But they've made something together."

"What? I've never seen it."

"No, because you don't bother noticing people properly, don't know what's happening to them, just don't take them in. That's probably what's wrong with your work now – why it's so routine and corny—"

"Who says it's routine and corny?" he shouted, furious at having his suspicions confirmed.

"I do. And I'm not the only one," she continued, with an infuriating gleam of triumph. "Ask some of your drinking chums, if you can get them to tell you the truth."

It was then that the dumpy woman in black returned, to beckon and mutter. She handed Luke a glass with liquor in it, and indicated that he should wait there, after which she took Betty through the doorway on the left. Evidently they were not to be turned out into the night, which was still drumming and roaring away. Luke tried the liquor and discovered that it was excellent old brandy. After a couple of sips there was a tiny patch of high summer inside him. He had a taste for fine objects and examined the glass itself with approval. It had that tulip shape which the French prefer for brandy, and clearly was old and of unsual quality, like the liquor it held.

By the time he had swallowed the last drop of the spirit, which seemed to release into his empty stomach a sunshine he had lost for years, he felt rather tight. Too uncomfortable in his wet clothes to sit down, he prowled round the hall, like a man left alone in a museum; but the light from the solitary small lamp was very dim. He still felt anger against Betty. If she were not with him, to show her resentment and to provoke his, it might not be bad here, a little adventure, a break in the dreary familiar pattern. But not with her under the same roof. She would keep the pattern unbroken all right. If he had not felt so wet, cold and empty, he might have hurried out into the night again, braving the rain, the darkness, the miles from anywhere, to enjoy some experience he could call his own. Slowly and resentfully he turned over these thoughts, like an idle and gloomy farm worker with a pitchfork.

The old woman came back, to lead him out as she had done Betty. But this time they used another door, which opened on to a passage as cold and nearly as narrow as the grave. At the end of this passage was a short flight of back stairs, for the use of servants and visiting riff-raff like himself. The room she showed him, the first they came to at the top of the stairs, was of no great size and appeared to be as sparsely furnished as the hall. It was lit by two tall candles, flickering in the draught. In the middle of the floor, clouding the dim gold of the candlelight with steam, was a hip bath. As soon as the woman had shown him soap and towels and had gone muttering out, Luke peeled off his sodden clothes and lowered himself into that steam. There were no other clothes in sight, not even a dressing-gown, but he did not care. Here was a chance to warm, clean and dry his protesting carcase. Like most young men he was usually a casual splashy fellow in a bath, never troubling to soap and scrub himself properly; but this time he was thorough, enjoying the hot water and finding the hip bath more encouraging to effort than the familiar kind of tub at home.

He began thinking about Betty again, not in anger now although his resentment was still there. He went back to their first encounters in the studio, then forward from them to their marriage. Had they been happy during those first months – or merely excited? Was there something wrong with her – or with him? Or were they both all right but simply no good in partnership? Or was it life itself that ought to take the blame? And now, with this question, his resentment shifted its ground. Perhaps the answer was that you asked for a colossal feature in Technicolor when all you could have was a documentary short in black and white with some lousy cheap sound effects. Life, real life, was strictly low budget.

"Come in," he shouted, without thinking, when he

heard the knock. But if these people couldn't spare a bathroom for him, they couldn't grumble if they found him stark naked. However, it was a man who entered, a portly middle-aged fellow carrying a bundle of clothes. "I thought you might like a razor too, my dear sir," he announced, holding out an old-fashioned cut-throat. "Supper in about half-an-hour. One of us will bring you down. Horrid weather. Listen to it." He waved a hand towards the shuttered window, against which the rain was beating hard. "Now don't hurry. There's plenty of time, always plenty of time."

"Thanks very much," Luke was stammering. "Very good of you to look after us like this."

"My dear sir, the least we could do." A smile, a majestic wave of the hand, and he was gone.

Sitting upright in his bath, Luke still stared at the door, wondering if the candlelight had been playing tricks with eyes that needed hundred-volt lamps. What about the clothes that had been left for him? Hurriedly he dried the upper part of himself, then jumped out and perfunctorily towelled his feet and legs. He took the clothes over to the candles. Yes, they were the same – black silk knee-breeches, long stockings, pumps, a ruffled shirt – except that this cut-away tailed coat was dark green and the one worn by the man who had just gone had been brown. In this house you were expected to wear fancy dress, Regency costume for the men. Well, if shelter, brandy, a bath, dry clothes, and supper to follow were the least these people could do, then the least Luke Gosforth could do was to put on their fancy costume and try to keep a straight face about it. So after giving his feet another rub, he began pulling on the long black stockings. "Mikes a nice chynge, ducks," he muttered, breaking into his comic Cockney act; which he favoured when things took a strange turn and he was not sure quite what was happening.

Betty held a candle in front of the long mirror, examined her reflection there critically at first, to make certain everything fitted and there were no embarrassing disclosures; and then stepped back a pace to wonder at and enjoy what she saw. Her hair wasn't right, of course – it hadn't a clue, though she ought to be able to improve it a bit – but the general effect was terrific. She wasn't Betty Gosforth at all, and yet at the same time she felt she looked more herself, the self she was certain she possessed, than she had done for ages. Thank goodness she had good arms and shoulders and needn't be afraid (though it was a bit much, among strangers too) of this tremendous bosomy effect! She turned one way and then the other, smiling at herself over her very nice bare shoulder. The high-waisted long dress made her look much taller, more dignified than usual but more dashing and voluptuous too – a sort of Napoleonic princess. But something would have to be done with her wretched hair. She took the candle over to the dressing-table, where there was another one, and after rubbing her hair again and then combing it, she found in the little drawer below the mirror several short lengths of broad ribbon, with which she began to experiment, lost to everything at the moment but the desire to perfect her toilet.

When at last she went rustling down the broad shallow stairs, she felt peculiar, all fancy dress and glamour outside but bewildered and rather shaky within; and very hungry too. There was a man standing below, as if waiting for her. When she drew nearer, he smiled and extended a hand. Without thinking what she was doing, she put her hand into his, and allowed him to bring her to the foot of the stairs.

"Welcome," he said, still smiling and still keeping her hand in his. He was middle-aged, perhaps about fifty, and his thick springy hair had some grey in it. His face, matching his rather bulky figure, was heavy but was lightened by a quick, clear glance, which she felt at once had something very masculine about it. He was wearing some sort of stock, a ruffled shirt, a dark brown cut-away coat, black knee-breeches and stockings; but did not give the impression that he was in fancy dress. She was certain he had always worn clothes like these. And just as she was asking herself what went on in this house, as if guessing her bewilderment he continued: "My niece will be joining us in a moment. And so, I trust, will your – er – companion – husband – lover—"

"Husband," she told him, smiling too. "It's very good of you—"

"No, no, we're delighted to have company on such a night," he said, cutting her short. "And don't let us stand on ceremony. Call me Sir Edward – or even Ned if you prefer it. What shall I call you?"

"Betty." It was out before she could stop it. She had meant to tell him she was Mrs Gosforth and to do a little more apologising, explain about the car and all that; but somehow she couldn't. And the next moment he was conducting her, with a hint of high ceremony, into a long panelled room where there was an uncommonly generous fire and several clusters of candles, so that it was filled with lovely warmth and light. At the far end of the room was a dining-table laid for four. Sir Edward placed her in a straight high-backed chair near the fire.

"I hope," he said, bending forward a little and looking deep into her eyes, "you will take a glass of sherry with me, Betty. You will? Excellent!" His voice was powerful, rich, like that of some famous actor; but it was oddly, and rather disturbingly, gentle too; quite different from the voices of Luke and his friends, which were much thinner and higher but also more aggressive. This man, she reflected as he went to the sideboard for the sherry, seemed to bend his voice and his look at you – not to throw them as Luke and his friends did – and if you were a woman, you could easily find this most disarmingly attractive. In spite of his age and queer costume, this Sir Edward was in fact a most attractive man.

"Allow me to observe," he said, looking down at her as they sipped the sherry, "that you look more than becoming in this dress."

"I adore it. Only of course my hair's all wrong."

"It's uncommonly short, Betty." He smiled at her. "Some new fashion – French, I'll be bound – that hasn't reached us before down here. But I've been admiring it. In this light, it looks like black midnight with a distant fire or two somewhere. If your eyes were dark," he continued, regarding her thoughtfully, "I might like your hair less. But you have grey eyes, I think—"

"Yes, they *are* grey." It occurred to her that nobody had bothered for ages about what colour her eyes were. It would have been much the same if she hadn't had eyes, only some electric seeing-apparatus. She smiled at this observant Sir Edward, using her eyes too.

"But a warm grey, surely, like a grey velvet in strong sunlight," he said slowly, his tone both gentler and richer than ever. He sounded rather wistful about it too, as if he had waited for years to stare into exactly this kind of eye and knew that it could be only a tantalising glimpse.

To hide her confusion, although it was not unpleasant, Betty drank some more sherry. It seemed much stronger than any sherry she had had for a long time. Now that Sir Edward was silent, though she knew he was still looking at her, this was the moment to explain about the car going into the ditch and perhaps to ask a cautious question or two about this house and its family and fancy dress. But somehow, when it came to the point, there did not seem any particular reason why she should.

"I call myself a gentleman," he said, almost with regret, "and so you may be sure I shan't abuse the laws of hospitality. But I must warn you, Betty, that I have a passion for Woman – and when she appears before me wearing dark hair and fine grey eyes – by Heaven – I begin to feel overmastered by that passion. So, take warning, my dear."

As she looked up at him, she asked herself if he was about to make a pass at her, and wondered wildly what she would do if he did. It just wasn't fair to a girl if a man with such a terrific line turned at once into a pouncing wolf. But all he did – and she could not have said if she felt relief or disappointment – was to give her a slow smile, and then saunter back to the sideboard to refill his glass. When he returned, he sat opposite to her, nursing his glass on his crossed knees. He looked anything but over-mastered by a passion, yet something, Betty felt, still danced and flashed between them in the firelight.

"Talk to me," she said, after waiting a little time. "Don't just think it – say it." As if she had known him for ages; but it was his fault.

His heavy face came to life again. "You have an odd abrupt trick of speech, Betty—"

"I'm sorry—"

"No, no. It has a certain charm, though if you were older and plain I might not think so." He smiled at her over the glass he was slowly raising.

"Tell me what you were thinking, please, Sir Edward." There again, it came out before she had time to remember they had just met.

"I was thinking," he began carefully, "that in middle life men either begin to die – and there are many Englishmen who are dead but not buried – or turn more and more, and with increasing passion, in the mind if not always in the body, to Woman. I suspect – except perhaps for priests and philosophers – we have no other choice – it is Death or Woman. You are astonished, I gather."

"Yes, I am." She regarded him gravely. "I always think of young men wanting women."

"Young men want women as they want beef and pudding. And it may be this is what most women prefer."

"I don't think so," said Betty.

"But men of my age," Sir Edward continued, "who are still alive and are not merely solid ghosts, cheating the graveyard, see Woman as the manifestation of a sublime mystery. She is both goddess and priestess out of a strange religion. She is the other side of things taking on exquisite shape and colouring, to attract us, and speaking our language to communicate with us. She carries a diplomatic passport from the Moon. She is the last survivor of Atlantis and all the lost kingdoms. There is more in her that is at once alien, fascinating, delicious, than there is in all China. Young men, still warm from their mothers' milk, do not perceive all this. It is only when we men are growing old ourselves that we understand that Woman, though she may be all bloom and springtime, is older than we are."

"You can't look at me like that," said Betty, "and really believe what you're saying."

"Certainly I can. And there is something in you that knows what I say is true. Something that does not belong simply to you, Betty. For Betty as Betty may be shy, humble, wondering if her hair is out of place, anxious to please her company, perhaps fearful of what the night may bring—"

"How do you know that?" she cried, but not in protest against it.

"But Betty as Woman is all I have said she is. And when you can enjoy, as I can, the contrast between the simple humility of the individual girl and the pride, grandeur, and mystery of the ancient empire of Woman, then you are doubly fascinated. Then add," he went on, regarding her with a mock severity that was not without tenderness, "hair of midnight and old fires, eyes of smoke and silver – and imagine the havoc—"

A girl came into the room. Betty didn't know if she was glad or sorry to see her. It was comforting to meet another girl in this peculiar house, but even though she was only Sir Edward's niece, this girl tumbled Betty off her perch as Woman the grand and mysterious. Also, this girl was beautiful, there could be no doubt about that. She had red-gold hair, artfully tumbling in curls from a centre parting, and wide eyes of a warm hazel. Her dress was like Betty's, white and in the Empire style, but had a cunning little frill, of a pastel blue shade, that went round her bare shoulders and curved its ends in a knot on her bosom, thus shaped like an inverted heart. She was also at least two or three years younger than Betty, who had to admit that she looked a nice girl. But she would have seemed a much nicer girl if she had not looked quite so devastating.

"Uncle Ned," she announced, smiling at them sweetly, "supper's coming in."

"Betty," said Sir Edward, who was now standing, "allow me to present my niece, Julia. I promised our other guest he would be brought down to supper. Julia, my dear, he's in the small room at the back. Run up there, please, and give him a knock."

Julia floated away, leaving Betty and Sir Edward standing together on the hearth. "She looks a charming girl," Betty murmured, looking up at him.

"She is indeed. Delightful." He waited a moment, regarding her smilingly. "But for once I'll confess I wish she weren't with me. Though of course I'm forgetting – there's your husband." He placed a finger delicately under her chin and gently tilted her face up an inch or two. "Are you in love with your husband, Betty?"

"I was. But I don't think I am now," she replied unsteadily.

"A pity."

"Yes, that's what I think. Still—" She stopped because she had no idea what else to say. She had a strong desire, which she resisted, to close her eyes, now so near to his, with their direct masculine challenge.

"The laws of hospitality," he said softly. "No need to be pedantic about them – humph?"

"Well—" And her eyes apparently closed of their own accord. What happened now was no business of hers at all.

She felt herself gently but masterfully enclosed in his arms. There was nothing violent and passionate about the kiss that followed, otherwise, passive and helpless though she felt, she might have resented it. Nevertheless, it seemed the most personal, the most directly communicating kiss she had had for a long while. It made her feel at once enormously herself and alive, and very precious too. She opened her eyes, and withdrew gently, her knees wobbling a little.

"Somewhere between the mere pecking of salutation and the groping of mouths on their way to darkness," Sir Edward observed, "is the kiss that a man and woman exchange when they are completely aware of one another's personalities and delight in them. It is the kiss of recognition, of acceptance, of tribute, beyond friendship but not yet hounded and blinded by passion. It is the kiss of love not yet ready to destroy itself in the night. Everything that can happen is there in it but kept within the bounds of what is individual and personal, this particular man, this particular woman. Do you agree, Betty?"

She did, and as she told him so, she found herself possessed by a queer thought that everything Sir Edward said to her was something she had wanted some man to say to her, although she could not have put the words into his mouth, and that he behaved as she had wanted some man to behave, even though what he did might seem to surprise her; so that in an unreasonable fashion it was all as if she had invented him, like a dream figure. Yet there was nothing hazy and dreamlike about him and this house: they were solidly before her, unexpected, fantastic, but not at all unreal. Indeed, it was the rest of the day, with its fuss and squalor, its journey through the rain and deepening darkness to nowhere, its meaningless squabbling, that now seemed unreal.

"Yes, Sir Edward," she was saying, "I've always felt that . . ."

The clothes were not a bad fit, and Luke rather fancied himself in the dark green coat. All that was wrong now was the stock or cravat or whatever it was called, which had defeated him for the last ten minutes. He was still holding it, sadly crumpled, when somebody knocked and he went to open the door. The girl looked so beautiful, it hurt.

"I'm Julia," she said, "and my uncle sent me to bring you down to supper. You must be very hungry, aren't you?"

He found some breath. "Yes, I am – rather," he stammered. "Er – my name's Luke Gosforth. Do you know how to tie one of these things? I was just giving it up."

She smiled. "I can try. Now stand quite still, please."

He did stand still but his mind was blazing and whirling. It was as if every other girl he had ever seen was nothing but a faint copy of this one, as if in fact he had never really seen a girl before. And he was the fellow who had been telling himself that life, real life, was strictly low budget. This girl burst any budget. Life had pulled something out of a bag he didn't know was there: "I'll show you, Gosforth," it had replied. By the time she had finished tying that thing, in a fragrant kaleidoscope of red-gold curls, eyes with flecks of green and gold in them, round white arms and shoulders, he felt half drunk.

"There!" She smiled at him, as if he were an emperor. "Now we'll go down. Will you bring a candle, please?"

Halfway along the passage below, no longer as cold

and narrow as the grave, he stopped her. "Just a minute, please, Julia," he began, holding the lighted candle high between them. "I'm calling you Julia because that's all the name you gave me, so I hope you don't mind. I want to say first that I'm very grateful for the wonderful way you're looking after us. Thank you very much, Julia."

She looked at him without smiling, her eyes enormous and rather dark in that wavering light. "You have no need to thank me, Luke. You wanted us, I think, and here we are."

The ghost of a thought visited him then, like a cold finger tapping his spine; but he beat it down, determined to keep everything on a sensible level. "Nice of you to put it like that, Julia. But I also wanted to say this. I might find it hard to start questioning your uncle – and don't want to embarrass anybody – so before we join the others, could you just give me a quick line on the set-up here?"

"A quick line – on the set-up?" She looked as bewildered as she sounded.

Again, some moth-wing of a thought brushed his mind, and again he took a firm grip on sense and reality. "You know what I mean," he said apologetically. "No business of mine, I agree. But it might stop me making a fool of myself later. So – tell me – why are we all wearing these clothes? What goes on here?"

"What do you want to go on here?" she said, no longer bewildered. "Is this the wrong way to live? Do you wish to show us a better way?" She waited a moment, and then, when he did not answer her: "They are waiting for us, I must remind you." She put out a hand.

When his hand closed over hers, he could have shouted for joy. Everything suddenly expanded; the world was rich and wide. "Okay, don't explain anything, Julia. I don't want to know. I'll tell you this, though. I couldn't show you a better way. I couldn't show anybody anything, though I'm supposed to. I've been living like a rat in a cage." He felt a little tug. "Yes, let's go. Sorry for the hold-up."

But he halted her again just as they reached the last door. "Look, Julia," he whispered, "don't think I'm out of my mind – though perhaps I am and it might be the sort of mind to be out of. But I must talk to you alone some time tonight. I couldn't leave here without talking to you. If I did, tomorrow would be even worse than today and yesterday."

"I knew at once you were unhappy," she said softly. "Why are you?"

"That's what I want to talk about, partly. So can we get together somewhere, just the two of us? It wouldn't be the same with anybody else there. Can we, Julia?"

She nodded. "After supper. And now we must go in."

The portly fellow in the brown coat was standing before the fire, and with him was another beautiful girl, dressed more or less like Julia, but quite different, a dark mysterious creature. There are some men who seem to claim the right to be surrounded by beautiful women, and evidently this fellow was one of them.

"Prompt to the moment," he cried jubilantly. "The food's on the table. The wine's in the decanter. Luke, isn't it? I'm Sir Edward – or Ned, if it takes your fancy and we don't quarrel. Now, Luke, give Julia an arm. Come, my dear." He said this, offering an arm, to the dark mysterious beauty; and as she turned, no longer withdrawn but as smiling and gracious as a young queen, Luke saw that it was Betty. She gave him a look that was even more disturbing than her changed appearance, for it was not an angry look, an anxious or questioning look, not any look she had ever given him before as a wife: it was serene and not unfriendly but without any feeling or even any curiosity.

So they went with some ceremony down the long room to the table at the end. Luke and Sir Edward sat facing one another; and Luke had Julia upon his right and a little closer to him than Betty was, the table having been laid in this way. No servant came in. Sir Edward served the rich soup and then carved the roast chicken. Luke ate slowly, which was unusual for him, and felt that for once he was enjoying each mouthful.

After Sir Edward had begged them formally to take wine with him and had filled their glasses, he began making a speech at them, which did not surprise Luke, who had already guessed that here was a man who loved the sound of his own voice. Betty never took her eyes off the man, and gave the impression that she was willing to sit there all night listening to him orate. But to Luke's joy there was a moment when Julia turned her peach-bloom face towards him and made a tiny grimace, as if she had guessed his thought and was showing her agreement with it. God's truth – she was the honey of the world!

"You and I, my dear Luke," Sir Edward was saying, "are fortunate men to have such ladies at our elbow. But they are here, I think, because we deserve them. Not entirely, of course, for that would be impossible, but so far as men can deserve such ladies, we deserve these. We have the eyes to observe their beauty, the minds to record, to remember and praise their charms. If they are Eros, then we are Logos. The word and the deed are with us, so we have magic too. We offer them strong arms, tender hearts, and, when the wine has gone round three or four times more, minds that shall seem enchanted kingdoms to them. For they can no more do without us than we can without them."

"No, of course not," cried Betty boldly, and held out her glass to him.

"Speak to us, friend Luke," Sir Edward continued, with one eye still on Betty. "You are still young, and a noble fellow. Poetry burns in you, I see it in your eye. Come, set these ladies delicately but surely on fire. Restore to me the green but blazing madness of my youth, before I turn complete philosopher and take this table and company into Greenland. Julia, command him."

He could not hear what she said, perhaps she said nothing but only made mocking but tender motions with her lips; but her glowing look was an invitation to a new life, as if he had fallen heir to some fabulous estate. Through his mind went pattering, like rats down a corridor, the familiar staccato phrases of disillusion and fear, the double talk of the world of double gins; but not in that fashion did he speak, when he found himself standing, looking down upon them, glass in hand. The words seemed to arrive, and be roundly spoken, of their own accord.

"Ladies – Sir Edward," he heard himself saying, "all my life I have wished to be here as I am tonight. It is not true that I am a noble fellow. I am a miserable fellow. But now I am not such a miserable fellow as I have long imagined myself to be. That is because I am here, speaking to you like this." He shot a glance at Julia and what he saw in her face turned his heart over. "I did not know this was what I wanted. I only knew, though I pretended not to know and hated my pretence, that days, months, years, were hurrying past while my life was merely being endured and not lived. I drew an evil magician's circle and existed within it, watching colour drain out of the rose and fire and gold leave the sun. I disinherited myself, planned my own starvation. I was afraid of joy, so joy never came. I believed the past to be a graveyard, the future a menace. That left me with a present time that was never anything but a tasteless wafer. My life lacked spacious dimensions; there was no room in it for style, ceremony, admiration, deep feeling, and the enchantment of long vistas. There was an artist in me and I put a rope round his neck. There was a friend, and I sneered him into banishment. There was a lover, but I could not feed him with wonder and faith. I could neither love God nor defy Him. I was too corrupt for Heaven and not lively enough for Hell. I have lived, a dusty midget, on the endless desert of cement. I would have been already half an insect, lost as a man, if some unquenched spark of soul had not for ever kept alive the resentment that burned in me. No, Sir Edward, my friend – no poetry burned in me, only resentment, though that may have been the defiance of the poet dying within me. I – and all my kind – we are the resenters; and there is a terrible despair in our resentment, for while we know we have been disinherited and cheated, we also know we have contrived to disinherit and cheat ourselves. But for once, here, tonight, I am where I might always have been. I was ready to resent you, Sir Edward – to question your generosity, to mock at your offer of friendship, to make your food seem unpalatable, your wine taste sour – but now I say you are indeed the noble fellow you said I was. That lady – so richly dark and delicately glowing – is my wife, and I know now that I have never really seen her before as she is – or as she might be; and she does well to turn away from me, to look at and listen to a better man, whose eyes and tongue do not rob her of her true inheritance. As for Julia – why should I hide what I feel? All my life I have loved her. Without seeing her, without being certain she existed, I have loved her. She is the very face of beauty – and all that is gentle and good besides – and now that I have seen her and she has spoken to me, she possesses my heart for ever."

He sat down, drained his glass, then met the dazzling look that Julia was giving him. Her hand came across the table and he raised it to his lips. Then it stayed within his grasp, small and still yet as marvellously filled with life as a bird. Were the candles dimming and turning flame into smoke, or was it the sunburst of happiness inside him that made the table seem darker? Soon he was asking himself other questions. Had he really made that elaborate speech, so far removed from his customary talk, or had he merely sat there imagining himself making such a speech? Did he kiss Julia's hand and then hold it? Once he had had a dream within a dream. Was this one of them?

Certainly, candle after candle guttered and smouldered and darkness crept along the table. It was hard to see Betty now – she seemed much further away too – and it was she who was talking to them. If you could call it talking, for the words, clear and high, seemed to come floating out of her. "I am a woman," he caught, then kept his attention steady, not to miss the rest, "and now at last, when I had begun to feel our life was all a cheat, I have met a Man, and for an hour I have begun to live as a woman should live. And as she expects to live. I do not know how it is with men – and perhaps there is less difference between us than we think – but we women grow up with expectations that owe nothing to our mothers, nurses, governesses, who tell us too little of these things. Then Nature starts us flowering, but we may wither still in bud unless the society of man ripens us. The hidden pattern of our unfolding is known to us somehow, so that we see it fragmentarily in dreams, are tantalised by it, and then driven to a terrible despair, in which we care nothing if we make life hateful to all around us. We feel we possess in secret essence, waiting to be released into the air, everything that could delight a man, whatever his mood, while it delights us too. But unless we ripen, we are nothing. We are flower and fruit that must have gardeners. Because we are so much closer to Nature than man is, we know that Nature is not enough. Man must complete us, not only in his capacity as the lover but also as the creator of a society, a style of life, in which we can grow. And now I have found that Man. To leave him would be unimaginable. Not to share a roof with him even for half a day would be a little death. Dear Ned, now I can never let you go."

All the wicks in the central candelabra seemed to be smoking, and beyond them Sir Edward's face was nothing but a blur of crimson: it might have been a great mask carried in some distant torchlight procession. What was the man saying? Luke tried to concentrate his attention. "For my part, my dear," he heard, "I believe what are most necessary are style, energy and good humour. Energy without style brings barbarism. Style without energy results in corruption and death. But even style with energy, energy with style, must have good humour too, otherwise we might be Asiatic conquerors or Caesar Borgia. I do not ask for saintliness, for I am thinking of this world, which is all I know, and not the next, which may not be there and even if it is can wait for us. I ask for a cheerful temper, for unwearied tolerance and kindness, without which we could erect a hell on earth in six months. Sheer good-nature is sadly under-valued. But there must be energy behind it or it becomes torpid. And good humour and energy must express themselves in a fine style of life."

"With light, if you'll allow me to say so," Luke called down the table, "more than we have here at this moment."

"To say nothing of coffee and brandy," cried Sir Edward. And Luke could just see him rising hastily. "We must serve ourselves, but I'll do it."

Betty had risen too. "I'm coming with you, Ned." There was some urgency in her tone.

"Why not, my dear Betty, why not?" He was jovial as he reached for a candlestick. "We'll go hand-in-hand."

"But they'll come back here," Luke said to Julia as soon as they were alone. "And remember your promise. After supper, you said."

She stood up, so white, so golden, that it appeared as if she needed no light to be seen, as if light came from her. "I have not forgotten. Dear Luke! Come, you must sit by the fire while you are waiting." She led him down the room. "I shall go for coffee and brandy too – if you would like some brandy – yes? But I shall take them up to the Library, which is always warm, and there you can talk

to me as long as you please. To find the Library you go
up the main staircase, not the little one where your room
is, turn to the right and go along the landing and then
you will see a short staircase at the end, on the left, and
at the top of that staircase is the Library. It has double
doors, and the inner one is covered with green baize.
Be there in half an hour, not sooner because there are
things I must do first. Now is there anything you want
here, Luke?"

"Yes," he replied ruefully, "tobacco. I smoke all the
time—"

"Sit there, and you shall have tobacco," she cried,
with all the bustling gaiety of a girl who is happy to
be waiting upon a man. It was incredible, but there it
was – she seemed as happy to be with him as he was
with her. "There." And she handed him a tobacco-box
and a long churchwarden clay pipe. "And don't smoke
yourself into a stupor or you won't be able to talk to
me. And remember – the Library in half an hour, and
it's at the top of the short staircase at the end of the
landing."

After she had gone he filled the churchwarden, rather
clumsily for he had never been a pipe-smoker, and lit it
with a brand from the dying fire. He pulled the narrow
high-backed chair closer, fitted himself into it snugly,
crossed his legs, and began puffing away at the fragrant
Virginia tobacco. He did not look like Luke Gosforth,
was not behaving like him, and now to crown all – and
to the astonishment of that central recording little self
which might be the essential Luke Gosforth or might
be some impersonal atom of pure intelligence – he no
longer thought like Luke Gosforth. His consciousness
was no longer like an angry cascading stream but more
like some broad placid river. The usual staccato phrases,
jeering, protesting, fearful, that went crackling through
his mind as he pulled at a cigarette, strode about a room
or humped himself into an easy chair, were no longer

tormenting him; and in their place were large serene thoughts that came floating along the river like nobly coloured barges. He discovered in himself no noticeable pieces of wisdom; yet he felt wise, and the master, not the agitated slave, of experience. It was a moment, he felt, for planning some great work that would take years and fill them with creation. He was no longer a rat in a cage, he was a man at the end of a good day . . .

When Betty left Sir Edward to go up to her room, where she remembered seeing a shawl she needed now, he told her not to return down there but to look for him in the Library, at the head of the short staircase that she would find at the end of the landing. Carrying a small brass candlestick, she found her room easily enough. In all her life, she felt, she had never before known such happiness as this. There were in fact three shawls and she amused herself trying them on in different ways. After deciding on the smallest but fleeciest, she unfastened the ribbon in her hair and used her comb again. The face she saw, not too well in the light of one small candle, was the face she had always wanted to see in every mirror, the face that had been waiting in some secret store for such a time as this, a face that was at the furthest remove from the angry hag's countenance she had worn in the car. She remembered what happened in the car and the unpleasant scene she had had with Luke after they arrived here; but now all that seemed part of a dream she had had, one of those dreams both confused and wildly improbable that can yet make the dreamer feel wretched. She did not understand the events of the last hour or so, how they could come about, what sensible explanation there was of them; but then so far she had never really tried to understand them, had no desire to live in that part of the mind which could begin to make ordinary sense out of them. She was alive now, whereas only a few

hours ago she had felt half dead. Why should she ask
questions when she had suddenly been transformed from
a hard, angry little thing into a fountain of joy? Vague
memories of fairy tales returned to her, tales in which the
over-curious, the obstinate enquirers, only cut themselves
off from the good magic.

Now, with no more she could usefully do to herself,
she was on fire again to be with Sir Edward, in whose
presence she felt herself to be lovely and gracious and
almost wise. She had more than once fancied herself to
be in love, not only with Luke but also before and after
she had married him, with men of his sort, brittle and
demanding; but always she had felt herself working up
an excitement to keep the affair going, like people at a
party, and had found herself hurrying away from various
doubts and hesitations, pretending they did not exist; so
that the whole of her was far from being completely
involved, absorbed. But with Sir Edward it was as if she
began from the true centre of her being, and none of the
delicious excitement had to be manufactured, while at the
heart of the relationship was a wonderful calm, the peace
of certainty. In whatever time and place he existed, she
belonged to him.

She stood still for a moment or two outside her room,
carefully shielding her candle from the draught. She could
hear the steady drumming of the rain and nothing else,
not a sound. The house seemed immense, cavernous. She
wondered whether Sir Edward had already gone up to
the Library; she had never heard him pass her room; but
then he might have used another staircase. This house no
longer seemed the compact Queen Anne type of small
mansion she had imagined it to be when she first arrived.
Most houses, she reflected uneasily, appear much larger at
a first glance than they seem to be on further acquaintance,
whereas this house, in a disturbing fashion, began to grow,
and the longer you were in it the bigger it seemed. This
staircase, descending into darkness, was not the staircase

the old woman had first shown her, though it led to and from the same room. Should she go and find the Library or look for Sir Edward below? Irresolutely she drifted down and halted at the foot of the stairs, hoping to hear a sound that would tell her he was still somewhere on the ground floor. Hearing nothing, then spurred by something like panic, she hurried upstairs, going as fast as her trailing skirts and the care of her precious candle-flame would allow her to go.

There was a terrifying scuttling somewhere along the landing, and after that nothing to be heard there except her heart behaving like a trapped bird. The floor was uncarpeted and its boards worn and uneven. The air along there was cold and seemingly thick with dust. Several of the bedroom doors were open, but she hurried past without so much as a glance inside. At the end she remembered to turn left up the short staircase, which brought her to a stout door that was half open, uncovering a green baize door that was closed. She knocked at this second door, waited a moment or two, then pushed it open, discovering at once that Sir Edward was not there, nothing but cold darkness. And there was a patch of cold darkness in her mind now. She went down to the landing again and heard a horrid slithering behind one of the open doors. Her happiness a bright wreck, she felt alone and afraid. She began to run; the flame she tried to shield wavered dangerously; she had to stop to allow it to burn upright again. If this inch of flame vanished, she felt she might be lost for ever.

At the head of the main staircase, which looked large enough now for some ruined opera house, she began calling to him, telling him where she was, begging him to come and find her. But all that came back were echoes, strange echoes like so much mockery. Her final call became a scream, a scream cut off by a sob. For she knew then, with a desolate finality, like a blow delivered at the heart, that it was useless to call for Sir Edward, that he was no longer in that house, no longer in any world or time where her cries could reach him.

After the first ten minutes or so had gone by, Luke thought that at any moment Betty and Sir Edward might return. He was not surprised, however, when they did not come back; they were probably making long speeches at one another in some kitchen or pantry. He was not carrying a watch and there seemed to be no clock in this long room; he had to guess at the half-hour Julia asked him to wait. Finally, taking two candles for good measure, he went off to find the Library. He took two wrong turnings, along narrow passages, before arriving at the main staircase, which he had not seen before. After that it was easy enough to follow Julia's instructions, turning to the right at the head of the staircase and then going along the landing until he found the short flight of stairs. And there were the double doors she had described; he could see the green baize on the inner door.

"Julia, I'm here," he cried, all joy and excitement, with a vision of the two of them talking for hours in this Library, so remote and yet so snug and companionable with its calf-lined walls. "Here I am," he shouted idiotically as he charged in, "here I am."

The room was empty, bare, and had the damp chill of an endless winter. It had been a library once, for there were still some shelves on two of the walls and even a few shabby books heaped together in one corner. Cold ashes and a litter of half-burnt paper filled the grate. Patches of damp had not merely stained the walls and ceiling but had eaten into them. There was not a single piece of furniture in the room, only an old packing case. Nobody could have read a book here for the last thirty years. It was a room that had forgotten what human beings are like. Luke felt sick with misery.

He could hear the rain and the creaking of a shutter somewhere, and that was all. It was impossible to believe now that the room he had left, still bright with the image of Julia, was only two flights of stairs away. Terrible suspicions, for which he refused to find words, came creeping into the back of his mind. What if – once you left that long room below – you could take a wrong turning in time? Where was Julia? Where was she waiting for him with that coffee and brandy? He knew – and desperately wished he didn't know – that this was the Library she meant. He began shivering: there was ice squeezing his heart.

Then he heard steps, slow dragging steps but coming nearer. He could not move, only listen. The stairs creaked. Tremulous candlelight appeared in the doorway. His welcoming shout of "Julia!" was hope against all sense, and the hope died before the last echo faded.

"Luke," said Betty as she came forward, pale, her eyes deep-set and smudged, still dressed as she had been at the supper table but without the beauty she had worn then, not even elegant any longer, just a girl wearing the wrong clothes, "Luke, I thought it must be you." She stared about her for a moment. "Yes, I knew it would look like this. I think that's why I didn't come in before. I knew somehow." She looked at him. "Were you going to meet her here?"

"Yes," he said, looking away, towards the empty shelves. "We'd arranged to talk after supper, and she told me to come up here."

"That's what he told me." She spoke without expression, as a sleepwalker might talk. "And I came as far as the door. I think I knew then."

"Knew what?"

"That he isn't here – not now. And she isn't here either, of course." She shook her head slowly. "I'm certain now

there's nobody here but us. Not even that old woman –
though of course she was quite different from them."

"What do you mean, Betty?" He was rather angry.

"I mean," she said carefully, "that we might see her in
the morning. But we shan't see them. Not ever. Luke,
don't be cross. I couldn't bear it."

"You won't have to. I'm trying to understand, that's
all. And it was a hell of a shock when I charged in here
expecting to see her—" He broke off.

She nodded. "You needn't tell me. It happened to me
too. And that's something, I suppose – that it happened to
both of us. We ought to remember that. It's important."

"Yes, but what happened? And if we're going to talk,
let's get out of this morgue. Let's go downstairs – where
we had supper. That room's warm." He stopped there,
stared at her, changed his tone. "Or isn't it? Perhaps
that's just a cold empty dump too with nothing in it but
a couple of packing cases. But look – damn it!" he cried
angrily, "I'm still wearing these clothes – *their* clothes.
So are you. And we had supper together, didn't we, the
four of us – you don't deny that?"

"No, I don't." She sounded tearful. "But, please, Luke,
don't be angry about it all. Don't let's start quarrelling
again. I really couldn't bear it now."

"All right, I won't, Betty. I'm not really angry, certainly
not with you. But we did have supper, all four of us –
and you and he and I made speeches. Or didn't we? Am
I making that up?"

"You and he did. I didn't. How could I?"

"I thought you did – about what women wanted—"

"No, I just listened to you two. And talked to him a
little. But that doesn't matter now. Let's go down. We
can't stay here."

As they moved to the door, carrying their candles, Luke
stopped and pointed. "Look at that."

"What? I don't see anything."

He jabbed a finger at the wall. "An electric light

switch. And I never noticed any before." He tried it but nothing happened. "There's no longer a fitting in here, and probably the electricity's been cut off anyhow. Let's save two of these candles. Keep close to me, I know the way down."

"Did this house seem to you to get bigger and bigger?" she asked as they went down. "It did to me – just when everything began to turn sinister and awful. I think it was when there wasn't a proper time – when it wasn't *then* and hadn't got back to *now*."

"Don't let's start on that yet." He was silent for a few moments as he led the way. "I believe you when you say they're not here. I feel they're not here now. But we're still wearing these clothes – and we had supper in that long room – that I'll swear. So let's wait for more evidence."

They entered the long room at the opposite end from the table. As soon as they were inside, Luke exclaimed: "There you are! This hasn't changed. Same furniture. The fire's not quite out yet. It's exactly as I remember it. I left those two candles burning – there they are. Now let's have a look at that supper table."

It was the same table but it was not the same meal that had been eaten there. Only two chairs had been drawn up to it, not four, and clearly only two people had used these plates and cutlery. On the table were some remaining bits of tinned meat, a dry hunk of cheese and half a loaf of bread. Near one place was a small teapot, jug of milk, cup and saucer, and at the other an empty beer bottle kept company with a glass still laced with froth.

"But I drank wine," Luke protested, "and had soup, roast chicken—"

"I had pâté and an omelette," cried Betty.

"You couldn't," Luke began; but then he checked himself. "Let's go over to the fire. No point in staring at this stuff."

"These are exactly the same chairs," said Betty when

they reached the hearth. "Everything here's just the same as it was. What are you looking for?"

"A round tobacco-box and a churchwarden pipe. They were here before. I used them. But they're not here now." He poked around for a minute, while Betty sat silent. "Hello! Just what I wanted."

"What have you found?" She looked towards the sideboard.

"Five cigarettes in a packet. Right at the back here. They must have been here some time – very dry and dusty – but they'll do. Want one?"

"Yes, please. Hope it isn't stealing."

"We'll make it right with somebody in the morning."

They smoked for a while without exchanging another word, both of them staring into what was left of the fire. They had the air of being survivors after some catastrophe.

"What did you want to talk to her about?" Betty asked finally.

"Anything. Everything. It didn't matter. I hadn't planned a discussion. I just wanted to be with her."

"I did with him."

"Yes, I know you did," said Luke not unamiably. "We're both in the same boat."

"That's the one thing that makes it better," she said. "It would have been much worse if it had happened just to one of us. You're not feeling jealous about him, are you?"

"Not yet, though I think I could be," he confessed.

"You're not because you're not thinking about me – you're still thinking about her."

"Do you mind?"

"No, not yet," she said. "I'm like you. It's the same for both of us. We've lost them. And I'm certain neither of them can ever be found again. So here we are, to make the best of it."

There was so little light either from the fire or the

spluttering candles that they might have been sitting in the dusk of some warm cave. The night still sounded wet and wild; it was easy to imagine a new Deluge beginning out there.

"They never seemed ghostly to me, you know," said Luke, after an interval.

"They weren't ghosts." She was decisive.

"What were they, then? People in another time? I've read and heard stories about people going back in time."

"I was thinking about that," she said eagerly.

"But then they merely saw and heard things," he continued slowly, "as spectators. They didn't join in as we did. Talking, holding hands, having supper together."

"Look at the remains of that supper there. What a swiz! Typical of us and our time too."

"No, listen, Betty," he said earnestly. "We must get this bit right. You might be able to slip along the fourth dimension or whatever it is – and don't take me up on this, I'm very hazy about it – and then perhaps see people living a hundred-and-fifty years ago. But you wouldn't be really there with them, couldn't join in as we did. Otherwise, it would mean two different times – then and now – overlapping in a third and quite different sort of time, if you see what I mean."

"No, I don't really, Luke. It's much too complicated."

"I know, that's what I'm saying. It's worse than those two women at Versailles. But what *did* happen then?"

She waited a moment, then began very carefully. "This is what I think. There were two people, Sir Edward Somebody and his niece, Julia, who once lived here, and who looked and behaved like the two we saw tonight. We arrived here very tired and on edge, wondering what was going to happen to us, and then when we relaxed and put these clothes on – well, Sir Edward and Julia happened. But – no, please, listen, Luke, this is the difficult part and if you interrupt I may lose the thread of it – but we were never *really* with them. I mean, they hadn't an independent life, as real people have. They looked themselves – we didn't make up their appearance – but what they said and did was what we wanted them to say and do, as if we were playwrights and they were characters in our play—"

"Now wait a minute, Betty," he protested. "You're not going to tell me that Julia—"

"Yes, I am," she cut in sharply. "And Sir Edward too, though I hate to say so. Didn't they always behave as we wanted them to behave? Just think, Luke. I felt some of this at the time."

"You mean you've always wanted a Sir Edward?" he asked, puzzled and displeased.

"Not consciously, no," she replied, a glint of amusement in her glance. "But he must have represented important things I did want, mostly without my knowing it. Just as Julia, who was probably rather a dull girl, a Regency version of the dumb blonde, was all marvellous and magical to you. He made me feel like that, because that's what I was wanting somebody to make me feel. Not always – that's too much to expect – but at times. And all the marvellous and magical feeling you had about Julia belonged to you, came from some part of you that was beginning to feel frustrated. Don't you see, darling," she continued in a tone she had not used with him for a long time, "that we arrived here not only wet and cold and lost but feeling utterly frustrated and miserable, just angry bits of ourselves that had been worked almost to death? And the Sir Edward and Julia we met, not the ones who really lived here, were those parts we'd neglected and forgotten. So we acted in a sort of play with them. It all started because we put these clothes on and not our own. We had to behave in a different way. But we couldn't do it with each other so we had to have those two as well, to help us out."

"That doesn't quite work," he said, "though I see what you mean. He brought me the clothes. Or I thought he did.

Spoke to me too – I was still in my bath then. Didn't talk about style – that was later. Did you hear that?"

"Yes," she cried eagerly, "but all that was something, I'm sure, that I hadn't quite thought out for myself but that I'd already felt. Don't you see?"

"What I do see," he said, with a defiant air, "is that it's all very well for some Regency buck to talk about style and the grand manner in living. He could cope with it, I can't. But then I haven't got my foot on anybody's face, have to pay my own way, and no kids get up in the dark to make money for me in cotton mills and coal mines. If that's what his style depends on, he can have it. I'll still go tatting round pubs and cafeterias wearing a dirty shirt and oily pants. And you'll still be in the fish queue and the two-bob seats at the cinema. But nobody can say we're living on other people's daylight. Style my foot!"

"Yes, yes, of course we couldn't live like that," she cried, "but it isn't *style your foot*. He didn't say those things. How could he? *We* said them. You said them to me. I said them to you. That was the only way we could do it – to express what we must have been feeling deep down about ourselves and our lives. And Luke – please – don't be tough and aggressive about it. We've both had enough of that, and it isn't us, but all a dreary fake anyhow. Just be quiet and think for a minute or two, remembering what we were like when we arrived here and what you felt afterwards."

"We came in wet and snarling," he said slowly, "and then soon it was different." As he tried to remember all that had happened – and much of it was confused, incredible – he was aware of Betty watching him intently, although her eyes were invisible and her face nothing but a pale oval in that dusk of the cave.

"If people ever look back on us – our generation, I mean – and try to give a verdict on us," he said finally, "they'll have to say we had a hell of a lot of faults but at least we were trying to be honest. No pretence at all costs – that's been our slogan. No doubt we've gone too far—"

"Much too far," she cried. "I'm sick of this honesty that leaves everything looking small, ugly and mean. And there's plenty of pretence too – neurotics pretending to be tough, tired frightened people getting rough and sexy on gin. Sheer laziness and sloppiness too – the men can't bother shaving and finding a clean shirt, the girls won't take a bath and change their underclothes. Yes, I know it's all more difficult – nobody need tell *me* that – but if we only tried to stop shuffling round and slopping about, jeering at and cheapening life – if we brought to it energy and good humour and some sense of style—" And here she broke off.

He stood in front of her and took her hands in his; her hands were cold, so he brought them together and began to warm them between his encircling palms. "You felt a shiver down your spine then, didn't you?" he said softly. "So did I. It's a good thing both of us experienced whatever happened tonight. If it had been only one of us—"

"It would have been hopeless," she told him hastily. "It's because it happened to both that there's some hope for us. But love isn't just grabbing sex when you need it and sharing a bath and a frying pan. All women know that. You have to work at it, to build something."

"The trouble is," he said, "a fellow wants to knock off, to take it easy. Yes, I know, Betty, then he expects more than he's a right to expect. You can't dress a relationship in rags and kick it around, and then ask it to satisfy a sudden demand for glamour and glory. And if we stop making these demands, we may soon find ourselves in an anthill—"

"Oh – Luke – I'm sure you said something like that," she cried. "Don't you remember?"

"I remember a little time – part of a dream or some time that doesn't really belong to us – when you were a beautiful and bewitching being and I was a noble fellow, burning with poetry and waiting to show you a mind that would seem like an enchanted kingdom to you. Yes," he continued, "I remember all that and more, and I'll try never to forget. And because I'll know that you're remembering too, you'll always seem different from any other woman—"

"Oh – yes, my darling – that's what I've been trying to say—"

"What we can do I don't know, and I'm certainly not going to work it out tonight. But from now on, at least, the names of Betty and Luke Gosforth will not be found in any heats of the rat race. And now – for I'm certain we have this place to ourselves – I must find you a bed, dear Mrs Gosforth—"

"There's a large one in that room where I dressed," said Betty, and kissed him. On the way up, she murmured sleepily: "I still don't understand about these clothes and the old woman. And they're in this world all right."

"They are," he said, "and so, with luck, tomorrow morning ought to be able to throw some light on them."

It was not a morning to throw much light on anything; not raining still, but with water everywhere, and even the sunlight struggling through an atmosphere that seemed as much water as air. But it brought them a Mrs Rogers, a beaky, bird-eyed woman, one of those who cover an immense interior good-nature and desire to help with an appearance of snapping fury. She had come up from the village of her own accord; she finished drying their clothes, gave them hot water, and even contrived a rough-and-ready breakfast for them; but she never stopped giving a performance as a woman who had been press-ganged into a hideous service.

"She's a blessing and all that," said Luke, over his

boiled egg, "but we'll never find out anything from her."

"Yes, we shall," Betty declared, out of her experience of the vast ruinous underworld of London chars. "Just leave it to me, darling."

"I'd have to do that anyhow. In five minutes I'm off to buy some cigarettes and to find somebody who'll pull the car out of that ditch. And give this Mrs Rogers a pound – here you are, while I remember – but suggest she might split it with last night's old woman, if she can be found. By the way, did you ever understand anything that old woman said?"

"Not much," Betty replied. "But I'll get it all out of this Mrs Rogers, you'll see."

An hour later, they met in the small square hall, and as he lit the cigarette she had immediately demanded, Luke said: "I've got the bags out of the car and arranged for it to be lifted and gone over. I sent a wire to the studio. And there's a taxi coming in ten minutes to take us to the station. What's your news, woman?"

"Straight from the Rogers Service, darling," she replied. "The old woman we saw last night – Mrs Grashki, or something like that – is a Czech. She looks after this house but lives with a daughter next door to Mrs Rogers. Last night she was working late, luckily for us – and was actually sorting out a mass of old things. This house has belonged for centuries to a family called Periton – all baronets. The present Bart – Sir Leslie – is in the diplomatic service, so he's always abroad. Well, Mrs Grashki, who's obviously a character, thought we looked terrible last night and thought how much nicer we'd look in some of the old things she'd been sorting out. So she put some out for us. Then after filling our baths – both the boiler and the electric light plant aren't functioning – and scraping together a bit of supper for us, probably having a peep and a giggle at us, she suddenly thought she'd gone too far, took fright, and ran home. She was thoroughly soaked of course, found herself laid up with rheumatism, and sent an S.O.S. to Mrs Rogers, who nobly responded. I'm just saying," said Betty as Mrs Rogers marched in, "you nobly responded to Mrs Grashki's call for help."

"I did what I could," cried Mrs Rogers angrily, "but if you ask me, that Mrs Grashki's not all there – playing tricks like that at her age – and not the first neither. Thinks she's still abroad, that's her trouble. But Sir Leslie took a fancy to her, being abroad a lot too. That one there's Sir Leslie's grandfather – Sir Eustace," she pointed to one of the portraits. "And I could tell you some tales of him too."

"Darling – look!" cried Betty rather shakily. She had gone to take a closer view of Sir Eustace. He went across to stand by her side, and then he felt her fingers digging into his arm until they hurt. "There – don't you see?" And in a moment he did. The portrait of Sir Edward Periton was excellent, although the sitter's brown coat did not come out too well. The portrait of Miss Julia Periton was smaller and less successful, but the tumbling red-gold curls were admirably suggested, and her white Empire dress, with its pastel blue frill that went round the bare shoulders, was not badly done at all.

"Yes," said Mrs Rogers with some complacency, as she joined them, "there's some more – and I could tell you some tales of these Peritons."

"So could I," said Luke.

THE GHOST GOES WEST

(London Films, 1935)
Starring: Robert Donat, Jean Parker &
Eugene Pallete
Directed by Rene Clair
From the short story 'Sir Tristram Goes West'
by Eric Keown

Just three years after the worldwide success of *The Old Dark House*, the leading British film making company, London Films, shot what is now regarded as the second classic ghost movie: *The Ghost Goes West*. Curiously, where Hollywood had chosen to use a story set in England, London Films looked in the other direction and made a story which takes places mainly across the Atlantic in Florida. The tale concerns a Scottish clan chief who sells his old family castle to an American millionaire planing to rebuild the mansion in the US. What the American had not bargained for was the family ghost who is tied to the castle by a 300-year-old curse and reappears when it is re-erected in Florida. However, in the New World the spook is finally able to break the curse and bring together the present clan chief and the millionaire's beautiful daughter.

The producer of *The Ghost Goes West* was Alexander Korda who earlier that year had masterminded the landmark British Science Fiction film, *Things To Come*, based on the story by H.G. Wells. Korda again called on the services of the top Hollywood special effects designer, Ned Mann, who had worked on the

SF movie to create the supernatural illusions for the new picture. Equally illustrious was the film's French director, Rene Clair, who had previously tackled supernaturalism in *Le Fantome du Moulin Rouge* (1925) and would later film the picture that inspired a TV series, *I Married A Witch* (1942). Famed for rarely shooting on location and using mostly studio-built exteriors, Clair still managed to make Denham Studios where the picture was shot look remarkably like parts of Florida! The picture also offered a special challenge for Robert Donat, the tall, handsome former Shakesperean actor who was then rapidly becoming one of the leading British stage and film actors. Donat played both the clan chief and the ghost and several times confronted himself in sequences orchestrated by Ned Mann. The film, scripted by Geoffrey Kerr, and lightened with some sly elements of satire on American imperialism, was a big success with British and American cinemagoers – though it did little to enhance the reputation of the original author, Eric Oliver Dilworth Keown (1902–1963), a freelance writer who contributed to *Punch* for a number of years as well as writing the scripts for several B-movies and biographies of Peggy Ashcroft (1955) and Margaret Rutherford (1956). This reprint of his story which inspired the movie (still regularly re-shown on late night television) marks its first reappearance in print for almost half a century . . .

Three men sat and talked at the long table in the library of Moat Place. Many dramatic conversations had occurred in that mellow and celebrated room, some of them radically affecting whole pages of English history; but none so vital as this to the old house itself. For its passport was being viséd to the United States.

Lord Mullion sighed gently. He was wondering whether, if a vote could be taken amongst his ancestors – most of those florid portraits had already crossed the Atlantic – they would condemn or approve his action. Old Red Roger, his grandfather, would have burnt the place round him rather than sell an inch of it. But then Red Roger had never been up against an economic crisis. And at that moment, the afternoon sun flooding suddenly the great oriel window, a vivid shaft of light stabbed the air like a rapier and illuminated Mr Julius Plugg's chequebook, which was lying militantly on the table.

"Would you go to forty thousand?" asked Lord Mullion.

Mr Plugg's bushy eyebrows climbed a good half-inch. When they rose further a tremor was usually discernible in Wall Street.

"I'll say it's a tall price for an old joint," he said. "Well – I might."

Lord Mullion turned to the Eminent Architect. "You're absolutely certain that the house can be successfully replanted in Mr Plugg's back garden, like a damned azalea?"

The Eminent Architect, whose passion happened to be Moat Place, also sighed. "Bigger houses than this have been moved. It'll be a cracking job, but there's no real snag. I recommend that for greater safety the library be sent by liner. The main structure can go by cargo-boat."

The shaft of sunlight was still playing suggestively on the golden cover of the chequebook. Sadly Lord Mullion inclined his head.

"Very well, Mr Plugg. It's yours," he said.

A gasp of childish delight escaped the Pokerface of American finance. "That's swell," he cried, "that's dandy! And, now it's fixed, would you give me the the low-down on a yarn I've heard about a family spook? Bunk?"

"On the contrary," said Lord Mullion, "he's quite the most amusing ghost in this part of the country. But I shouldn't think he'll bother you."

"Anyone ever seen him?"

"I saw him yesterday, sitting over there by the window."

Mr Plugg sprang round apprehensively. "Doing what?" he demanded.

"Just dreaming. He was a poet, you know."

"A poet? Hey, Earl, are you getting funny?"

"Not a bit, We know all about him. Sir Tristram Mullion, laid out by a Roundhead pike at Naseby. He must have been pretty absent-minded; probably he forgot about the battle until somebody hit him, and then it was too late. The story goes that his father, a fire-eating old Royalist, got so bored at always finding his eldest son mooning about the library when he might have been out trailing Cromwell that when he was dying he laid a curse on Tristram which could only be expunged by a single-handed act of valour. Tristram rode straight off to Naseby and got it in the neck in the first minute. So he's still here, wandering about this library, never getting a chance to do anything more heroic than a couplet. And he wasn't even a particularly good poet."

Mr Plugg had regained command of himself. "I seem to have read somewhere of a ghost crossing the Atlantic with a shack," he said, "but that won't rattle a tough baby like me, and I doubt if your spook and I'd have much in common. How about having the lawyers in and signing things up?"

The S.S. *Extravaganza* was carving her way steadily through the calm and moonlit surface of the Atlantic. The thousand portholes in her steep sides blazed, and the air was sickly with the drone of saxophones. It was as though a portion of the new Park Lane had taken to the water.

Down in the dim light of No. 3 Hold a notable event had just taken place. Sir Tristram Mullion had emerged from nowhere and was standing there, very nearly opaque with surprise and irritation. His activities had been confined to the Moat Place library for so long that he could think of no good reason why he should suddenly materialize in this strange dungeon. That it was a dungeon he had little doubt. Its sole furniture was a number of large packing-cases marked "JULIUS PLUGG, ARARAT, U.S.A.", and they were too high for even a ghost to sit upon with comfort. Tristram decided to explore.

The first person he encountered in the upper reaches of the ship was Alfred Bimsting, a young steward, who cried, "The Fancy Dress ain't on till tomorrow, Sir," and then pardonably fainted as he saw Tristram pass clean through a steel partition . . .

Sitting up on high stools at the bar, Professor Gupp, the historian, and an unknown Colonel were getting all argumentative over the *Extravaganza's* special brown sherry.

"My dear fellow," the Professor was saying, "whatever you may say about Marston Moor, Naseby showed Rupert to be a very great cavalry leader. Very great indeed."

"Nonsense!" growled the Colonel. "A hot-headed young fool. Fairfax was the better soldier in every way."

"I tell you—" the Professor began when he became aware of a presence at his elbow – a handsome young man in the clothes of a Cavalier.

"Frightfully sorry to interrupt," said Tristram (for acquaintance with the young Mullions had kept his idiom level with the fashion), "but as a matter of fact I used to know Rupert and Fairfax pretty well, and you can take it from me they were a couple of insufferable bores. Rupert was a shockin' hearty, always slappin' you on the back, and Fairfax was a pompous old fool. As for Naseby, it was a hell of a mess."

Professor Gupp hiccupped. "Young man," he said reprovingly, "I am driven to conclude that you have been drinking to excess. It may interest you to know that I am the author of the standard monograph on Naseby."

"It may interest *you* to know," Tristram cried rather dramatically, "that I was killed there." And he faded through the black glass wall of the refrigerator with such startling ease that neither Professor Gupp nor the Colonel could ever face Very Old Solera again . . .

After the dazzle of strip-lights and chromium Tristram was glad to find himself out on the promenade deck, which was deserted. It was nearly three hundred years since he had been to sea, returning from the French Court in considerable disgrace, having lost his dispatches; but, aided by the traditional adaptability of the ghost and the aristocrat, he noted with unconcern the tremendous pace at which the waves were flying past and the vast scarlet funnels towering above, which seemed to him to salute the moon so insuitably (he was a poet, remember) with great streamers of heavy black smoke. As he paced the deck he meditated the opening rhymes of a brief ode to the heavens . . .

Meanwhile, in the the convenient shadow of Lifeboat 5, a stout politician was surprised to find himself proposing marriage to his secretary, who with a more practised eye had seen it coming ever since Southampton. He was warming up to it nicely. Not for nothing had he devoted a lifetime to the mastery of circumambient speech.

"And though I cannot offer you, my dear, either the frivolities of youth or the glamour of an hereditary title, I am asking you to share a position which I believe to carry a certain distinction—" Here he broke off abruptly as Tristram appeared in the immediate neighbourhood and leaned dreamily over the rail.

There was an embarrassing silence, of which the secretary took advantage to repair the ravages of the politician's first kiss.

"Would you oblige me, Sir, by going away?" he boomed in the full round voice that regularly hypnotised East Dimbury into electing him.

Tristram made no answer. He was trying hard to remember if "tune" made an impeccable rhyme to "moon".

"Confound you, Sir," cried the Politician, "are you aware that you are intruding upon a sacred privacy?"

Tristram genuinely didn't hear. He was preparing to let "boon" have it, or, if necessary, "loon".

The Politician heaved his bulk out of his deck chair and fetched Tristram a slap on the shoulder. But of course as you can't do that with a properly disembodied matured-in-the-wood ghost, all that happened was that the Politician's hand sank through Tristram like a razor through dripping and was severely bruised on the rail. It was left to the secretary to console him, for Tristram was gone.

And then, rumours of Tristram's strange interludes percolating through the ship, all at once he became the centre of a series of alarming enfilading movements. The young Tuppenny-Berkeleys and their friends, who had been holding a sausage-and-*peignoir* party in the swimming-bath, bore down upon him waving *Leberwursts* and crowing "Tally-ho! The jolly old Laughing Cavalier!" Cavalierly was the way he treated them. Sweeping off his hat to young Lady Catherine, he nodded coldly to the others and walked straight through his brother, a young Guardsman, who was to dine out on the experience for nearly half a century.

The main staircase was already blocked with excited passengers. At the top of it stood the Chief Stewardess, a vast and imposing figure. Just for fun (for he was beginning to enjoy his little outing – and so would you if you had been stuck in a mouldy library for three hundred years) Tristram flung his arms gallantly round her neck and cried, "Your servant, Madam!" The poor woman collapsed mountainously into the arms of a Bolivian millionaire, who consequently collapsed too, in company with the three poorer millionaires who were behind him.

At this point the Captain arrived and advanced majestically. To the delight of the company Tristram picked up a large potted palm and thrust it dustily into his arms.[1] Then, with a courtly bow to the crowd and a valedictory gesture of osculation, he disappeared backwards through a massive portrait of Albert The Good.

On the way back to No. 3 Hold he sped through the Athenian Suite. In it the new lord of Moat Place lay on his bed in his pink silken underwear, pondering on the triumph with which in a few months he would spring upon the markets the child of his dreams, his new inhumane killer for demolishing the out-of-date buildings of the world, Plugg's Pneumatic Pulveriser.

Tristram took one look at him and disliked him at sight. On the bed table lay a basin of predigested gruel. Inverting it quickly over Mr Plugg's head, he passed on to disappear into the bowels of the ship.

Blowzy Bolloni and Redgat Ike sat at a marble-topped table sinking synthetic gin with quiet efficiency. They had spent the afternoon emptying several machine-guns into a friend, so they were rather tired.

"I've given Bug and Toledo the line-up," Bolloin said. "It's a wow. Toledo's in cahoots with one of Plugg's maids and she spilled the beans. The stuff's in his new

[1]N.B. – Can't a ghost grip? I say it can.

safe in the library – see? Any hop-head could fetch it out. Is that oke?"

"Mebbe it'll mean a grand all round, eh?" asked Redgat.

"Or two." And Bolloni winked.

"That'll be mighty nice. You want my ukulele?"

"Yeah. But I got a hunch heaters'll be enough."

They called for another snort of hooch, testing its strength in the approved gangster way by dipping a finger in it. The nail remaining undissolved, they drank confidently.

In the library of the reassembled Moat Place, Julius Plugg squirmed on a divan and cursed his folly in not entrusting the secret plans of his Pulveriser to the strong-room of his factory. Only a simp would have asked for it by bringing them home, he told himself bluntly. But it was too late now to do anything about them, for he was roped down as tightly as a thrown steer. Also he was gagged with his own handkerchief, a circumstance which gave him literally a pain in the neck.

Mrs Plugg, similarly captive in the big armchair had shed her normal dignity in a way which would have startled the Ararat Branch of the Women's Watch and Ward Fellowship, over which she presided. Her head was completely obscured by a large wicker wastepaper-basket, and through it there filtered strange canine noises.

As for Hiram Plugg, the leader of sophomore fashion, he was lashed so firmly to the suit of armour in the corner that it positively hurt him to blink; for before the high rewards of ace-gunning had attracted Blowzy Bolloni to the civilization of the West he had helped his father with his fishing-nets in Sicily, and it was now his boast that he could tie a victim up quicker and more unpleasantly than any other gangster in the States.

At the back of the library Redgat Ike lounged gracefully

on the table with a finger curled ready round the trigger of a Thompson sub-machine-gun, trained on the door. He grinned amiably as he thought how bug-house the servants had looked as they went down before his little chloroform-squirt, the cook clutching a rolling-pin and the butler muttering he'd rung the cops already – the poor bozo not knowing the wire had been cut an hour before. Oh, it was a couple of grands for nothing, a show like this. Redgat couldn't think why every one wasn't a gangster.

Bolloni and Toledo and the Bug, who had been searching the panels for signs of the safe, gave it up and gathered round the prostrate form of Mr Plugg, who snarled at them as fiercely as he could manage through his nose.

"Come on, Mister," said Bolloni, "we ain't playing Hunt the Slipper any more. You'd better squawk where that tin box is *and* its combination. Otherwise my boy-friend over there might kinda touch his toy by mistake, and that's goodbye to that teapot dome of yours." He smiled evilly at Redgat, who smiled back and swung the machine-gun into line with Mr Plugg's bald head.

"Have his comforter out and see what he says," suggested Toledo. But, shorn of much pungent criticism of the gangsters and their heredity, all Mr Plugg said was, "There's no safe here, you big bunch of saps."

Most sailormen are practical and many are crude. Bolloni was both. Replacing the gag in Mr Plugg's champing jaws, he drew from his pocket a twelve-bore shot-gun sawn off at the breech and pressed it persuasively against Mr Plugg's ample stomach. With his other hand he took a firm grip of the magnate's moustache and began to heave.

"When you sorta remember about the safe," he said, "give three toots on your nose."

Who would blame Mr Plugg? Gathering together his

remaining breath, he let out a first toot which would have done honour to a Thames tug. He was filling up with air for a second one when suddenly the three gangsters sprang round as if stung. Painfully he turned his head, to see a strange figure standing by the bookshelves. (You've got it first guess. It *was*.)

Tristram hadn't noticed the others. He was poring over a set of Spenser when Redgat slid back his trigger, and it was not until a heavy .45 bullet tore the book from his hand that he realized that something was happening. A stream of lead was hurtling through him and turning a priceless edition of Boccaccio to pulp, but he felt nothing. He was filled only with resentment at such ill-mannered interruption.

None of the gangsters had ever seen a man take fifty bullets in the chest and remain perpendicular. The sight unnerved them. Redgat continued to fire as accurately as before, but the other three stood irresolute.

Before Bolloni could dodge him Tristram had picked up what was left of *The Faëry Queen* and brought it down with terrific force on his head, dropping him like a skittle. Boiling with rage, Tristram grabbed up *The Anatomy of Melancholy* and set about Toledo and the Bug. One of them discharged the shotgun full in his face, but not with any great hope – Gee! a ritzy guy in fancy-dress who only got fresher after a whole drum of slugs!

It was soon over. Redgat clung to his beloved machine-gun to the end, unable to believe that a second drum wouldn't take effect. But he, too, went down to a thundering crack on the jaw from an illustrated *Apocrypha* . . .

Tristram began to feel very odd. For a moment he surveyed the scene, not quite comprehending what it all meant. Mrs Plugg had swooned, which merely caused the wastepaper-basket on her head to drop from the vertical to the horizontal. Her son was clearly about to be sick. Julius Plugg, himself supine but undaunted, was making wild signals with his famous eyebrows to be released.

Then, something in his nebulous inside going queerly click, Tristram realized what was happening. At last he had been a hero. At last he was free. The hail of bullets had smashed up not only Boccaccio but his father's curse . . .

Debating, with the exquisite detachment of the poet, whether the Pluggs would be free before the gangsters recovered, he faded imperceptibly and left them to it.

TOPPER

(MGM, 1937)
Starring: Roland Young, Constance Bennett &
Cary Grant
Directed by Norman Z. McLeod
Story 'A Smoky Lady in Knickers' by Thorne Smith

Few series of ghost films were more popular during
the late Thirties and early Forties than those featuring
Cosmo Topper, the hapless American banker plagued
by the spirits of two departed friends, George and
Marion Kerby. Topper, a meek and henpecked little
man, was no match for the trendy and mischievous
couple – in particular the pretty, seductive wife –
and found himself drawn into one compromising
situation after another by the two ghosts. The first
picture in the series, *Topper*, was released in 1937
with the British-born actor Roland Young who had
made a speciality of playing whimsical, bemused
characters in the title role; the two spirits were
played by the wisecracking Constance Bennett and
the new heart-throb of Hollywood, Cary Grant. Under
Norman Z. McLeod's well-paced direction, the picture
was a huge box office hit and earned Roland Young an
Oscar nomination. Two years later a sequel, *Topper
Takes A Trip*, set on the French Riviera, was made
by United Artists which reunited the same team
with the exception of Cary Grant whose fees had
increased enormously during the interim. (He did,
though, appear briefly at the start of the picture in
footage cleverly lifted from the previous film!) Even

without Grant, the film was successful enough to generate a third in the series, *Topper Returns*, in which only Roland Young re-appeared, with ghostly Joan Blondell helping him to solve a murder. Described as "a splendid sendup of the Old Dark House Thrillers", *Topper Returns* was again excellently directed by Roy del Ruth. A decade later, the concept was revised once more for television by CBS who made 78 half-hour episodes in 1953–54 starring Leo G. Carroll (who became famous ten years later in *The Man From Uncle*), Robert Sterling and Anne Jeffrey. Both the original films and videos of the series have been shown in recent years.

Despite the number of Topper stories, the original creator, Thorne Smith (1893–1934), actually only wrote two books about the character: *The Jovial Ghosts* (1926) and *Topper Takes A Trip* (1932). Smith, the son of a US Navy Commodore, was for some years a journalist and struggling comedy writer, until the success of the Topper books. A number of his other novels have also been filmed including *Night Life of the Gods* (1931) and *Turnabout* (1932); while an unfinished manuscript, *Passionate Witch*, which was completed by Norman Matson and published in 1941, was adapted for the screen and filmed by United Artists as *I Married a Witch* with Frederic March, Veronica Lake and Robert Benchley, and directed by Rene Clair. The following episode, 'A Smoky Lady in Knickers' is from *The Jovial Ghosts* and recounts one of the early encounters between Topper and the beautiful ghost which launched a comic legend on the screen.

Mr Topper was in an unspeakable frame of mind. He shook himself free from the invisible grasp that had made a retreat of his departure, and fumed up the street, escape his one desire. And every time he passed a drug store a slight tugging at his sleeve informed him that he was not alone, that for him escape was impossible.

"Stop doing things to my sleeve," he growled. "Stop pushing."

"But I want you to buy me a soda," came the whispered reply.

"After all you've done to me you ask me that?" exclaimed the outraged man, for the moment forgetting his fear of being caught talking to himself in the streets. "Fiddling with my hat and stick. Giving my secretary a nervous fit. Why didn't you bawl and scream?"

"But you took such a long time in that horrid old place," the voice pleaded. "And that ridiculous woman looked at you so familiarly. I wanted to pull her ribbons off, but . . ."

"Let me understand this," interrupted Mr Topper, seeking refuge in a nearby doorway. "Am I no longer to dictate to my secretary? Do you object? By what right? I've never compromised you, although God knows you've ruined my reputation – you and your husband. Why don't you torture him and leave me alone?"

"He's left me," the voice replied with just a hint of moisture. "He's gone to sea for a change."

"He needs one," said Mr Topper. "Haven't you any friends?"

"None that I like as well as you. Please don't go on any more. It would be funny to see tears dropping from no place in particular."

The woman was actually hugging him in broad daylight. Mr Topper swayed forward, then with a supreme effort regained both his balance and his composure.

"Don't do that again, ever," he commanded.

"Let's be glad," Marion pleaded. "I didn't mean any harm. George was gone and I didn't have anything to do, so I just went down to the station to see the trains come in and then I saw you and I wanted to go along. It's awfully lonely being a low-planed spirit. You don't know."

Now there had been very little wheedling practised on Mr Topper in the course of his married life. Mrs Topper had arranged everything and Topper had followed the arrangements. On those rare occasions when he had balked Mrs Topper had instantly assumed the rôle of a martyred woman and in pallid silence cherished her indigestion. It was a strange, fearful and fascinating sensation that Mr Topper now experienced as Marion Kerby clung to his neck and asked him to buy her a soda. He forgot the humiliation of the office out of sheer sympathy for the poor, parched spirit who had been the cause of it.

"But hang it, Marion," he said in a softer voice, "be reasonable. How can I buy you a soda?"

"You can pretend to be drinking it," she replied eagerly, "and when you hold your glass aside to look at your newspaper I can sip through the straw. No one will notice it. Just hold your glass a little to one side and I'll come close to you and sip through the straw – little, quiet sips. But you must only pretend to be drinking it. Don't forget yourself."

"I'd rather risk the chance of a scandal and have you materialise," said Mr Topper thoughtfully.

"All right," replied Marion. "I'll do that in a jiffy."

"Not here!" Mr Topper protested. "For once show some restraint. Can't you go somewhere to materialise and then come back to me?"

"How about that shop?" suggested Marion.

The shop she referred to was a small notion shop which owed its existence to the fact that women, regardless of their means, must be clad in silk or near silk against the ever-present dangers of being run over, unexpectedly married or caught in a sudden gale. The shop seemed suitable to Topper for the business of materialisation. He said as much and Marion Kerby departed, declaring that she would be right back in a minute. Mr Topper waited ten before he became impatient, then he walked slowly past the shop and peered through the door. As he did so a hatless woman came bounding forth with stark terror gleaming in her eyes. She was speedily followed by a small boy, who in turn was closely pursued by a man whose features were working frantically. Before Mr Topper could recover from his surprise three girls dashed from the shop and joined their companions in flight, now huddled compactly at a safe distance from the shop. Mr Topper felt like running, too, but curiosity overcame his fear. He approached the group and asked questions. One of the girls looked at him and began to cry.

"Mamma!" she gulped. "Mamma!"

He quickly transferred his gaze to the man.

"What's happened in there?" asked Mr Topper.

"Don't go in, sir," pleaded the man, for the first time in his life discouraging a prospective customer from entering his place of business. "For God's sake, sir, stay here with us."

Topper looked at the boy.

"Little boy," he said, "tell me what frightened all these people."

"I'm not frightened," declared the boy, "but they all started to run and I just got ahead."

"Yes, but why did they start to run?" continued Mr Topper patiently.

"Because of her," said the boy, pointing to the shop.

"Of whom?" demanded Topper.

"The smoky lady who was trying on knickers and everything," answered the boy.

At this point the woman who had been the first to seek comfort in flight found her tongue. A crowd had begun to gather and she addressed herself to the crowd.

"She was all smoky," the woman announced. "And you could see right through her. How I first came to notice her was when I pulled back a curtain to show one of these girls some knickers. There she was, as calm as life, trying on a pair of knickers, a pair of our best knickers, and she was all smoky and transparent so that only the knickers seemed real. When she saw us she got scared and went bounding round the shop so that it looked like a pair of knickers come to life and gone mad. I started to run . . ."

"And I made a grab for the knickers," interrupted the man, "but the smoky woman wouldn't let go, so I just decided that, before any trouble started, I'd run out and see what had happened to Lil."

"It was awful," proclaimed one of the girls. "I'll never forget those knickers dancing round the shop."

"Our best knickers," said the woman.

"A good pair," added the man.

"Perhaps they are not a total loss," Mr Topper suggested. "Why not go back and find out? I'll buy the knickers if this smoky woman hasn't walked off with them."

As attractive as the offer was to the proprietor he seemed reluctant to accept.

"Come on," said Mr Topper. "I'll lead the way."

"But, sir, you don't understand," the man protested earnestly. "Have you ever seen a transparent woman dancing about in a real pair of knickers?"

"That depends on what you mean by transparent," replied Mr Topper judiciously. "Anyway, it's much better than seeing a real woman dancing about in a transparent pair of knickers."

At this remark the young lady who had been sobbing for mamma suddenly giggled and looked archly at Mr Topper. The proprietor seemed unconvinced.

"No, it isn't," he said, with a shake of his head. "Nowadays you can see that at most any good show, but not the other, thank God. It isn't what I call natural entertainment – not for me at any rate."

"And while you're standing here talking," Mr Topper

reminded him, "the smoky lady is probably trying on every blessed thing in your shop."

"Well, I'm not going back to watch her," the proprietor proclaimed to the crowd. "If any of you gents want to see a smoky woman trying on underwear you can step right in, but I don't budge without a cop – two cops," he added as an afterthought.

Mr Topper felt a soft, flimsy article being thrust stealthily into his coat pocket. His hand flew to the spot and shoved the thing out of sight. A gentle pressure on the arm indicated that it was time to depart, and a policeman, pushing through the crowd, strengthened Mr Topper in his belief. He permitted himself to be led away by his invisible guide. After several blocks of silent companionship he could no longer restrain his annoyance.

"Now what the devil do you mean by trying on a pair of those things?" he demanded.

"What a crude question!" Marion murmured.

"Your conduct has given me the privilege to ask it," replied Mr Topper.

"Cosmo," she whispered, leaning heavily against him, "I just love nice things."

"You should leave all that stuff behind you now that you're dead," he answered.

"Even spirits have to be modest," said Marion. "And anyway they frightened me. I was getting along fine until that woman pulled back the curtain. I was pretty nearly completely materialised, but that made me so startled I couldn't finish it."

"That was fortunate, to say the least," replied Mr Topper, "considering the condition you were in."

Topper heard a low laugh.

"You're vile all the way through," said Marion Kerby. "Here's a soda shop. Come on in – chocolate with vanilla ice cream."

Mr Topper felt himself being pulled in the direction of

the soda shop. He resisted feebly feeling that he had gone through enough for one day.

"Must you have that soda?" he asked.

"Oh, no," Marion replied in a resigned voice. "I can do without it. I'm used to being miserable. One more disappointment will make no difference. Keep me hanging round your office all morning, then send me in to a place to be scared to death, and after that refuse to buy me a soda. Go on, I like harsh treatment. You remind me of my husband, the low creature."

With the chattering courage of a man being placed in the electric chair, Mr Topper walked into the soda shop and seated himself at the counter.

"Vanilla soda with a chocolate ice," he muttered darkly in the direction of a white-clad individual.

"No! No!" whispered Marion excitedly. "You've got it all wrong. Tell him quick. It's chocolate soda with a vanilla ice."

Mr Topper could feel her fluttering on his lap.

"Be still," he whispered, then smiling ingratiatingly at the clerk he added, "I'm afraid, old man, I got that wrong. I want it the other way 'round."

The clerk looked long at Mr Topper, then walked to the other end of the counter and engaged a colleague in a whispered conversation. From time to time they stopped talking to look back at Mr Topper, whose anxiety was mounting with each look.

Marion Kerby in her eagerness was pinching Topper's hand. He pulled his newspaper from his pocket and hid behind it.

"You and your sodas," he growled. "Why can't you keep quiet?"

"But you had it all wrong," protested Marion. "Look out, here he comes now."

When the attendant had placed the glass on the counter Mr Topper idly reached for it with the air of one too deeply engrossed in the news of the day to be interested in a trivial beverage. Leisurely he placed the glass to his lips, then held it aside.

"The straws," whispered Marion. "Must have straws."

"My God," murmured Mr Topper. "Won't you ever be satisfied?"

He procured two straws, plunged them viciously into the soda, then held the glass behind his paper. The liquid immediately began to descend in the glass. From the rapidity of its descent Mr Topper decided that George Kerby had bought his wife very few sodas during her earthly existence.

"Now dig out the ice cream with the spoon," she whispered. "Pretend to be eating it. I'll nibble it off."

"This is going to be pretty," murmured Mr Topper with as much sarcasm as can be packed into a murmur. "You'll have to do better than nibble. You'll fairly have to snap it off."

The nibbling or snapping operation required the use of both of Mr Topper's hands and forced him to abandon the protection of his paper. With an earnest expression, which was perfectly sincere, he endeavoured to give the impression of a man publicly lusting after ice cream. The spoon flew to his avid mouth, but, just before his lips concealed their prize, the ice cream mysteriously vanished. It must be said in favour of Marion Kerby that she met the demands of the occasion. Not once did she fail to claim her own. Not once was Mr Topper allowed to sample that which he most abhorred. When the ice cream had run its course Mr Topper resumed his paper and waited, with a knowledge bred of experience, for the dregs of the soda to be drawn. He had little time to wait. Hollow, expiring, gurgling sounds loudly proclaimed the welcome ending of the soda. With a sigh of relief Mr Topper was about to return the hateful vessel to the counter when he met the eyes of the clerk peering at him over the top margin of the newspaper. They were cold, worldly eyes, yet curious, and they fixed themselves on Mr Topper like two weary suns regarding a newborn star. A nervous muscular reaction contorted Mr Topper's mouth into a smile.

"Do that again," the clerk said. "Do that trick again without me guessing it and I'll give you this."

He dangled some crumpled bills alluringly in Mr Topper's face.

"I can't," replied Mr Topper. "It's hard enough to drink one of your nauseating concoctions, much less two."

"You didn't drink the first one," said the attendant. "What's your game, anyway? I was watching you all the time. Trying to be funny?"

"Not funny," Mr Topper answered, delicately slipping from his seat. "You're wrong there. That was one of the most serious sodas in my life – one of the worst."

"You're one of those funny guys," said the attendant menacingly. "Come back here and I'll tell you exactly what you are."

But Mr Topper did not wait to be told. He hurried from the store and mingled with the crowd.

"It's awful to be cut off from sodas," breathed Marion Kerby.

"I have no sympathy to waste on you," said Mr Topper.

He was hungry, yet he dared not eat. If she had behaved so excitedly in the presence of a soda, what would she do at the sight of food. Mr Topper shuddered. He was thinking of a plate of soup. No, it would never do. He would have to forego luncheon. This was an overwhelming decision. It left Mr Topper shaken. Never had he missed a meal save when his adenoids had been surreptitiously removed many years before. Mr Topper gazed up at the lean cascades of the Woolworth tower through the tragic eyes of a deflated stomach. There was no fortitude in him. He was the abject slave of a passion he longed but feared to indulge. All his friends were eating luncheon now. He wondered what they were having. Menus danced before his eyes. The 'blue plate' of the day brought savoury odours to his nose. Strangely enough it was in this dismal crisis that Marion Kerby came to his aid.

"Isn't it time for your luncheon?" she suggested.

"Past time," said Mr Topper, "but how can I eat with you with me?"

"Food means nothing to me," she replied. "I can take it or leave it as I choose, but you're different. You must eat."

"I feel that way about it myself," admitted Mr Topper. "For once I think you're right, but, frankly, I'm afraid to enter a public place with you. My nerves can't stand it. Too much has happened."

"Come," she said in a changed voice, taking him forcibly by the arm. "I'm going to see that you get your luncheon. Don't bother at all about me. I'm different now. The city went to my head at first. I'll admit it. Those knickers and the ice cream soda got the best of me. I lost control of myself, but now you don't have to worry. Just a cup of tea – nothing more."

"That ends it," declared Mr Topper. "That's enough. I don't eat. I dare say you fully expect me to crouch under a table and hold a plate of tea while you make strangling noises."

Marion Kerby laughed softly.

"I was only joking about the tea," she said. "Honestly, now, I don't really want it. That's true. I should want it, but I don't. There was only one person I ever knew, not counting myself, who couldn't stand tea, and he was a fine but fanatical drunkard. Graze with the herd and I'll keep quiet."

So Mr Topper had his luncheon. It was a tense luncheon, a suspicious, waiting sort of luncheon, one filled with false starts and empty alarms. In spite of everything it was a good luncheon and Marion Kerby behaved splendidly. Once, when Mr Topper used the pepper too violently, a fit of sneezing came from the opposite chair. The waiter was momentarily startled, but immediately adjusted himself to the situation. He realised, as does everyone who knows anything at all about sneezing, that there are no two sneezes alike and that most anything can be expected of a sneezer. He regarded Mr Topper with the commiseration of one whose sneezes were infrequent and well under control, and departed in stately search of a pie à la mode. Nevertheless, he considered Mr Topper as being not quite the usual customer. He had noticed certain little things. Nothing you could put your finger on, but still a trifle different. For instance, why had the tray containing bread risen to meet Mr Topper's outstretched hand? And why had the salt stand behaved so obligingly? How could one account for a menu tilted in space? And, if that was perfectly natural, why had Mr Topper made such strange fluttering movements with his hands? Deep within himself the waiter sensed that all was not well with his table, but the clatter of plates, the demands of his occupation, and the deep-rooted instinct of all people to deny the existence of the unusual successfully maintained him in his poise of sharply chiselled indifference. The generous size of the tip he washed up in his obsequious hands completely restored his faith in the normal order of things. There had been nothing unusual. Mr Topper was a man who desired to dine. The waiter hoped he would do so more frequently at his table. The waiter was one of those people whose tolerance increases with the size of the tip. For a ten-dollar bill he would have respectfully tidied up after a murder and made excuses for the toughness of the corpse.

Later that afternoon Mr Topper was trying on a cap. He was a diffident man about such things, but on this occasion his heart was in his task. The brownish thing that was making his head ridiculous had vague, temporising lines in it of a nervous blue, but to Mr Topper the cap was lovely. To a man or to a woman he would have said harshly that the cap 'would do,' but to himself he had to admit it was lovely. He admired it hugely. It was a good cap. Mr Topper had no difficulty in convincing the salesman that it was a good cap. With suitable apologies the man agreed that it was a very good cap and that it suited Mr Topper well. Mr Topper found himself admiring the salesman. He knew his business, this man – one of the few salesmen with unimpeachable taste. The cap was practically Topper's. All the salesman had to do was to snatch it from Mr Topper's vainglorious head and wrap it up. Mr Topper was willing. He had never purchased such a cap in his life. With the eager timidity of a virgin he hoped to demolish the record of years. He was brazen about it, yet he was shy almost to the point of tenderness. The cap was in the salesman's hands. Mr Topper was reaching for money. The salesman's free hand was politely waiting for the object of Mr Topper's reaching. Then something happened. A new and different cap appeared in the salesman's outstretched hand. With the instinct of his calling he automatically began to sell the new cap. Then he stopped in confusion and looked helplessly at Mr Topper, who was convulsively clutching a roll of bills. Mr Topper refused to meet the salesman's gaze. Instead he glared at the new cap. It was a terrible cap, an obscene, gloating, desperate cap. Its red checks displayed the brazen indifference of deep depravity. Mr Topper was revolted.

"Take it away," he said. "I don't want it."

At this remark the new cap shook threateningly in the salesman's hand. He tried to give it to Mr Topper, but was unsuccessful. Mr Topper backed away.

"I don't want it," he repeated. "I don't like that cap. Please take it away."

The salesman was deeply moved.

"I'm not trying to sell it to you, sir," he said in a low voice, "but somehow I can't help it."

A Smoky Lady in Knickers

He stood before Mr Topper with a cap in either hand. One cap he held almost lovingly, the other he clung to in spite of himself, like a man with a live coal in a nest of dynamite. His lips trembled slightly. He tried to smile. He was mortally afraid that at any moment Mr Topper would depart with a bad opinion of the shop. He could never permit that to happen. With an effort he turned away, but before he had gone many yards he abruptly swung around and came back at a dog-trot. To Mr Topper he gave the appearance of a man who was being held by the scruff of his neck and the seat of his trousers by someone intent on motivating him from the rear. He stopped suddenly in front of Mr Topper and, in an attitude of supplication, offered him the red checked cap. Mr Topper again refused it.

"I must apologise," the man said rather breathlessly, "but I really think you had better take this cap."

In spite of his irritation Mr Topper regarded the salesman with quick sympathy.

"Why have you changed your mind?" he asked. "I've already told you that I hate that cap. It isn't a nice cap. I don't like it."

The salesman was almost chattering. He shook himself like a dog and glanced quickly over his shoulder. Then he approached Mr Topper.

"I haven't changed my mind," he whispered. "I've lost my mind. It isn't the shop. It's me. I'm mad."

Mr Topper was beginning to feel extremely sorry for the salesman. He wanted to do what he could, but he refused to be bullied into buying a cap he utterly loathed, a cap that went against all his instincts.

"It's too bad about your mind," said Mr Topper, "but I don't want that cap. I won't buy it. And if I do buy it I won't wear it. I'm honest about that."

"Listen," whispered the salesman. "I'll give you the cap if you'll only take it away."

"If you're as anxious as all that to get rid of the

cap," Mr Topper replied, "I'll buy them both. How much are they?"

"Practically nothing," said the salesman, his face clearing. "I'll wrap them up myself."

He hurried away.

"But I won't wear it," said Mr Topper, addressing space. "You won't be able to force the thing on my head."

"Here they are," announced the salesman, returning with the package. "You've been very nice about it, I'm sure."

As the elevator bearing Mr Topper to the ground floor began its descent a low gasp was heard in the car.

"I can't stand these things," whispered Marion Kerby. "They always take my breath."

At each floor the gasp was repeated, whereat Mr Topper cringed under the curious eye of the operator. Mr Topper pretended to gasp in order to protect himself. He smiled sickly at the operator and said:

"Did it affect you that way at first? It always does me."

The operator continued to look at him, but made no answer. He was glad to see the last of Mr Topper. He was afraid that the man was going to swoon in his car.

On the train that evening Mr Topper tried to hide himself in his newspaper, but was unsuccessful. Marion Kerby insisted on turning back the pages and scanning the advertisements. At last Mr Topper abandoned the newspaper and looked out of the window. Presently he became conscious of the fact that several passengers were regarding the vacant seat beside him with undisguised interest. The newspaper was slanted against the air as though it were being held by unseen hands. Mr Topper seized the paper and thrust it into his pocket.

"Rotter!" whispered Marion Kerby.

"Fiend!" muttered Mr Topper.

A heavy personage attempted to occupy the seat,

but arose with a grunt of surprise. For a moment he regarded Mr Topper bitterly, but that distraught gentleman was gazing at the landscape with the greedy eyes of a tourist.

At the end of the trip he hurried home. His day had been crammed with desperate events. There would be nothing for him at home save Scollops, but at present Mr Topper preferred a sleepy cat to an active spirit. He yearned for repose.

"Goodbye," said Marion Kerby as he was turning into the driveway. "I've had an awfully nice time and I want to thank you."

"Why did you make me buy that cap?" demanded Mr Topper.

"Because I knew it would look well on you," she answered. "George had one once and everybody liked it."

"Well, I don't, and I won't wear it," said Mr Topper. "Goodbye."

Marion Kerby clung to his arm.

"Don't be angry," she pleaded. "I've got to go back now and it's going to be lonely out there without even George to haggle with. Say goodbye nicely and call me Marion."

Mr Topper had a twinge of conscience. He was going away in the morning without even telling her about it. He was running away from her. Although he realised that he was in no way bound to Marion Kerby, he nevertheless felt guilty in abandoning her, particularly in the absence of her irresponsible husband. However, if he confided in her everything would be ruined. She would be sure to come along. He knew he would never be able to drive her off. After all, why should he not take her along? Then he remembered the events of the day and decided that there was every reason in the world for leaving her behind. He was going away for a rest and not a riot. With Marion Kerby with him rest would be out of the question.

"Well," he said in a mollified voice, "it's not going to be any too crisp for me at home, but I'll look you up in a few days. We'll take a ride together."

"Goodbye," she said, her voice sounding strangely thin and far away. "Don't forget. I'll be waiting for you."

The house had lost none of its funereal atmosphere during Mr Topper's absence. Mrs Topper was sitting in the shadows with her hands folded in her lap. She was the picture of resignation.

"Are you feeling better, my dear?" asked Mr Topper.

"I haven't been thinking about myself," she replied. "There are other things on my mind."

Mr Topper discreetly refrained from asking her what they were. He sat down and read the paper until the maid announced dinner, then he followed his wife into the dining-room, where the evening meal was consumed in silence. He felt like a convict being entertained by a member of a Christian Endeavour Society. Mrs Topper made it a point to see that he was properly served. She seemed to derive a sort of mournful pleasure in watching him chew his food.

When they were once more in the sitting-room Mr Topper announced the fact that he was going away for a trip. It was a difficult announcement to make and Mrs Topper was not helpful. She listened in silence until he was through, then she said without looking at him:

"I hope that for my sake you'll try to keep out of jail."

"It's not a habit," replied Mr Topper. "It was an accident, an unfortunate misunderstanding."

Mrs Topper bent over her sewing and compressed her lips.

"I'll never forget it to my dying day," she said. "The shame and humiliation of it."

"You could forget it if you wanted to," answered Mr Topper. "If you liked me instead of yourself you could forget a lot of things."

A Smoky Lady in Knickers

Mrs Topper regarded her husband with melancholy eyes.

"You ask me to forget that?" she asked.

"Come, Mary," replied Mr Topper in an earnest voice. "I don't know what got into me. I was all wrong, but just the same . . ."

He stopped and, pulling the knickers from his pocket, began to mop his face with them. They were orchid-coloured knickers heightened in attractiveness by crimson butterflies and lace insertion. They gave Mr Topper a foppish appearance. As he stood before his wife with his face nonchalantly buried in the silken fabric Mr Topper looked almost giddy. A new light came into Mrs Topper's eyes. It was the light of despair masking behind outraged modesty. At the height of his mopping Mr Topper must have realised the situation, for he suddenly withdrew his face from its tender concealment and peered at Mrs Topper over the knickers. Mrs Topper had risen. As she confronted her husband she was trembling slightly. He tried to speak, but she held up a restraining hand.

"I refuse to remain in the room and have you flaunt your infidelity in my face," she said. "Don't speak to me. Don't try to explain. Everything is perfectly clear."

"But I bought them for you," gasped Mr Topper. "They were to be a surprise."

"They were a surprise," replied Mrs Topper as she left the room recoiling from the offending garment. "They were a *shock!*"

THE UNINVITED

(Paramount, 1944)
Starring: Ray Milland, Ruth Hussey & Gail Russell
Directed by Lewis Allen
Story 'Samhain' by Dorothy Macardle

When premiered in the last full year of the Second World War, *The Uninvited* was the first major horror picture to have been released by a top Hollywood studio since the mid-Thirties. For some curious reason it was advertised by Paramount as 'The story of a love that is out of this world', but it was the terrifying shot of a glowing ectoplasmic apparition at the top of a flight of stairs towards the climax of the picture which sat audiences bolt upright in their cinema seats and later sent them away shivering into the night. The story of a brother and sister who buy an eerie old house on the Cornish coast and only discover after they have moved in the reason for it being so cheap – it is haunted by the ghost of a woman that can be sensed, smelt, heard and seen. Only with the help of a beautiful young medium are the pair able to tackle the malevolent spirit. The success of the picture owed much to the restrained acting of Ray Milland, Ruth Hussey and Gail Russell under the serious-minded direction of Lewis Allen, a British director then working in Hollywood, who sadly never quite reached the same ghostly heights again. Not even in the follow-up movie ordered the next year by Paramount entitled *The Unseen* which he co-wrote with Raymond Chandler and which also

starred **Gail Russell** along with **Joel McCrea** and
Herbert Marshall.

The screenplay for *The Uninvited* by **Frank Partos**
and **Dodie Smith** (the playwright famous for *Dear
Octopus*, 1938, and *I Capture The Castle*, 1952) was
faithful to both the contemporary evidence about the
nature of ghosts and the supernatural as well as the
original novel from which it have been adapted,
Uneasy Freehold by the Irish authoress, **Dorothy
Marguerita Callan Macardle (1889–1958)**. A lady of
fierce political beliefs whose involvement in the Irish
Nationalist Movement led to her being imprisoned in
Mountjoy Jail in 1922, Dorothy used her confinement
to good effect by writing a series of ghost stories and
launching her career as a writer. Apart from *Uneasy
Freehold*, she also wrote two other highly regarded
mystery thrillers, *The Unforseen* (1946) and *Dark
Enchantment* (1953), not forgetting a major study
of the political conditions in Ireland at that time,
The Irish Republic (1951). Dorothy first began to
explore the supernatural in the manner that made
The Uninvited such a success on the screen and as a
book (it sold over half a million copies in hardcovers
alone) in the short stories she wrote while in the
Irish prison. 'Samhain' is one of the best from that
now rare collection and with its presentiment of the
great novel to come, makes an ideal inclusion in this
volume . . .

It was only on rare and premeditated occasions that the
studio was visited by Una's old friend Andrew Fitzgerald.
He had been burrowing through his great work on Celtic
Etymology for so many years that "by the law of inertia,"
he said, he could not stop. But once or twice in a season
he would emerge, blinking, into the light and visit his
young friends. He came one April evening to meet Doctor

Christiansen, the Norwegian folklorist, and he was as happy as a Leprechaun talking of trolls and pooka and the Sidhe and Norse monuments in Ireland and the ship symbol in Brugh-na-Boinne.

Doctor Christiansen had been exploring the Gaeltacht and was full of delight in the people he had met.

"What is to me most charming," he said, "is their good friendship with their dead. I hoped much to meet a revenant, or a woman of the Sidhe – but alas, to a Norseman, she would not appear!"

Una looked at him reproachfully. "You are laughing at us," she said.

"Indeed no!" he replied quickly. "I have learned so much, I no longer venture to disbelieve. To me, magics and religions all are one, and all very full with what is true. And those people – they speak in good faith. It was in Kerry, more than anywhere in the world," he went on, "that poor, beautiful country, that they told me mysteries of the dead."

"Still, you thought the people credulous," FitzGerald said gently; "but you will not suspect a lexicographer of being fantastical. I, too, could tell you of strange happenings in Kerry – a mystery of the dead."

"Daddy Fitz!" Frank exclaimed, "how well you never told us you had seen a ghost!"

"But I saw no ghost, Avic," he replied, his crumpled old face sweet with a reminiscent smile. "If I had seen him, I think, truly, I should now be far away. I will tell you, if you like, what I heard."

"If you please!" begged Dr Christiansen eagerly.

"Please!" said Una. "Was it long ago?"

"Long ago indeed – when I was young. I was learning Irish at that time and I went to live in a small fishing village in West Kerry where the people had the language still – and had very little else.

I made the best friend of my life there; 'twas Father Patrick O'Rahilly, the parish priest, a middle-aged man, but white-haired, very delicate – the nearest creature to a saint I have ever known.

No life could be more lonely, I suppose, than that of an Irish priest in those desert regions of the west and south. This man had been a student and traveler in his youth – he had a very subtle, originating mind – and there he was, marooned among the poorest fisher-folk in existence – too poor himself to buy books. My coming, heretic though he found me – I was a sort of agnostic then – was a godsend to him; he made no secret of it from the first, and I was as welcome to the Presbytery as if it had been my home.

I rejoiced in the man and in his queer, desultory house; there was charm, life about it, though 'twas not old. It had been built a generation ago by a Father Howe. He had chosen the site for the sake of the grand view. Over Dingle Bay, you looked, through a gap in the trees, across to the mountains – mountains like mother-o'-pearl. To secure that he did what the folk said was a wrongful thing; he built on an old pathway that ran from the chapel to the ancient graveyard on the hill. That path had been disused altogether since the opening of the military road. He harmed no living soul, building on it; moreover he lived jovially, and died piously in his bed; all the same the people never gave up blaming his choice. "'Twas bad," they said, "to go meddling with an old path; there's them might be wishful to be using it still."

There was one old woman who used to beg Father Patrick with tears in her eyes, every time she met him, to take a house somewhere else. I remember the day his patience gave out.

"Maura O'Shea," he said sternly, "are you suggesting that a priest of God has cause to dread the vengeance of the living or of the dead?"

And "Ah, Father Patrick, dear," she replied in distress, "don't you know we'd stay out of Heaven itself, and Saint Peter bidding us step in, to do a good turn to you, alive or dead?"

They are people who know how to love and to speak out of the heart as well as out of the mind.

My coming brought the bad luck, so it seemed. All that Summer and Autumn one disaster after another broke on those unfortunate people, until, towards Samhain time, the last blow came – Father Patrick fell ill."

"Sah-wen?" Max repeated enquiringly. His tongue tangled always over Irish words. Dr Christiansen looked up, smiling:

"Your Festival of the Dead?"

"It corresponds, doesn't it, to the Feast of Balor?" FitzGerald went on: "Mananaan, the god of the under-world was potent then and it is a time of strange happenings in Gaelic countries still. It is then, in Ireland, that the living pray for the dead, invoking the prayers of the holy saints; it is then, old people will tell you, that the drowned come up out of the sea – they come to draw away living souls; there are footfalls you must not follow, knocking to which you dare not open; dead voices call . . .

The trouble began about July; 'twas the wettest July Corney O'Grady remembered, and he was ninety-five years old.

August was a month of storm; day after day passed and the little boats dared not venture out, while the pirating French trawlers, hardier vessels, came plundering the spawn-beds – destroying the harvest of the sea. The farms, no more than potato patches among the stones, which were the fisher-folks' last resource, failed them, too; the potatoes came black and rotten from the summer rains.

It was one of those seasons of heart-breaking tragedy which are recurrent on those Irish coasts where the people dwell in the Valley of the Shadow all their lives. By the end of Summer the spectre of famine had come.

I think that but for Father Patrick many of those poor souls would have boarded up their windows, as in the old days, and lain down in their bare huts to die; but he was with them like an inspired and inspiring spirit, giving them courage, energy and hope. He got an instructress from Cork to start a knitting industry and the girls worked hard, but they could get no price for the garments they made. And all the time the sky was pitiless. "You'd think," old Corney said bitterly, "God grudged Ireland the light of the sun."

The men began to get desperate. They saw the children growing wizened and sickly before their eyes. They were without milk, without flour, without even Indian meal. I don't think they cried or complained, the children, but they had not the strength to climb the steep road to the school. You'd see them creeping among the potato ridges, turning over the sods, in the hope that a good potato might remain.

The men took to going out in any weather at all – going twenty miles out to sea in their canoes, and they'd come home without having netted a fish. Many a time, at the pleading of a distracted wife or mother, Father Patrick went down to them to protest, but even he could not hold them now. "Sure, Father," they would answer, "there is death only before us anyway, and isn't it better go look for it on the water than bide waiting it on the black land? What good are we to the childer, and we walking the roads?"

The best boat in the village was owned by a grand old fellow named MacCarthy, his two sons and his son-in-law, Dermot Roche. There was a tribe of young children dependent on this crew, and I watched the demons of misery give place to the demons of recklessness in the sombre eyes of the men.

I troubled most about Dermot. The man attracted me strongly and had taken me under his protection from the first. He was a creature of fierce attachments; he loved me, I think, for my love of the Irish; he never let a word of English across his tongue. To my imagination he incarnated the spirit of that savage, primitive, gentle place; hard and gaunt he was as the rocks, protective as the hills; he seemed to know its terrible history "in his bones." I never saw him smile, but I have seen him glow with a kind of angry joy. He used to take me out fishing in the early morning to teach me the old ranns and proverbs that he knew I loved, and he would sing to me on the water wild old traditional songs in a rich voice that had a drone in it like the wind. He had a shy, smiling little wife, and half-a-dozen black-haired youngsters who seemed to live like sea-creatures among the rocks. Father Patrick had been good to the children, and for Father Patrick, Dermot would have faced the legions of Hell. In those famine days the man's face became terrible; his wife was expecting another child.

I was sitting at the round table in the Presbytery, that black September evening, reading with Father Patrick the ancient annals which were his delight and mine, when Dermot unlatched the door and came striding in – a man angry with his God. Father Patrick's gentle welcome was too much for him; he sat down and laid his head on the table and wept. Annie had given birth to a seventh child and died.

Father Patrick asked me to stay in the house in case any call should come, and went down with Dermot. He came back in the morning worn out, his habitual tranquillity gone.

"The men are losing hold of themselves," he said. "'Tis not right. Dermot's left the neighbors to wake Annie, and gone off with MacCarthy in the boat."

All that day a diabolical gale was raging. The boat did not come home. By dusk the people were huddling together, silent and ghastly, at the little pier; as long as daylight lasted there was nothing visible but the grey, murderous sea. At dawn they launched the life-boat and it came back at noon. Mat Kearney climbed out of it and passed up through the crowd. He answered me with a heavy gesture of his hand: "They're all away." His own son was in it – one of the crew of eight. They had found the boat upside down.

If Father Patrick had laboured before, he laboured after this like forty men; day and night, in wind and wet, he was in and out of the broken hovels, bringing what comfort there was to bring to forlorn old mothers and derelict young widows and starving families that had no man.

I sent an appeal to the Dublin press and to friends in Boston which brought us enough to keep Dermot's orphans and the MacCarthy's for a few weeks; after that, neighbours who had forgotten what it was not to be hungry took the children to their own homes.

Our language studies were all laid aside. When Father Patrick was not visiting he would be brooding and writing and calculating, trying to work out schemes. He knew little of the commercial world and I thought most of his suggestions impracticable; but one seemed sound. He began corresponding with traders in Cork and Dublin, trying to work up a market for carrigeen moss – a kind of edible seaweed which grows in the rock pools and can be gathered at low tide. He hoped to have a sale for it very soon. It could never, of course, bring in much to the poor creatures, but the work and planning kept them from black despair.

But all the time Father Patrick was struggling against illness, himself obsessed by a fear of breaking down. His people had no one else.

Then, near and far along the coast, washed up by the tide, the bodies of the drowned fishermen came in. One by one we laid them with the multitude of their fathers, seafaring generations, in the windswept graveyard beyond the house. And from each burial Father Patrick came home bowed as though under another load of care. Grief weakened him no less than the endless toil. I would have given all I had to take him away from it, to the South.

It was on the evening we buried Dermot that the

sickness came. I found him huddled in the chair in his parlour, unable to speak or move. His old housekeeper and I helped him upstairs and put him to bed and carried the red sods up to his room.

The doctor had to ride out to us over Brandon Mountain. It was that dreaded scourge of the poor, typhoid; a desperate attack. Every day for a week he came, and he and Brigid and I were fighting avenging nature for that dear life. On the last day of October he told me there was no more hope and that I should send for the priest. I went down the village street with him, looking for a boy to ride out with the message; the men were at the street corners, the women at their doors, waiting, dumbly, for the doctor's word. "Pray for him; pray for him!" was all he said. I heard men sobbing as they turned away.

Late in the evening the young priest came and gave the Viaticum to my dying friend. When he had gone and I went in to Father Patrick I found him lying very quiet with a happy radiance on his face. He held out his hand for mine. "Stay by me tonight, Andreas," he whispered. "'Twould be good to have you near when I set out."

You can imagine I felt desolate enough. For months this man had made the whole kindness of my world; I knew I'd never see his like again. And I had no resource. Bitterly I envied the good Catholic people with their boundless faith in prayer. They were praying for him that night, I knew well, in every cottage, and invoking prayers more powerful than their own – All Saints' – all Souls.

When I drew the curtains and lit the lamp at nightfall he asked was it Samhain night. "It is," I answered, and he sighed distressfully: "I ought to be praying for the dead."

There was a little oratory behind the bedroom where he used sometimes to say Mass. "Would you light the altar candles for me, Andreas?" he said. "That way they'll know I didn't forget . . ."

I lit a candle and walking down the draughty passage,

opened the oratory door. It was a bare little room with no adornment; there were only a few benches and the altar with its Tabernacle, four brass candlesticks and white cloth, but it was full, to my imagination, of rest. I lit the candles and then, surrendering to a sudden whim, it may be of faith, I prayed. I suppose it was a pagan sort of prayer.

When I went back to Father Patrick his eyes were closed and his breathing was so faint that I thought he had died, until I saw his fingers move feebly along his rosary beads.

There was nothing that I could do but sit in the old chair by the fire putting fresh sods on from time to time, giving him a drink when I saw that he was awake. About midnight he began moaning; his face had grown grey and wan, and his fingers were groping about the quilt. I could see that he was in high fever. "What will they do at all?" he kept murmuring unhappily, and "I ought to be praying for the dead . . ." Then: "Pray that I'll be spared to them awhile, Andreas;" and again, moaning: "God pity him, he can't pray!"

I knew that he could scarcely live till dawn.

Then the trance-like silence fell again, broken only by the long, wailing gusts of a wind that seemed to blow out of infinity and into infinity again, like a human soul.

We forget, thank God, those intensities of desolation. I only know that the sense of Eternity, always appalling, fell on me in that quiet room – and to me, Eternity was a void. The weak, insane moment in which I had prayed was over . . . the bright flame that had been my friend's spirit was going out . . . after life there was only the Abyss . . . and I could not hold him back; I knew no way . . .

It was an hour or two after midnight, I suppose, when I roused myself and drank some black coffee and went over to my patient to see whether he slept.

He was awake; his eyes were open; he was listening –

listening to something which I did not hear. He did not look up at me or speak or move.

I stood, wondering, beside the bed, and presently a sound came to my ears – faintly – a low, rhythmic murmur, like a multitude of voices at prayer. I listened and gradually I heard clearly, much more clearly – a soothing and entrancing sound. It came from the room behind the bedroom – the oratory. I leaned, listening, against the wall. It was prayer; I heard the prayers and responses – but not in Latin – it was Irish – I knew the soft, rich sounds.

I suppose the language was my only passion – maybe I loved it better, even, than my friend; anyhow, in the mere joy and wonder of hearing it I became oblivious of everything else. Soon every syllable came to me, full and clear; I heard a long unfamiliar litany, full of noble phrases and ancient names – "Naov Finghin . . . Naov Breandan . . . Naov Colmcille . . ." and, after the litany, prayers, long and ceremonious – the whole Mass.

While it lasted I stood spellbound, but when silence came I felt shaken with awful fear; I knelt down, suddenly, by the bed and stared at Father Patrick's face. His eyes were wide open; his lips were moving in quiet prayer; the flush of fever had gone; he seemed to have forgotten me; he said "Amen!"

From the oratory too, I heard a long "Amen," like a contented sigh. I heard the sound of people rising from their knees, and their footsteps, soft and light, as of an innumerable multitude, went past the door. I heard them after a moment on the gravel outside, and low voices began caoining mournfully until a man's voice called quietly, "Na bi ag caoineadh anois" – "Do not be caoining now!" That voice was strangely familiar; caught by it, as one's whole being may be caught by intolerable agony or joy, I waited, in a kind of rigour, for it to come again. I heard it, then – calling my own name, strongly and insistently, three times.

I would have risen; I would have opened the door and rushed out, but Father Patrick's arm was around me, his hand pressed over my mouth. "Don't answer," he whispered urgently, and held me until the noises had passed away.

He lay back on his pillow then, and smiled at me happily, and fell asleep."

FitzGerald, too, smiled happily as he ended his tale. He was tired. Doctor Christiansen's blue eyes were alight. "It was poor Dermot," he asked gently – "He who called?"

FitzGerald answered, "It was his voice."

"He would have loved to take you, instead of that other? If you had answered – is it not so – you would have followed within a year?"

"So Father Patrick said."

"And he recovered – your good friend?"

"Thank God," FitzGerald answered, "he is living still."

Doctor Christiansen spoke wonderingly, "They prayed for him well, those Dead."

DEAD OF NIGHT

(Ealing Films, 1945)
Starring: Mervyn Johns, Michael Redgrave
& Sally Ann Howes
Directed by Alberto Cavalcanti
Story 'The Extraordinarily Horrible Dummy'
by Gerald Kersh

Just as there had been a hiatus of supernatural films in America between the mid-Thirties and early Forties, so the same was true in Britain. And by coincidence, the gap was also filled in 1944 with the making of *The Halfway House*, a foreboding and strongly atmospheric ghost story from Ealing Studios about a father and daughter, killed when their inn in Wales was bombed, whose spirits help a group of world-weary travellers to a greater acceptance of their lot. Although clearly intended to inspire audiences in wartime Britain to self-sacrifice and the preservation of human values, it also – to quote one later evaluation – "works simply as one of the cinema's small group of effective ghost stories". Directed by Basil Dearden and starring the real-life father and daughter, Mervyn and Glynis Johns as the innkeepers who cast no shadows, it also foreshadowed a picture from the same studio the following year, *Dead of Night*, which has since became a cult classic and the first of the 'anthology films' which feature groups of interconnected stories. Both Mervyn Johns and Sally Ann Howes, who played one of the stranded travellers in Wales, reappeared in the 1945 production, of which critic Philip Jenkinson has written unequivocally, "It is one of the best supernatural movies and certainly the most ingenious at dovetailing five different stories into a neat – and finally chilling – package."

The various stories in *Dead of Night* were linked by Mervyn Johns as a guest at a country house who is plunged into a living nightmare when he discovers that everyone else staying there has a sinister connection with his past. Indeed, such was the unsettling nature of the film that there were fears that it might be banned because audiences had already suffered a great deal of real trauma during the war. As it was the Censor gave *Dead of Night* a certificate for showing to 'Adults Only' and it soon began to earn widespread critical acclaim. Writing of the picture's influence, cinema historian A.R. Morlan has said, "This wonderful film not only predated anthology/supernatural shows like *Twilight Zone*, *Alfred Hitchcock Presents*, *Thriller* and *Night Gallery*, but established the basic format of the horror/supernatural anthology." Each episode in *Dead of Night* was, in fact, based on a short story by a leading writer of fantasy fiction including H.G. Wells, John Baines, E.F. Benson, Angus MacPhail and Gerald Kersh (1911–1968). Kersh, who had served as a Coldstream Guardsman during the war and made his literary reputation with *They Die With Their Boots Clean* (1942), was also an accomplished writer of supernatural stories which were later collected in volumes such as *The Brighton Monster* (1953), *Men Without Bones* (1955) and *Nightshade and Damnations* (1968). His tale, "The Extraordinarily Horrible Dummy", published in 1944, provided the inspiration for undoubtedly the best episode in *Dead of Night*, a heavily expressionistic sequence in which Michael Redgrave played a ventriloquist dominated by his dummy. It makes just as unforgettable reading on the printed page as is did on the screen underscored by George Auric's ominous soundtrack . . .

Gerald Kersh

*

An uneasy conviction tells me that this story is true, but I hate to believe it. It was told to me by Ecco, the ventriloquist, who occupied a room next to mine in Busto's apartment-house. I hope he lied. Or perhaps he was mad? The world is so full of liars and lunatics, that one never knows what is true and what is false.

All the same, if ever a man had a haunted look, that man was Ecco. He was small and furtive. He had unnerving habits: five minutes of his company would have set your nerves on edge. For example: he would stop in the middle of a sentence, say *Ssh!* in a compelling whisper, look timorously over his shoulder, and listen to something: The slightest noise made him jump. Like all Busto's tenants, he had come down in the world. There had been a time when he topped bills and drew fifty pounds a week. Now, he lived by performing to theatre queues.

And yet he was the best ventriloquist I have ever heard. His talent was uncanny. Repartee cracked back and forth without pause, and in two distinct voices. There were even people who swore that his dummy was no dummy, but a dwarf or small boy with painted cheeks, trained in ventriloquial backchat. But this was not true. No dummy was ever more palpably stuffed with sawdust. Ecco called it Micky; and his act, *Micky and Ecco*.

All ventriloquists' dummies are ugly, but I have yet to see one uglier than Micky. It had a home-made look. There was something disgustingly avid in the stare of its bulging blue eyes, the lids of which clicked as it winked; and an extraordinarily horrible ghoulishness in the smacking of its great, grinning, red wooden lips. Ecco carried Micky with him wherever he went, and even slept with it. You would have felt cold at the sight of Ecco, walking upstairs, holding Micky at arm's length. The dummy was large and robust; the man was small and wraith-like; and in a

104

bad light you would have thought: *The dummy is leading the man!*

I said he lived in the next room to mine. But in London, you may live and die in a room, and the man next door may never know. I should never have spoken to Ecco, but for his habit of practising ventroliquism by night. It was nerve-racking. At the best of times it was hard to find rest under Busto's roof; but Ecco made night hideous, really hideous. You know the shrill, false voice of the ventriloquist's dummy? Micky's voice was not like that. It was shrill, but querulous; thin, but real – not Ecco's voice distorted, but a *different* voice. You would have sworn that there were two people quarrelling. *This man is good*, I thought. Then: *But this man is perfect!* And at last, there crept into my mind this sickening idea: *There are two men!*

In the dead of night, voices would break out:

"Come on, try again!" – "I can't!" – "You must." – "I want to go to sleep." – "Not yet; try again!" – "I'm tired, I tell you; I can't!" – "And I say try again". Then there would be peculiar singing noises, and at length Ecco's voice would cry: "You devil! You devil! Let me alone, in the name of God!"

One night, when this had gone on for three hours, I went to Ecco's door, and knocked. There was no answer. I opened the door. Ecco was sitting there, grey in the face, with Micky on his knee. "Yes?" he said. He did not look at me, but the great, painted eyes of the dummy stared straight into mine.

I said: "I don't want to seem unreasonable, but this noise . . ."

Ecco turned to the dummy, and said: "We're annoying the gentleman. Shall we stop."

Micky's dead red lips snapped as he replied: "Yes. Put me to bed."

Ecco lifted him. The stuffed legs of the dummy flapped lifelessly as the man laid him on the divan, and covered him with a blanket. He pressed a spring. *Snap!* – the eyes closed. Ecco drew a deep breath, and wiped sweat from his forehead.

"Curious bedfellow," I said.

"Yes," said Ecco. "But . . . please—" And he looked at Micky, frowned at me, and laid a finger to his lips. "*Ssh!*" he whispered.

"How about some coffee," I suggested.

He nodded. "Yes: my throat is very dry," he said. I beckoned. That disgusting stuffed dummy seemed to charge the atmosphere with tension. He followed me on tiptoe, and closed his door silently. As I boiled water on my gas-ring, I watched him. From time to time he hunched his shoulders, raised his eyebrows, and listened. Then, after a few minutes of silence, he said, suddenly: "You think I'm mad."

"No," I said, "not at all; only you seem remarkably devoted to that dummy of yours."

"I hate him," said Ecco, and listened again.

"Then why don't you burn the thing?"

"For God's sake!" cried Ecco, and clasped a hand over my mouth. I was uneasy – it was the presence of this terribly nervous little man that made me so. We drank our coffee, while I tried to make conversation.

"You must be an extraordinarily fine ventriloquist," I said.

"Me? No, not very. My father, yes. He was great. You've heard of Professor Vox? Yes, well he was my father."

"Was he, indeed?"

"He taught me all I know; and even now . . . I mean . . . without him, you understand – nothing! He was a genius. Me, I could never control the nerves of my face and throat. So you see, I was a great disappointment to him. He . . . well, you know; he could eat a beefsteak, while Micky, sitting at the same table, sang *Je crois entendre encore*. That was genius. He used to make me practise, day in and day out – *Bee, Eff, Em, En, Pe, Ve, Doubleyou*, without moving the lips. But I was no good. I couldn't do it. I simply couldn't. He used to give me hell. When I was a child, yes, my mother used to protect me a little. But afterwards! Bruises – I was black with them. He was a terrible man. Everybody was afraid of him. You're too young to remember: he looked like – well, look."

Ecco took a wallet out and extracted a photograph. It was brown and faded, but the features of the face were still vivid. Vox had a bad face; strong but evil – fat, swarthy, bearded and forbidding. His huge lips were pressed firmly together under a heavy black moustache, which grew right up to the sides of a massive flat nose. He had immense eyebrows, which ran together in the middle; and great, round, glittering eyes.

"You can't get the impression," said Ecco, "but when he came on to the stage in a black cloak lined with red silk, he looked just like the devil. He took Micky with him wherever he went – they used to talk in public. But he was a great ventriloquist – the greatest ever. He used to say: 'I'll make a ventriloquist of you if it's the last thing I ever do'. I had to go with him wherever he went, all over the world; and stand in the wings, and watch him; and go home with him at night and practise again – *Bee, Eff, Em, En, Pe, Ve, Doubleyou* – over and over again, sometimes till dawn. You'll think I'm crazy."

"Why should I?"

"Well . . . This went on and on, until – *ssh* – did you hear something?"

"No, there was nothing. Go on."

"One night I . . . I mean, there was an accident. I – he fell down the lift-shaft in the Hotel Dordogne, in Marseilles. Somebody left the gate open. He was killed." Ecco wiped sweat from this face. "And that night I slept well, for the first time in my life. I was twenty years old then. I went to sleep, and slept well. And then I had a horrible dream. He was back again, see? Only not he, in the flesh; but only his voice. And he was saying: 'Get up, get up, get up and try again, damn you; get up I say – I'll make a ventriloquist of you if it's the last thing I ever do. Wake up!'

"I woke up. You will think I'm mad.

"I swear. I still heard the voice; and it was coming from . . ."

Ecco paused and gulped. I said: "Micky?" He nodded. There was a pause; then I said: "Well?"

"That's about all," he said. "It was coming from Micky. It has been going on ever since; day and night. He won't let me alone. It isn't I who makes Micky talk. Micky makes me talk. He makes me practise still . . . day and night. I daren't leave him. He might tell the . . . he might . . . oh, God; anyway, I can't leave him . . . I can't."

I thought: *This poor man is undoubtedly mad. He has got the habit of talking to himself, and he thinks—*

At that moment, I heard a voice; a little, thin, querulous, mocking voice, which seemed to come from Ecco's room. It said:

"Ecco!"

Ecco leapt up, gibbering with fright. "There!" he said. "There he is again. I must go. I'm not mad; not really mad. I must—"

He ran out. I heard his door open and close. Then there came again the sound of conversation, and once I thought I heard Ecco's voice, shaking with sobs, saying: *"Bee, Eff, Em, En, Pe, Ve, Doubleyou . . ."*

He is crazy, I thought; *yes, the man must be crazy . . . And before he was throwing his voice . . . calling himself . . .*

But it took me two hours to convince myself of that; and I left the light burning all that night, and I swear to you that I have never been more glad to see the dawn.

NIGHT OF THE DEMON

(Columbia, 1958)
Starring: Dana Andrews, Peggy Cummins &
Niall MacGinnis
Directed by Jacques Tourneur
Based on 'Casting The Runes' by M.R. James

The success of *Dead of Night* prompted a sequence of ghost movies based on literary classics in the early post war years. The first of these was MGM's adaptation of the Oscar Wilde comedy novella, *The Canterville Ghost* (1945), followed by the first supernatural film to be made in technicolour, a version of Noel Coward's stage play, *Blithe Spirit*, about a writer whose second marriage is threatened by the appearance of his first wife's ghost, which starred Rex Harrison, Kay Hammond and Constance Cummins. Two years after this, no less than four supernatural pictures were released in Britain: *The Ghosts of Berkeley Square* from the novel by Caryl Brahms and S.J. Simon about two 18th century military ghosts played by Robert Morley and Felix Aylmer; *Night Comes Too Soon* based on Bulwer Lytton's 19th Century classic *The Haunted and the Haunters*; *Things Happen At Night* from Frank Harvey's contemporary thriller, *The Poltergeist*; and *The Ghost and Mrs Muir* from R.A. Dick's novel about a 'spiritual love affair' between a lonely young widow (Gene Tierney) and the ghost of an old sea captain (Rex Harrison again!). With the success of these pictures at the box office it is a surprise that it was not until the late Fifties that a movie based on the work of England's pre-eminent ghost story writer, M.R. James, finally made it to the screen.

Night of the Demon was adapted by Charles Bennett and Hal Chester from James's story 'Casting The Runes' about an ancient parchment inscribed with runic symbols which can be used to summon demonic beings from beyond time and space. The movie was directed with subtlety and sophistication by the French-born director, Jacques Tourneur, who had learnt his craft in Hollywood working with the cinema's great *horror-meister*, Val Lewton. Although it was Tourneur's intention never to show the demon on the screen – but leave it to the viewer's imagination – Columbia insisted on the insertion of a glimpse of the monster. And, according to cinema historian Geoff Brown, "They ran up a demon costume, plonked a man inside it, and devised lurid close-ups of its feet and claws – shots which seem to belong to another film entirely." Nevertheless, the stylish acting of Dana Andrews and Peggy Cummins (something of a ghost story veteran after her splendid appearance in *Blithe Spirit*) kept audiences on the edges of their seats. Unfortunately, the author, Montague Rhodes James (1862–1936), the former Provost of Eton who began devising tales of the supernatural to entertain friends at Christmas gatherings and has since come to be regarded as arguably the finest ghost story writer of this century, was not alive to pass his judgement on the picture. Curiously, despite the success of *Night of the Demon*, no other film company has made a story by James, although his work has frequently been adapted for television and shown – most appropriately – at Christmas.

'April 15th, 190—.
DEAR SIR,
I am requested by the Council of the — Association to return to you the draft of a paper on *The Truth of Alchemy*, which you have been good enough to offer to read at our forthcoming meeting, and to inform you that the Council do not see their way to including it in the programme.
I am,

Yours faithfully,
— *Secretary.'*

'April 18th.

DEAR SIR,
I am sorry to say that my engagements do not permit of my affording you an interview on the subject of your proposed paper. Nor do our laws allow of your discussing the matter with a Committee of our Council, as you suggest. Please allow me to assure you that the fullest consideration was given to the draft which you submitted, and that it was not declined without having been referred to the judgment of a most competent authority. No personal question (it can hardly be necessary for me to add) can have had the slightest influence on the decision of the Council.

Believe me (*ut supra*).'

'April 20th.

The Secretary of the Association begs respectfully to inform Mr Karswell that it is impossible for him to communicate the name of any person or persons to whom the draft of Mr Karswell's paper may have been submitted; and further desires to intimate that he cannot undertake to reply to any further letters on this subject.'

*

"And who *is* Mr Karswell?" inquired the Secretary's wife. She had called at his office, and (perhaps unwarrantably) had picked up the last of these three letters, which the typist has just brought in.

"Why, my dear, just at present Mr Karswell is a very angry man. But I don't know much about him otherwise, except that he is a person of wealth, his address is Lufford Abbey, Warwickshire, and he's an alchemist, apparently, and wants to tell us all about it; and that's about all – except that I don't want to meet him for the next week or two. Now, if you're ready to leave this place, I am."

"What have you been doing to make him angry?" asked Mrs Secretary.

"The usual thing, my dear, the usual thing: he sent in a draft of a paper he wanted to read at the next meeting, and we referred it to Edward Dunning – about the only man in England who knows about these things – and he said it was perfectly hopeless, so we declined it. So Karswell has been pelting me with letters ever since. The last thing he wanted was the name of the man we referred his nonsense to; you saw my answer to that. But don't you say anything about it, for goodness' sake."

"I should think not, indeed. Did I ever do such a thing? I do hope, though, he won't get to know that it was poor Mr Dunning."

"Poor Mr Dunning? I don't know why you call him that; he's a very happy man, is Dunning. Lots of hobbies and a comfortable home, and all his time to himself."

"I only meant I should be sorry for him if this man got hold of his name, and came and bothered him."

"Oh, ah! yes, I daresay he would be poor Mr Dunning then."

*

The Secretary and his wife were lunching out, and the friends to whose house they were bound were Warwickshire people. So Mrs Secretary had already settled it in her own mind that she would question them judiciously about Mr Karswell. But she was saved the trouble of leading up to the subject, for the hostess said to the host, before many minutes had passed, "I saw the Abbot of Lufford this morning." The host whistled. *"Did* you? What in the world brings him up to town?" "Goodness knows; he was coming out of the British Museum gate as I drove past." It was not unnatural that Mrs Secretary should inquire whether this was a real Abbot who was being spoken of. "Oh no, my dear: only a neighbour of ours in the country who bought Lufford Abbey a few years ago. His real name is Karswell." "Is he a friend of yours?" asked Mr Secretary, with a private wink to his wife. The question let loose a torrent of declamation. There was really nothing to be said for Mr Karswell. Nobody knew what he did with himself: his servants were a horrible set of people; he had invented a new religion for himself, and practised no one could tell what appalling rites; he was very easily offended, and never forgave anybody: he had a dreadful face (so the lady insisted, her husband somewhat demurring); he never did a kind action, and whatever influence he did exert was mischievous. "Do the poor man justice, dear," the husband interrupted. "You forget the treat he gave the school children." "Forget it, indeed! But I'm glad you mentioned it, because it gives an idea of the man. Now, Florence, listen to this. The first winter he was at Lufford this delightful neighbour of ours wrote to the clergyman of his parish (he's not ours, but we know him very well) and offered to show the school children some magic-lantern slides. He said he had some new kinds, which he thought would interest them. Well, the clergyman was rather surprised, because Mr Karswell had shown himself inclined to be unpleasant to the children – complaining of their trespassing, or something of the sort; but of course he accepted, and the evening was fixed, and our friend went himself to see that everything went right. He said he never had been so thankful for anything as that his own children were all prevented from being there: they were at a children's party at our house, as a matter of fact. Because this Mr Karswell had evidently set out with the intention of frightening these poor village children out of their wits, and I do believe, if he had been allowed to go on, he would actually have done so. He began with some comparatively mild things. Red Riding Hood was one, and even then, Mr Farrer said, the wolf was so dreadful that several of the smaller children had to be taken out: and he said Mr Karswell began the story by producing a noise like a wolf howling in the distance, which was the most gruesome thing he had ever heard. All the slides he showed, Mr Farrer said, were most clever; they were absolutely realistic, and where he had got them or how he worked them he could not imagine. Well, the show went on, and the stories kept on becoming a little more terrifying each time, and the children were mesmerised into complete silence. At last he produced a series which represented a little boy passing through his own park – Lufford, I mean – in the evening. Every child in the room could recognise the place from the pictures. And this poor boy was followed, and at last pursued and overtaken, and either torn in pieces or somehow made away with, by a horrible hopping creature in white, which you saw first dodging about among the trees, and gradually it appeared more and more plainly. Mr Farrer said it gave him one of the worst nightmares he ever remembered, and what it must have meant to the children doesn't bear thinking of. Of course this was too much, and he spoke very sharply indeed to Mr Karswell, and said it couldn't go on. All *he* said was: 'Oh, you think it's time to bring our little show to an end and send them home to their beds? *Very* well!' and then, if you please, he switched on another slide, which showed a great mass of snakes, centipedes, and disgusting creatures with wings, and somehow or other he made it seem as if they were climbing out of the picture and getting in amongst the audience; and this was accompanied by a sort of dry rustling noise which sent the children nearly mad, and of course they stampeded. A good many of them were rather hurt in getting out of the room, and I don't suppose one of them closed an eye that night. There was the most dreadful trouble in the village afterwards. Of course the mothers threw a good part of the blame on poor Mr Farrer, and, if they could have got past the gates, I believe the fathers would have broken every window in the Abbey. Well, now, that's Mr Karswell: that's the Abbot of Lufford, my dear, and you can imagine how we covet *his* society."

"Yes, I think he has all the possibilities of a distinguished criminal, has Karswell," said the host. "I should be sorry for anyone who got into his bad books."

"Is he the man, or am I mixing him up with someone else?" asked the Secretary (who for some minutes had been wearing the frown of the man who is trying to recollect something). "Is he the man who brought out a *History of Witchcraft* some time back – ten years or more?"

"That's the man; do you remember the reviews of it?"

"Certainly I do; and what's equally to the point, I knew the author of the most incisive of the lot.

So did you: you must remember John Harrington; he was at John's in our time."

"Oh, very well indeed, though I don't think I saw or heard anything of him between the time I went down and the day I read the account of the inquest on him."

"Inquest?" said one of the ladies. "What has happened to him?"

"Why, what happened was that he fell out of a tree and broke his neck. But the puzzle was, what could have induced him to get up there. It was a mysterious business, I must say. Here was this man – not an athletic fellow, was he? and with no eccentric twist about him that was ever noticed – walking home along a country road late in the evening – no tramps about – well known and liked in the place – and he suddenly begins to run like mad, loses his hat and stick, and finally shins up a tree – quite a difficult tree – growing in the hedgerow: a dead branch gives way, and he comes down with it and breaks his neck, and there he's found next morning with the most dreadful face of fear on him that could be imagined. It was pretty evident, of course, that he had been chased by something, and people talked of savage dogs, and beasts escaped out of menageries; but there was nothing to be made of that. That was in '89, and I believe his brother Henry (whom I remember as well at Cambridge, but *you* probably don't) has been trying to get on the track of an explanation ever since. He, of course, insists there was malice in it, but I don't know. It's difficult to see how it could have come in."

After a time the talk reverted to the *History of Witchcraft*. "Did you ever look into it?" asked the host.

"Yes, I did," said the Secretary. "I went so far as to read it."

"Was it as bad as it was made out to be?"

"Oh, in point of style and form, quite hopeless. It deserved all the pulverising it got. But, besides that, it was an evil book. The man believed every word of what he was saying, and I'm very much mistaken if he hadn't tried the greater part of his receipts."

"Well, I only remember Harrington's review of it, and I must say if I'd been the author it would have quenched my literary ambition for good. I should never have held up my head again."

"It hasn't had that effect in the present case. But come, it's half-past three; I must be off."

On the way home the Secretary's wife said, "I do hope that horrible man won't find out that Mr Dunning had anything to do with the rejection of his paper." "I don't think there's much chance of that," said the Secretary. "Dunning won't mention it himself, for these matters are confidential, and none of us will for the same reason. Karswell won't know his name, for Dunning hasn't published anything on the same subject yet. The only danger is that Karswell might find out, if he was to ask the British Museum people who was in the habit of consulting alchemical manuscripts: I can't very well tell them not to mention Dunning, can I? It would set them talking at once. Let's hope it won't occur to him."

However, Mr Karswell was an astute man.

*

This much is in the way of prologue. On an evening rather later in the same week, Mr Edward Dunning was returning from the British Museum, where he had been engaged in Research, to the comfortable house in a suburb where he lived alone, tended by two excellent women who had been long with him. There is nothing to be added by way of description of him to what we have heard already. Let us follow him as he takes his sober course homewards.

A train took him to within a mile or two of his house, and an electric tram a stage further. The line ended at a point some three hundred yards from his front door. He had had enough of reading when he got into the car, and indeed the light was not such as to allow him to do more than study the advertisements on the panes of glass that faced him as he sat. As was not unnatural, the advertisements in this particular line of cars were objects of his frequent contemplation, and, with the possible exception, of the brilliant and convincing dialogue between Mr Lamplough and an eminent K.C. on the subject of Pyretic Saline, none of them afforded much scope to his imagination. I am wrong: there was one at the corner of the car furthest from him which did not seem familiar. It was in blue letters on a yellow ground, and all that he could read of it was a name – John Harrington – and something like a date. It could be of no interest to him to know more; but for all that, as the car emptied, he was just curious enough to move along the seat until he could read it well. He felt to a slight extent repaid for his trouble; the advertisement was *not* of the usual type. It ran thus: "In memory of John Harrington, F.S.A., of The Laurels, Ashbrooke. Died Sept. 18th, 1889. Three months were allowed."

The car stopped. Mr Dunning, still contemplating the blue letters on the yellow ground, had to be stimulated to rise by a word from the conductor. "I beg your pardon," he said, "I was looking at that advertisement; it's a very odd one, isn't it?" The conductor read it slowly. "Well, my word," he said, "I never see that one before. Well, that is a cure, ain't it? Some one bin up to their jokes 'ere, I should think." He got out a duster and applied it, not without saliva, to the pane and then to the outside. "No," he said, returning, "that ain't no transfer; seems to me as if it was reg'lar *in* the glass, what I mean in the substance, as you may say. Don't you think so, sir?" Mr Dunning examined it and rubbed it with his glove, and agreed. "Who looks after these advertisements, and gives leave for them to be put up? I wish you would inquire. I will just take a note of the words." At this moment there came a call from the driver: "Look alive, George, time's up." "All right, all right; there's somethink else what's up at this end. You come and look at this 'ere glass." "What's gorn with the glass?" said the driver, approaching. "Well, and oo's 'Arrington? What's it all about?" "I was just asking who was responsible for putting the advertisements up in your cars, and saying it would be as well to make some inquiry about this one." "Well, sir, that's all done at the Company's orfice, that work is: it's our Mr Timms, I believe, looks into that. When we put up tonight I'll leave word, and per'aps I'll be able to tell you tomorrer if you 'appen to be coming this way."

This was all that passed that evening. Mr Dunning did just go to the trouble of looking up Ashbrooke, and found that it was in Warwickshire.

Next day he went to town again. The car (it was the same car) was too full in the morning to allow of his getting a word with the conductor: he could only be sure that the curious advertisement had been made away with. The close of the day brought a further element of mystery into the transaction. He had missed the tram, or else preferred walking home, but at a rather late hour, while he was at work in his study, one of the maids came to say that two men from the tramways was very anxious to speak to him. This was a reminder of the advertisement, which he had, he says, nearly forgotten. He had the men in –

they were the conductor and driver of the car – and when the matter of refreshment had been attended to, asked what Mr Timms had had to say about the advertisement. "Well sir, that's what we took the liberty to step round about," said the conductor. "Mr Timm's 'e give William 'ere the rough side of his tongue about that: 'cordin' to 'im there warn't no advertisement of that description sent in, nor ordered, nor paid for, nor put up, nor nothink, let alone not bein' there, and we was playing the fool takin' up his time. 'Well,' I says, 'if that's the case, all I ask of you, Mr Timms,' I says, 'is to take and look at it for yourself,' I says. 'Of course if it ain't there,' I says, 'you may take and call me what you like.' 'Right,' he says, 'I will': and we went straight off. Now, I leave it to you, sir, if that ad., as we term 'em, with 'Arrington on it warn't as plain as ever you see anything – blue letters on yeller glass, and as I says at the time, and you borne me out, reg'lar in the glass, because, if you remember, you recollect of me swabbing it with my duster." "To be sure I do, quite clearly – well?" "You may say well, I don't think. Mr Timms he gets in that car with a light – no, he told William to 'old the light outside. 'Now,' he says, 'where's your precious ad. what we've 'eard so much about?' ''Ere it is,' I says, 'Mr Timms,' and I laid my 'and on it." The conductor paused.

"Well," said Mr Dunning, "it was gone, I suppose. Broken?"

"Broke! – not it. There warn't, if you'll believe me, no more trace of them letters – blue letters they was – on that piece o' glass, than – well, it's no good *me* talkin'. *I* never see such a thing. I leave it to William here if – but there, as I says, where's the benefit in me going on about it?"

"And what did Mr Timms say?"

"Why'e did what I give 'im leave to – called us

pretty much anything he liked, and I don't know as I blame him so much neither. But what we thought, William and me did, was as we seen you take down a bit of a note about that – well, that letterin'—"

"I certainly did that, and I have it now. Did you wish me to speak to Mr Timms myself, and show it to him? Was that what you came in about?"

"There, didn't I say as much?" said William. "Deal with a gent if you can get on the track of one, that's my word. Now perhaps, George, you'll allow as I ain't took you very far wrong to-night."

"Very well, William, very well; no need for you to go on as if you'd 'ad to frog's-march me 'ere. I come quiet, didn't I? All the same for that, we 'adn't ought to take up your time this way, sir; but if it so 'appened you could find time to step round to the Company's orfice in the morning and tell Mr Timms what you seen for yourself, we should lay under a very 'igh obligation to you for the trouble. You see it ain't bein' called – well, one thing and another, as we mind, but if they got it into their 'ead at the orfice as we seen things as warn't there, why, one thing leads to another, and where we should be a twelvemunce 'ence – well, you can understand what I mean."

Amid further elucidations of the proposition, George, conducted by William, left the room.

The incredulity of Mr Timms (who had a nodding acquaintance with Mr Dunning) was greatly modified on the following day by what the latter could tell and show him; and any bad mark that might have been attached to the names of William and George was not suffered to remain on the Company's books; but explanation there was none.

Mr Dunning's interest in the matter was kept alive by an incident of the following afternoon. He was walking from his club to the train, and he noticed some way ahead a man with a handful of leaflets such as are distributed to passers-by by agents of enterprising firms. This agent had not chosen a very crowded street for his operations: in fact, Mr Dunning did not see him get rid of a single leaflet before he himself reached the spot. One was thrust into his hand as he passed: the hand that gave it touched his, and he experienced a sort of little shock as it did so. It seemed unnaturally rough and hot. He looked in passing at the giver, but the impression he got was so unclear that, however much he tried to reckon it up subsequently, nothing would come. He was walking quickly, and as he went on glanced at the paper. It was a blue one. The name of Harrington in large capitals caught his eye. He stopped, startled, and felt for his glasses. The next instant the leaflet was twitched out of his hand by a man who hurried past, and was irrecoverably gone. He ran back a few paces, but where was the passer-by? and where the distributor?

It was in a somewhat pensive frame of mind that Mr Dunning passed on the following day into the Select Manuscript Room of the British Museum, and filled up tickets for Harley 3586, and some other volumes. After a few minutes they were brought to him, and he was settling the one he wanted first upon the desk, when he thought he heard his own name whispered behind him. He turned round hastily, and, in doing so, brushed his little portfolio of loose papers on to the floor. He saw no one he recognised except one of the staff in charge of the room, who nodded to him, and he proceeded to pick up his papers. He thought he had them all, and was turning to begin work, when a stout gentleman at the table behind him, who was just rising to leave, and had collected his own belongings, touched him on the shoulder, saying, "May I give you this? I think it should be yours," and handed him a missing quire. "It is mine, thank you," said Mr Dunning. In another moment the man had left the room. Upon finishing his work for the afternoon, Mr Dunning had some conversation with the assistant in charge, and took occasion to ask who the stout gentleman was. "Oh, he's a man named Karswell," said the assistant, "he was asking me a week ago who were the great authorities on alchemy, and of course I told him you were the only one in the country. I'll see if I can't catch him: he'd like to meet you, I'm sure."

"For heaven's sake don't dream of it!" said Mr Dunning, "I'm particularly anxious to avoid him."

"Oh! very well," said the assistant, "he doesn't come here often: I daresay you won't meet him."

More than once on the way home that day Mr Dunning confessed to himself that he did not look forward with his usual cheerfulness to a solitary evening. It seemed to him that something ill-defined and impalpable had stepped in between him and his fellow-men – had taken him in charge, as it were. He wanted to sit close up to his neighbours in the train and in the tram, but as luck would have it both train and car were markedly empty. The conductor George was thoughtful and appeared to be absorbed in calculations as to the number of passengers. On arriving at his house he found Dr Watson, his medical man, on his doorstep. "I've had to upset your household arrangements, I'm sorry to say, Dunning. Both your servants hors de combat. In fact, I've had to send them to the Nursing Home."

"Good heavens! what's the matter?"

"It's something like ptomaine poisoning, I should think: you've not suffered yourself, I can see, or you wouldn't be walking about. I think they'll pull through all right."

"Dear, dear! Have you any idea what brought it on?"

"Well, they tell me they bought some shellfish from a hawker at their dinnertime. It's odd. I've made inquiries, but I can't find that any hawker has been to other houses in the street. I couldn't send word to you; they won't be back for a bit yet. You come and dine with me tonight, anyhow, and we can make arrangements for going on. Eight o'clock. Don't be too anxious."

The solitary evening was thus obviated; at the expense of some distress and inconvenience, it is true. Mr Dunning spent the time pleasantly enough with the doctor (a rather recent settler), and returned to his lonely home at about 11.30. The night he passed is not one on which he looks back with any satisfaction. He was in bed and the light was out. He was wondering if the charwoman would come early enough to get him hot water next morning, when he heard the unmistakable sound of his study door opening. No step followed it on the passage floor, but the sound must mean mischief, for he knew that he had shut the door that evening after putting his papers away in his desk. It was rather shame than courage that induced him to slip out into the passage and lean over the banister in his nightgown, listening. No light was visible; no further sound came: only a gust of warm, or even hot air played for an instant round his shins. He went back and decided to lock himself into his room. There was more unpleasantness, however. Either an economical suburban company had decided that their light would not be required in the small hours, and had stopped working, or else something was wrong with the meter; the effect was in any case that the electric light was off. The obvious course was to find a match, and also to consult his watch: he might as well know how many hours of discomfort awaited him. So he put his hand into the well-known nook under the pillow: only, it did not get so far. What he touched was, according to his account, a mouth, with teeth, and with hair about it, and, he declares, not the mouth of a human being. I do not think it is any use to guess what he said or did; but he was in a spare room with the door locked and his ear to it before he was clearly conscious again. And there he spent the rest of a most miserable night, looking every moment for some fumbling at the door: but nothing came.

The venturing back to his own room in the morning was attended with many listenings and quiverings. The door stood open, fortunately, and the blinds were up (the servants had been out of the house before the hour of drawing them down); there was, to be short, no trace of an inhabitant. The watch, too, was in its usual place; nothing was disturbed, only the wardrobe door had swung open, in accordance with its confirmed habit. A ring at the back door now announced the charwoman, who had been ordered the night before, and nerved Mr Dunning, after letting her in, to continue his search in other parts of the house. It was equally fruitless.

The day thus begun, went on dismally enough. He dared not go to the Museum: in spite of what the assistant had said, Karswell might turn up there, and Dunning felt he could not cope with a probably hostile stranger. His own house was odious; he hated sponging on the doctor. He spent some little time in a call at the Nursing Home, where he was slightly cheered by a good report of his housekeeper and maid. Towards lunchtime he betook himself to his club, again experiencing a gleam of satisfaction at seeing the Secretary of the Association. At luncheon Dunning told his friend the more material of his woes, but could not bring himself to speak of those that weighed most heavily on his spirits. "My poor dear man," said the Secretary, "what an upset! Look here: we're alone at home, absolutely. You must put up with us. Yes! no excuse: send your things in this afternoon." Dunning was unable to stand out: he was, in truth, becoming acutely anxious, as the hours went on, as to what that night might have waiting for him. He was almost happy as he hurried home to pack up.

His friends, when they had time to take stock of him, were rather shocked at his lorn appearance, and did their best to keep him up to the mark. Not altogether without success: but, when the two men were smoking alone later, Dunning became dull again. Suddenly he said, "Gayton, I believe that alchemist man knows it was I who got his paper rejected." Gayton whistled. "What makes you think that?" he said. Dunning told of his conversation with the Museum assistant, and Gayton could only agree that the guess seemed likely to be correct. "Not that I care much," Dunning went on, "only it might be a nuisance if we were to meet. He's a bad-tempered party, I imagine." Conversation dropped again; Gayton became more and more strongly impressed with the desolateness that came over Dunning's face and bearing, and finally – though with a considerable effort – he asked him point-blank whether something serious was not bothering him. Dunning gave an exclamation of relief. "I was perishing to get it off my mind," he said. "Do you know anything about a man named John Harrington?" Gayton was thoroughly startled, and at the moment could only ask why. Then the complete story of Dunning's experiences came out – what had happened in the tramcar, in his own house, and in the street, the troubling of spirit that had crept over him, and still held him; and he ended with the question he had begun with. Gayton was at a loss how to answer him. To tell the story of Harrington's end would perhaps be right; only, Dunning was in a nervous state, the story was a grim one, and he could not help asking himself whether there were not a connecting link between these two cases, in the person of Karswell. It was a difficult concession for a scientific man, but it could be eased by the phrase "hypnotic suggestion". In the end he decided that his answer tonight should be guarded; he would talk the situation over with his wife. So he said that he had known Harrington at Cambridge, and believe he had died suddenly in 1889, adding a few details about the man and his published work. He did talk over the matter with Mrs Gayton, and, as he had anticipated, she leapt at once to the conclusion which had been hovering before him. It was she who reminded him of the surviving brother, Henry Harrington, and she also who suggested that he might be got hold of by means of their hosts of the day before. "He might be a hopeless crank," objected Gayton. "That could be ascertained from the Bennetts, who knew him," Mrs Gayton retorted; and she undertook to see the Bennetts the very next day.

*

It is not necessary to tell in further detail the steps by which Henry Harrington and Dunning were brought together.

*

The next scene that requires to be narrated is a conversation that took place between the two. Dunning had told Harrington of the strange ways in which the dead man's name had been brought before him, and had said something, besides, of his own subsequent experiences. Then he had asked if Harrington was disposed, in return, to recall any of the circumstances connected with his brother's death. It is not necessary to dwell on Harrington's surprise at what he had heard: but his reply was readily given.

"John," he said, "was in a very odd state, undeniably, from time to time, during some weeks before, though not immediately before, the catastrophe. There were several things – the principal notion he had was that he thought he was being followed. No doubt he was an impressionable man, but he never had had such fancies as this before. I cannot get it out of my mind that there was ill-will at work, and what you tell me about yourself reminds me very much of my brother. Can you think of any possible connecting link?"

"There is just one that has been taking shape vaguely in my mind. I've been told that your brother reviewed a book very severely not long before he died, and just lately I have happened to cross the path of the man who wrote that book in a way he would resent."

"Don't tell me the man was called Karswell."

"Why not? that is exactly his name."

Henry Harrington leant back. "That is final to my mind. Now I must explain further. From something he said, I feel sure that my brother John was beginning to believe – very much against his will – that Karswell was at the bottom of his trouble. I want to tell you what seems to me to have a bearing on this situation. My brother was a great musician, and used to run up to concerts in town. He came back, three months before he died, from one of these, and gave me his programme to look at – an analytical programme: he always kept them. 'I nearly missed this one' he said. 'I suppose I must have dropped it: anyhow I was looking for it under my seat and in my pockets and so on, and my neighbour offered me his: said 'might he give it me, he had no further use for it,' and he went away just afterwards. I don't know who he was – a stout, clean-shaven man. I should have been sorry to miss it; of course I could have bought another, but this cost me nothing." At another time he told me that he had been very uncomfortable both on the way to his hotel and during the night. I piece things together now in thinking it over. Then, not very long after, he was going over these programmes, putting them in order to have them bound up, and in this particular one (which by the way I had hardly glanced at), he found quite near the beginning a strip of paper with some very odd writing on it in red and black – most carefully done – it looked to me more like Runic letters than anything else. "Why," he said, "this must belong to my fat neighbour. It looks as if it might be worth returning to him; it may be a copy of something; evidently someone has taken trouble over it. How can I find his address?" We talked it over for a little and agreed that it wasn't worth advertising about, and that my brother had better look out for the man at the next concert, to which he was going very soon. The paper was lying on the book and we were both by the fire; it was a cold, windy summer evening. I suppose the door blew open, though I didn't notice it: at any rate a gust – a warm gust it was – came quite suddenly between us, took the paper and blew it straight into the fire: it was light, thin paper, and flared and went up the chimney in a single ash. 'Well,' I said, 'you can't give it back now.' He said nothing for a minute: then rather crossly, 'No, I can't; but why you should keep on saying so I don't know.' I remarked that I didn't say it more than once. 'Not more than four times, you mean,' was all he said. I remember all that very clearly, without any good reason; and now to come to the point. I don't know if you looked at that book of Karswell's which my unfortunate brother reviewed. It's not likely that you should: but I did, both before his death and after it. The first time we made game of it together. It was written in no style at all – split infinitives, and every sort of thing that makes an Oxford gorge rise. Then there was nothing that the man didn't swallow: mixing up classical myths, and stories out of the *Golden Legend* with reports of savage customs of today – all very proper, no doubt, if you know how to use them, but he didn't: he seemed to put the *Golden Legend* and the *Golden Bough* exactly on a par, and to believe both: a pitiable exhibition, in short. Well, after the misfortune, I looked over the book again. It was no better than before, but the impression which it left this time on my mind was different. I suspected – as I told you – that Karswell had borne ill-will to my brother – even that he was in some way responsible for what had happened – and now his book seemed to me to be a very sinister performance indeed. One chapter in particular struck me, in which he spoke of 'casting the Runes' on people, either for the purpose of gaining their affection or of getting them out of the way – perhaps more especially the latter: he spoke of all this in a way that really seemed to me to imply actual knowledge. I've not time to go into details, but the upshot is that I am pretty sure from information received that the civil man at the concert was Karswell: I suspect – I more than suspect – that the paper was of importance: and I do believe that if my brother had been able to give it back, he might have been alive now. Therefore, it occurs to me to ask you whether you have anything to put beside what I have told you."

By way of answer, Dunning had the episode in the Manuscript Room at the British Museum to relate. "Then he did actually hand you some papers; have you examined them? No? because we must, if you'll allow it, look at them at once, and very carefully."

They went to the still empty house – empty, for the two servants were not yet able to return to work. Dunning's portfolio of papers was gathering dust on the writing-table. In it were the quires of small-sized scribbling paper which he used for his transcripts: and from one of these, as he took it up, there slipped and fluttered out into the room with uncanny quickness, a strip of thin light paper. The window was open, but Harrington slammed it to, just in time to intercept the paper, which he caught. "I thought so," he said; "it might be the identical thing that was given to my brother. You have to look out, Dunning; this may mean something quite serious for you."

A long consultation took place. The paper was narrowly examined. As Harrington had said, the characters on it were more like Runes than anything else, but not decipherable by either man, and both hesitated to copy them, for fear, as they confessed, of perpetuating whatever evil purpose they might conceal. So it has remained impossible (if I may anticipate a little) to ascertain what was conveyed in this curious message or commission. Both Dunning and Harrington are firmly convinced that it had the effect of bringing its possessors into very undesirable company. That it must be returned to the source whence it came they were agreed, and further, that the only safe and certain way was that of personal service; and here contrivance would be necessary, for Dunning was known by sight to Karswell. He must, for one thing, alter his appearance by shaving his beard. But then might not the blow fall first? Harrington thought they could time it. He knew the date of the concert at which the 'black spot' had been put on his brother: it was June 18th. The death had followed on Sept. 18th. Dunning reminded him that three months had been mentioned on the inscription on the car-window. "Perhaps," he added, with a cheerless laugh, "mine may be a bill at three months too. I believe I can fix it by my diary. Yes, April 23rd was the day at the Museum; that brings us to July 23rd. Now, you know, it becomes extremely important to me to know anything you will tell me about the progress of your brother's trouble, if it is possible for you to speak of it." "Of course. Well, the sense of being watched whenever he was alone was the most distressing thing to him. After a time I took to sleeping in his room, and he was the better for that: still, he talked a great deal in his sleep. What about? Is it wise to dwell on that, at least before things are straightened out? I think not, but I can tell you this: two things came for him by post during those weeks, both with a London postmark, and addressed in a commercial hand. One was a woodcut of Bewick's, roughly torn out of the page: one which shows a moonlit road and a man walking along it, followed by an awful demon creature. Under it were written the lines out of the 'Ancient Mariner' (which I suppose the cut illustrates) about one who, having once looked round—

"Walks on, and turns no more his head,
Because he knows a grisly fiend doth close behind
    him tread."

The other was a calendar, such as tradesmen often send. My brother paid no attention to this, but I looked at it after his death, and found that everything after Sept. 18 had been torn out. You may be surprised at his having gone out alone the evening he was killed, but the fact is that during the last ten days or so of his life he had been quite free from the sense of being followed or watched."

The end of the consultation was this. Harrington, who knew a neighbour of Karswell's, thought he saw a way of keeping a watch on his movements. It would be Dunning's part to be in readiness to try to cross Karswell's path at any moment, to keep the paper safe and in a place of ready access.

They parted. The next weeks were no doubt a severe strain upon Dunning's nerves: the intangible barrier which had seemed to rise about him on the day when he received the paper, gradually developed into a brooding blackness that cut him off from all the means of escape to which one might have thought he would resort. No one was at hand who was likely to suggest them to him, and he seemed robbed of all initiative. He waited with inexpressible anxiety as May, June, and early July passed on, for a mandate from Harrington. But all this time Karswell remained immovable at Lufford.

At last, in less than a week before the date he had come to look upon as the end of his earthly activities, came a telegram: "Leaves Victoria by boat train Thursday night. Do not miss. I come to you tonight. Harrington."

He arrived accordingly, and they concocted plans. The train left Victoria at nine and its last stop before Dover was Croydon West. Harrington would mark down Karswell at Victoria, and look out for Dunning at Croydon, calling to him if need were by a name agreed upon. Dunning, disguised as far as might be, was to have no label or initials on any hand luggage, and must at all costs have the paper with him.

Dunning's suspense as he waited on the Croydon platform I need not attempt to describe. His sense of danger during the last days had only been sharpened by the fact that the cloud about him had perceptibly been lighter; but relief was an ominous symptom, and, if Karswell eluded him now, hope was gone: and there were so many chances of that. The rumour of the journey might be itself a device. The twenty minutes in which he paced the platform and persecuted every porter with inquiries as to the boat train were as bitter as any he had spent. Still, the train came, and Harrington was at the window. It was important, of course, that there should be no recognition: so Dunning got in at the further end of the corridor carriage, and only gradually made his way to the compartment where Harrington and Karswell were. He was pleased, on the whole, to see that the train was far from full.

Karswell was on the alert, but gave no sign of recognition. Dunning took the seat not immediately facing him, and attempted, vainly at first, then with increasing command of his faculties, to reckon the possibilities of making the desired transfer. Opposite to Karswell, and next to Dunning, was a heap of Karswell's coats on the seat. It would be of no use to slip the paper into these – he would not be safe, or would not feel so, unless in some way it could be proffered by him and accepted by the other. There was a handbag, open, and with papers in it. Could he manage to conceal this (so that perhaps Karswell might leave the carriage without it), and then find and give it to him? This was the plan that suggested itself. If he could only have counselled with Harrington! but that could not be. The minutes went on. More than once Karswell rose and went out into the corridor. The second time Dunning was on the point of attempting to make the bag fall off the seat, but he caught Harrington's eye, and read in it a warning. Karswell, from the corridor, was watching: probably to see if the two men recognised each other. He returned, but was evidently restless: and, when he rose the third time, hope dawned, for something did slip off his seat and fall with hardly a sound to the floor.

Karswell went out once more, and passed out of range of the corridor window. Dunning picked up what had fallen, and saw that the key was in his hands in the form of one of Cook's ticket-cases, with tickets in it. These cases have a pocket in the cover, and within very few seconds the paper of which we have heard was in the pocket of this one. To make the operation more secure, Harrington stood in the doorway of the compartment and fiddled with the blind. It was done, and done at the right time, for the train was now slowing down towards Dover.

In a moment more Karswell re-entered the compartment. As he did so, Dunning, managing, he knew not how, to suppress the tremble in his voice, handed him the ticket-case, saying, "May I give you this, sir? I believe it is yours." After a brief glance at the ticket inside, Karswell uttered the hoped-for response, "Yes, it is; much obliged to you, sir," and he placed it in his breast pocket.

Even in the few moments that remained – moments of tense anxiety, for they knew not to what a premature finding of the paper might lead – both men noticed that the carriage seemed to darken about them and to grow warmer; that Karswell was fidgety and oppressed; that he drew the heap of loose coats near to him and cast it back as if it repelled him; and that he then sat upright and glanced anxiously at both. They, with sickening anxiety, busied themselves in collecting their belongings; but they both thought that Karswell was on the point of speaking when the train stopped at Dover Town. It was natural that in the short space between town and pier they should both go into the corridor.

At the pier they got out, but so empty was the train that they were forced to linger on the platform until Karswell should have passed ahead of them with his porter on the way to the boat, and only then was it safe for them to exchange a pressure of the hand and a word of concentrated congratulation. The effect upon Dunning was to make him almost faint. Harrington made him lean up against the wall, while he himself went forward a few yards within sight of the gangway to the boat, at which Karswell had now arrived. The man at the head of it examined his ticket, and, laden with coats, he passed down into the boat. Suddenly the official called after him, "You, sir, beg pardon, did the other gentleman show his ticket?" "What the devil do you mean by the other gentleman?" Karswell's snarling voice called back from the deck. The man bent over and looked at him. "The devil? Well, I don't know, I'm sure," Harrington heard him say to himself, and then aloud, "My mistake, sir; must have been your rugs! ask your pardon." And then, to a subordinate near him, "'Ad he got a dog with him, or what? Funny thing: I could 'a' swore 'e wasn't alone. Well, whatever it was, they'll 'ave to see to it aboard. She's off now. Another week and we shall be gettin' the 'oliday customers." In five minutes more there was nothing but the lessening lights of the boat, the long line of the Dover lamps, the night breeze, and the moon.

Long and long the two sat in their room at the Lord Warden. In spite of the removal of their greatest anxiety, they were oppressed with a doubt, not of the lightest. Had they been justified in sending a man to his death, as they believed they had? Ought they not to warn him, at least? "No," said Harrington; "if he is the murderer I think him, we have done no more than is just. Still, if you think it better – but how and where can you warn him?" "He was booked to Abbeville only," said Dunning. "I saw that. If I wired to the hotels there in Joanne's Guide, 'Examine your ticket-case, Dunning,' I should feel happier. This is the 21st: he will have a day. But I am afraid he has gone into the dark." So telegrams were left at the hotel office.

It is not clear whether these reached their destination, or whether, if they did, they were understood. All that is known is that, on the afternoon of the 23rd, an English traveller, examining the front of St Wulfram's Church at Abbeville, then under extensive repair, was struck on the head and instantly killed by a stone falling from the scaffold erected round the south-western tower, there being, as was clearly proved, no workman on the scaffold at that moment: and the traveller's paper identified him as Mr Karswell.

Only one detail shall be added. At Karswell's sale a set of Bewick, sold with all faults, was acquired by Harrington. The page with the woodcut of the traveller and the demon was, as he had expected, mutilated. Also, after a judicious interval, Harrington repeated to Dunning something of what he had heard his brother say in his sleep: but it was not long before Dunning stopped him.

THE HAUNTING

(MGM, 1963)
Starring: Julie Harris, Richard Johnson &
Claire Bloom
Directed by Robert Wise
Story 'The Bus' by Shirley Jackson

Aparently inspired by the success of Jacques Tourneur's
Night of the Demon, several Hollywood film studios
produced a little spate of ghost movies in the Sixties
which began with *Night of the Eagle* (1962), based on
the popular novel *Conjure Wife* by Fritz Leiber. This
picture, which contained a scene very reminiscent to
one in Lewton's adaptation, in which the hero was
chased through a forest by a monstrous supernatural presence, had been adapted from Leiber's book
by Richard Matheson and Charles Beaumont, and
starred Peter Wyngarde, Janet Blair and Margaret
Johnston. Matheson, who has since become one of
Hollywood's leading scriptwriters of fantasy and horror movies – in particular several based on the
stories of Edgar Allan Poe and filmed by Roger
Corman – also wrote *The Legend of Hell House* (1973)
with Roddy McDowall, Pamela Franklin and Clive
Revill. This visceral thriller about a group of psychic
investigators in a haunted house had strong echoes of
the film which had already become acknowledged as a
classic of the supernatural genre, *The Haunting*, from
the best-selling novel, *The Haunting of Hill House*,
written in 1959 by the American authoress, Shirley
Jackson (1919–1965).

Shirley's famous story concerns a notoriously haunted house which has remained unchanged since the 1880s until the arrival of a psychic researcher, Dr Montague (James?), who begins to piece together the terrible history of the building and experiences some of the horrifying effects it can generate. Hill House has been described as "perhaps the most vividly haunted house in literature" and demanded all the skill of director Robert Wise (who had also worked with Val Lewton) and special effects man Tom Howard to bring it convincingly to the screen. Filmed in black and white wide-screen, *The Haunting* was applauded by one reviewer for its, "Brooding corridors, long shadows that could be something terrifying, and most of all you never see what's behind the creaking, bending door." Tragically, Shirley Jackson who suffered from obesity, asthma and acute anxiety, was to die only two years after the making of the picture at the age of 45 when her reputation as one of the most talented writers of psychological horror fiction promised so much more. A woman who once jokingly claimed to be "the only practising witch in New England specialising in small-scale magic," Shirley came to public notice with her scandalising story, 'The Lottery' (1948) about a small American community and its cruel annual tradition of stoning a victim to death. Then after a series of short story collections and novels – including *Hangsaman* (1951), *The Bird's Nest* (1952) and *The Sundial* (1958) – she became an international best-seller with *The Haunting of Hill House* (1959) and *We Have Always Lived in the Castle* (1962) about three victims of poisoning who live on as ghosts. In fact – as several critics have pointed out – Shirley Jackson had been working towards her novel about Hill House in several earlier short stories which also feature strange and sinister buildings. Perhaps the one of these which most

clearly foreshadows *The Haunting* is 'The Bus' which is reprinted hereunder . . .

Old Miss Harper was going home, although the night was wet and nasty. Miss Harper disliked traveling at any time, and she particularly disliked traveling on this dirty small bus which was her only way of getting home; she had frequently complained to the bus company about their service because it seemed that no matter where she wanted to go, they had no respectable bus to carry her. Getting away from home was bad enough – Miss Harper was fond of pointing out to the bus company – but getting home always seemed very close to impossible. Tonight Miss Harper had no choice: if she did not go home by this particular bus she could not go for another day. Annoyed, tired, depressed, she tapped irritably on the counter of the little tobacco store which served also as the bus station. Sir, she was thinking, beginning her letter of complaint, although I am an elderly lady of modest circumstances and must curtail my fondness for travel, let me point out that your bus service falls far below . . .

Outside, the bus stirred noisily, clearly not anxious to be moving; Miss Harper thought she could already hear the weary sound of its springs sinking out of shape. I just can't make this trip again, Miss Harper thought, even seeing Stephanie isn't worth it, they really go out of their way to make you uncomfortable. "Can I get my ticket, please?" she said sharply, and the old man at the other end of the counter put down his paper and gave her a look of hatred.

Miss Harper ordered her ticket, deploring her own cross voice, and the old man slapped it down on the counter in front of her and said, "You got three minutes before the bus leaves."

He'd love to tell me I missed it, Miss Harper thought, and made a point of counting her change.

The Bus

The rain was beating down, and Miss Harper hurried the few exposed steps to the door of the bus. The driver was slow in opening the door and as Miss Harper climbed in she was thinking, Sir, I shall never travel with your company again. Your ticket salesmen are ugly, your drivers are surly, your vehicles indescribably filthy . . .

There were already several people sitting in the bus, and Miss Harper wondered where they could possibly be going; were there really this many small towns served only by this bus? Were there really other people who would endure this kind of trip to get somewhere, even home? I'm very out of sorts, Miss Harper thought, very out of sorts; it's too strenuous a visit for a woman of my age; I need to get home. She thought of a hot bath and a cup of tea and her own bed, and sighed. No one offered to help her put her suitcase on the rack, and she glanced over her shoulder at the driver sitting with his back turned and thought, he'd probably rather put me off the bus than help me, and then, perceiving her own ill nature, smiled. The bus company might write a letter of complaint about *me*, she told herself and felt better. She had providentially taken a sleeping pill before leaving for the bus station, hoping to sleep through as much of the trip as possible, and at last, sitting near the back, she promised herself that it would not be unbearably long before she had a bath and a cup of tea, and tried to compose the bus company's letter of complaint. Madam, a lady of your experience and advanced age ought surely to be aware of the problems confronting a poor but honest little company which wants only . . .

She was aware that the bus had started, because she was rocked and bounced in her seat, and the feeling of rattling and throbbing beneath the soles of her shoes stayed with her even when she slept at last. She lay back uneasily, her head resting on the seat back, moving back and forth with the motion of the bus, and around her other people slept, or spoke softly, or stared blankly out the windows at the passing lights and the rain.

Sometime during her sleep Miss Harper was jostled by someone moving into the seat behind her, her head was pushed and her hat disarranged; for a minute, bewildered by sleep, Miss Harper clutched at her hat, and said vaguely, "Who?"

"Go back to sleep," a young voice said, and giggled. "I'm just running away from home, that's all."

Miss Harper was not awake, but she opened her eyes a little and looked up to the ceiling of the bus. "That's wrong," Miss Harper said as clearly as she could. "That's wrong. Go back."

There was another giggle. "Too late," the voice said. "Go back to sleep."

Miss Harper did. She slept uncomfortably and awkwardly, her mouth a little open. Sometime, perhaps an hour later, her head was jostled again and the voice said, "I think I'm going to get off here. 'By now."

"You'll be sorry," Miss Harper said, asleep. "Go back."

Then, still later, the bus driver was shaking her. "Look, lady," he was saying, "I'm not an alarm clock. Wake up and get off the bus."

"What?" Miss Harper stirred, opened her eyes, felt for her pocketbook.

"I'm not an alarm clock," the driver said. His voice was harsh and tired. "I'm not an alarm clock. Get off the bus."

"What?" said Miss Harper again.

"This is as far as you go. You got a ticket to here. You've arrived. And I am not an alarm clock waking up people to tell them when it's time to get off; you got here, lady, and it's not part of my job to carry you off the bus. I'm not—"

"I intend to report you," Miss Harper said, awake. She felt for her pocketbook and found it in her lap, moved her feet, straightened her hat. She was stiff and moving was difficult.

"Report me. But from somewhere else. I got a bus to run. Now will you please get off so I can go on my way?"

His voice was loud, and Miss Harper was sickeningly aware of faces turned toward her from along the bus, grins, amused comments. The driver turned and stamped off down the bus to his seat, saying, "She thinks I'm an alarm clock," and Miss Harper, without assistance and moving clumsily, took down her suitcase and struggled with it down the aisle. Her suitcase banged against seats, and she knew that people were staring at her; she was terribly afraid that she might stumble and fall.

"I'll certainly report you," she said to the driver, who shrugged.

"Come on, lady," he said. "It's the middle of the night and I got a bus to run."

"You ought to be *ashamed* of yourself," Miss Harper said wildly, wanting to cry.

"Lady," the driver said with elaborate patience, "please get off my bus."

The door was open, and Miss Harper eased herself and her suitcase onto the steep step. "She thinks everyone's an alarm clock, got to see she gets off the bus," the driver said behind her, and Miss Harper stepped onto the ground. Suitcase, pocketbook, gloves, hat; she had them all. She had barely taken stock when the bus started with a jerk, almost throwing her backward, and Miss Harper, for the first time in her life, wanted to run and shake her fist at someone. I'll report him, she thought, I'll see that he loses his job, and then she realized that she was in the wrong place.

Standing quite still in the rain and the darkness Miss Harper became aware that she was not at the bus corner of her town where the bus should have left her. She was on an empty crossroads in the rain. There were no stores, no lights, no taxis, no people. There was nothing, in fact, but a wet dirt road under her feet and a signpost where two roads came together. Don't panic, Miss Harper told herself, almost whispering, don't panic; it's all right, it's all right, you'll see that it's all right, don't be frightened.

She took a few steps in the direction the bus had gone, but it was out of sight and when Miss Harper called falteringly, "Come back," and, "Help," there was no answer to the shocking sound of her own voice out loud except the steady drive of the rain. I sound old, she thought, but I will not panic. She turned in a circle, her suitcase in her hand, and told herself, don't panic, it's all right.

There was no shelter in sight, but the signpost said RICKET'S LANDING; so that's where I am, Miss Harper thought, I've come to Ricket's Landing and I don't like it here. She set her suitcase down next to the signpost and tried to see down the road; perhaps there might be a house, or even some kind of a barn or shed where she could get out of the rain. She was crying a little, and lost and hopeless, saying Please, won't someone come? when she saw headlights far off down the road and realized that someone was really coming to help her. She ran to the middle of the road and stood waving, her gloves wet and her pocketbook draggled. "Here," she called, "here I am, please come and help me."

Through the sound of the rain she could hear the motor, and then the headlights caught her and, suddenly embarrassed, she put her pocketbook in front of her face while the lights were on her. The lights belonged to a small truck, and it came to an abrupt stop beside her and the window near her was rolled down and a man's voice said furiously, "You want to get killed? You trying to get killed or something? What you doing in the middle of the road, trying to get killed?" The young man turned and spoke to the driver. "It's some dame. Running out in the road like that."

"Please," Miss Harper said, as he seemed almost about to close the window again, "please help me. The bus put me off here when it wasn't my stop and I'm lost."

"Lost?" The young man laughed richly. "First I ever heard anyone getting lost in Ricket's Landing. Mostly they have trouble *finding* it." He laughed again, and the driver, leaning forward over the steering wheel to look curiously at Miss Harper, laughed too. Miss Harper put on a willing smile, and said, "Can you take me somewhere? Perhaps a bus station?"

"No bus station." The young man shook his head profoundly. "Bus comes through here every night, stops if he's got any passengers."

"Well," Miss Harper's voice rose in spite of herself; she was suddenly afraid of antagonizing these young men; perhaps they might even leave her here where they found her, in the wet and dark. "Please," she said, "can I get in with you, out of the rain?"

The two young men looked at each other. "Take her down to the old lady's," one of them said.

"She's pretty wet to get in the truck," the other one said.

"Please," Miss Harper said, "I'll be glad to pay you what I can."

"We'll take you to the old lady," the driver said. "Come on, move over," he said to the other young man.

"Wait, my suitcase." Miss Harper ran back to the signpost, no longer caring how she must look, stumbling about in the rain, and brought her suitcase over to the truck.

"That's awful wet," the young man said. He opened the door and took the suitcase from Miss Harper. "I'll just throw it in the back," he said, and turned and tossed the suitcase into the back of the truck; Miss Harper heard the sodden thud of its landing, and wondered what things would look like when she unpacked; my bottle of cologne, she thought despairingly. "Get *in*," the young man said, and, "My God, you're wet."

Miss Harper had never climbed up into a truck before, and her skirt was tight and her gloves slippery from the rain. Without help from the young man she put one knee on the high step and somehow hoisted herself in; this cannot be happening to me, she thought clearly. The young man pulled away fastidiously as Miss Harper slid onto the seat next to him.

"You are pretty wet," the driver said, leaning over the wheel to look around at Miss Harper. "Why were you out in the rain like that?"

"The bus driver." Miss Harper began to peel off her gloves; somehow she had to make an attempt to dry herself. "He told me it was my stop."

"That would be Johnny Talbot," the driver said to the other young man. "He drives that bus."

"Well, I'm going to report him," Miss Harper said. There was a little silence in the truck, and then the driver said, "Johnny's a good guy. He means all right."

"He's a bad bus driver," Miss Harper said sharply.

The truck did not move. "You don't want to report old Johnny," the driver said.

"I most certainly—" Miss Harper began, and then stopped. Where am I? she thought, what is happening to me? "No," she said at last, "I won't report old Johnny."

The driver started the truck, and they moved slowly down the road, through the mud and the rain. The windshield wipers swept back and forth hypnotically, there was a narrow line of light ahead from their headlights, and Miss Harper thought, what is happening to me? She stirred, and the young man next to her caught his breath irritably and drew back. "She's soaking wet," he said to the driver. "I'm wet already."

"We're going down to the old lady's," the driver said. "She'll know what to do."

The Bus

"What old lady?" Miss Harper did not dare to move, even turn her head. "Is there any kind of a bus station? Or even a taxi?"

"You could," the driver said consideringly, "you could wait and catch that same bus tomorrow night when it goes through. Johnny'll be driving her."

"I just want to get home as soon as possible," Miss Harper said. The truck seat was dreadfully uncomfortable, she felt steamy and sticky and chilled through, and home seemed so far away that perhaps it did not exist at all.

"Just down the road a mile or so," the driver said reassuringly.

"I've never heard of Ricket's Landing," Miss Harper said. "I can't imagine how he came to put me off there."

"Maybe somebody else was supposed to get off there and he thought it was you by mistake." This deduction seemed to tax the young man's mind to the utmost, because he said, "See, someone else might of been supposed to get off instead of you."

"Then *he's* still on the bus," said the driver, and they were both silent, appalled.

Ahead of them a light flickered, showing dimly through the rain, and the driver pointed and said, "There, that's where we're going." As they came closer Miss Harper was aware of a growing dismay. The light belonged to what seemed to be a roadhouse, and Miss Harper had never been inside a roadhouse in her life. The house itself was only a dim shape looming in the darkness, and the light, over the side door, illuminated only a sign, hanging crooked, which read *Beer Bar & Grill*.

"Is there anywhere else I could go?" Miss Harper asked timidly, clutching her pocketbook. "I'm not at all sure, you know, that I ought—"

"Not many people here tonight," the driver said, turning the truck into the driveway and pulling up in the parking lot which had once, Miss Harper was sad to see, been a garden. "Rain, probably."

Peering through the window and the rain, Miss Harper felt, suddenly, a warm stir of recognition, of welcome; it's the house, she thought, why, of course, the house is lovely. It had clearly been an old mansion once, solidly and handsomely built, with the balance and style that belonged to a good house of an older time. "Why?" Miss Harper asked, wanting to know why such a good house should have a light tacked on over the side door, and a sign hanging crooked but saying *Beer Bar & Grill*; "Why?" asked Miss Harper, but the driver said, "This is where you wanted to go. Get her suitcase," he told the other young man.

"In here?" asked Miss Harper, feeling a kind of indignation on behalf of the fine old house, "into this saloon?" Why, I used to live in a house like this, she thought, what are they doing to our old houses?

The driver laughed. "You'll be safe," he said.

Carrying her suitcase and her pocketbook Miss Harper followed the two young men to the lighted door and passed under the crooked sign. Shameful, she thought, they haven't even bothered to take care of the place; it needs paint and tightening all around and probably a new roof, and then the driver said, "Come on, come on," and pushed open the heavy door.

"I used to live in a house like this," Miss Harper said, and the young men laughed.

"I bet you did," one of them said, and Miss Harper stopped in the doorway, staring, and realized how strange she must have sounded. Where there had certainly once been comfortable rooms, high-ceilinged and square, with tall doors and polished floors, there was now one large dirty room, with a counter running along one side and half a dozen battered tables; there was a jukebox in a corner and torn linoleum on the floor. "Oh, no," Miss Harper said. The room smelled unpleasant, and the rain slapped against the bare windows.

Sitting around the tables and standing around the

148

jukebox were perhaps a dozen young people, resembling the two who had brought Miss Harper here, all looking oddly alike, all talking and laughing flatly. Miss Harper leaned back against the door; for a minute she thought they were laughing about her. She was wet and disheartened and these noisy people did not belong at all in the old house. Then the driver turned and gestured to her. "Come and meet the old lady," he said, and then, to the room at large, "Look, we brought company."

"Please," Miss Harper said, but no one had given her more than a glance. With her suitcase and her pocketbook she followed the two young men across to the counter; her suitcase bumped against her legs and she thought, I must not fall down.

"Belle, Belle," the driver said, "look at the stray cat we found."

An enormous woman swung around in her seat at the end of the counter, and looked at Miss Harper; looking up and down, looking at the suitcase and Miss Harper's wet hat and wet shoes, looking at Miss Harper's pocketbook and gloves squeezed in her hand, the woman seemed hardly to move her eyes; it was almost as though she absorbed Miss Harper without any particular effort. "Hell you say," the woman said at last. Her voice was surprisingly soft. "Hell you say."

"She's wet," the second young man said; the two young men stood one on either side of Miss Harper, presenting her, and the enormous woman looked her up and down. "Please," Miss Harper said; here was a woman at least, someone who might understand and sympathize, "please, they put me off my bus at the wrong stop and I can't seem to find my way home. Please."

"Hell you say," the woman said, and laughed, a gentle laugh. "She sure is wet," she said.

"Please," Miss Harper said.

"You'll take care of her?" the driver asked. He turned

and smiled down at Miss Harper, obviously waiting, and, remembering, Miss Harper fumbled in her pocketbook for her wallet. How much, she was wondering, not wanting to ask, it was such a short ride, but if they hadn't come I might have gotten pneumonia, and paid all those doctor's bills; I have caught cold, she thought with great clarity, and chose two five-dollar bills from her wallet. They can't argue over five dollars each, she thought, and sneezed. The two young men and the large woman were watching her with great interest, and all of them saw that after Miss Harper took out the two five-dollar bills there were a single and two tens left in the wallet. The money was not wet. I suppose I should be grateful for that, Miss Harper thought, moving slowly. She handed a five-dollar bill to each young man and felt that they glanced at one another over her head.

"Thanks," the driver said; I could have gotten away with a dollar each, Miss Harper thought. "Thanks," the driver said again, and the other young man said, "Say, thanks."

"Thank *you*," Miss Harper said formally.

"I'll put you up for the night," the woman said. "You can sleep here. Go tomorrow." She looked Miss Harper up and down again. "Dry off a little," she said.

"Is there anywhere else?" Then, afraid that this might seem ungracious, Miss Harper said, "I mean, is there any way of going on tonight? I don't want to impose."

"We got rooms for rent." The woman half turned back to the counter. "Cost you ten for the night."

She's leaving me bus fare home, Miss Harper thought; I suppose I should be grateful. "I'd better, I guess," she said, taking out her wallet again. "I mean, thank you."

The woman accepted the bill and half turned back to the counter. "Upstairs," she said. "Take your choice. No one's around." She glanced sideways at Miss Harper. "I'll see you get a cup of coffee in the morning. I wouldn't turn a dog out without a cup of coffee."

"Thank you." Miss Harper knew where the staircase would be, and she turned and, carrying her suitcase and her pocketbook, went to what had once been the front hall and there was the staircase, so lovely in its still proportions that she caught her breath. She turned back and saw the large woman staring at her, and said, "I used to live in a house like this. Built about the same time, I guess. One of those good old houses that were made to stand forever, and where people—"

"Hell you say," the woman said, and turned back to the counter.

The young people scattered around the big room were talking; in one corner a group surrounded the two who had brought Miss Harper and now and then they laughed. Miss Harper was touched with a little sadness now, looking at them, so at home in the big ugly room which had once been so beautiful. It would be nice, she thought, to speak to these young people, perhaps even become their friend, talk and laugh with them; perhaps they might like to know that this spot where they came together had been a lady's drawing room. Hesitating a little, Miss Harper wondered if she might call "Good night," or "Thank you" again, or even "God bless you all." Then, since no one looked at her, she started up the stairs. Halfway there was a landing with a stained-glass window, and Miss Harper stopped, holding her breath. When she had been a child the stained-glass window on the stair landing in her house had caught the sunlight, and scattered it on the stairs in a hundred colors. Fairyland colors, Miss Harper thought, remembering; I wonder why we don't live in these houses now. I'm lonely, Miss Harper thought, and then she thought, but I must get out of these wet clothes; I really am catching cold.

Without thinking she turned at the top of the stairs and went to the front room on the left; that had always been her room. The door was open and she glanced in; this was clearly a bedroom for rent, and it was ugly and drab and cheap. The light turned on with a cord hanging beside the door, and Miss Harper stood in the doorway, saddened by the peeling wallpaper and the sagging floor; what have they done to the house, she thought; how can I sleep here tonight?

At last she moved to cross the room and set her suitcase on the bed. I must get dry, she told herself, I must make the best of things. The bed was correctly placed, between the two front windows, but the mattress was stiff and lumpy, and Miss Harper was frightened at the faint smell of dark couplings and a remote echo in the springs; I will not think about such things, Miss Harper thought, I will not let myself dwell on any such thing; this might be the room where I slept as a girl. The windows were almost right – two across the front, two at the side – and the door was placed correctly; how they did build these old places to a square-cut pattern, Miss Harper thought, how they did put them together; there must be a thousand houses all over the country built exactly like this. The closet, however, was on the wrong side. Some oddness of construction had set the closet to Miss Harper's right as she sat on the bed, when it ought really to have been on her left; when she was a girl the big closet had been her playhouse and her hiding place, but it had been on the left.

The bathroom was wrong, too, but that was less important. Miss Harper had thought wistfully of a hot tub before she slept, but a glance at the bathtub discouraged her; she could simply wait until she got home. She washed her face and hands, and the warm water comforted her. She was further comforted to find that her bottle of cologne had not broken in her suitcase and that nothing inside had gotten wet. At least she could sleep in a dry nightgown, although in a cold bed.

She shivered once in the cold sheets, remembering a child's bed. She lay in the darkness with her eyes open, wondering at last where she was and how she had gotten here: first the bus and then the truck, and now she lay in the darkness and no one knew where she was or what was to become of her. She had only her suitcase and a little money in her pocketbook; she did not know where she was. She was very tired and she thought that perhaps the sleeping pill she had taken much earlier had still not quite worn off; perhaps the sleeping pill had been affecting all her actions, since she had been following docilely, bemused, wherever she was taken; in the morning, she told herself sleepily, I'll show them I can make decisions for myself.

The noise downstairs which had been a jukebox and adolescent laughter faded softly into a distant melody; my mother is singing in the drawing room, Miss Harper thought, and the company is sitting on the stiff little chairs listening; my father is playing the piano. She could not quite distinguish the song, but it was one she had heard her mother sing many times; I could creep out to the top of the stairs and listen, she thought, and then became aware that there was a rustling in the closet, but the closet was on the wrong side, on the right instead of the left. It is more a rattling than rustling, Miss Harper thought, wanting to listen to her mother singing, it is as though something wooden were being shaken around. Shall I get out of bed and quiet it so I can hear the singing? Am I too warm and comfortable, am I too sleepy?

The closet was on the wrong side, but the rattling continued, just loud enough to be irritating, and at last, knowing she would never sleep until it stopped, Miss Harper swung her legs over the side of the bed and, sleepily, padded barefoot over to the closet door, reminding herself to go to the right instead of the left.

"What are you doing in there?" she asked aloud, and opened the door. There was just enough light for her to see that it was a wooden snake, head lifted, stirring and rattling itself against the other toys. Miss Harper laughed. "It's my snake," she said aloud, "it's my old snake, and it's come alive." In the back of the closet she could see her old toy clown, bright and cheerful, and as she watched, enchanted, the toy clown flopped languidly forward and back, coming alive. At Miss Harper's feet the snake moved blindly, clattering against a doll house where the tiny people inside stirred, and against a set of blocks, which fell and crashed. Then Miss Harper saw the big beautiful doll sitting on a small chair, the doll with long golden curls and wide-lashed blue eyes and a stiff organdy party dress; as Miss Harper held out her hands in joy the doll opened her eyes and stood up.

"Rosabelle," Miss Harper cried out, "Rosabelle, it's me."

The doll turned, looking widely at her, smile painted on. The red lips opened and the doll quacked, outrageously, a flat slapping voice coming out of that fair mouth. "Go away, old lady," the doll said, "go away, old lady, go away."

Miss Harper backed away, staring. The clown tumbled and danced, mouthing at Miss Harper, the snake flung its eyeless head viciously at her ankles, and the doll turned, holding her skirts, and her mouth opened and shut. "Go away," she quacked, "go away, old lady, go away."

The inside of the closet was all alive; a small doll ran madly from side to side, the animals paraded solemnly down the gangplank of Noah's ark, a stuffed bear wheezed asthmatically. The noise was louder and louder, and then Miss Harper realized that they were all looking at her hatefully and moving toward her. The doll said "Old lady, old lady," and stepped forward; Miss Harper slammed the closet door and leaned against it. Behind her the snake crashed against the door and the doll's voice went on and on. Crying out, Miss Harper turned and fled, but the closet was on the wrong side and she turned the wrong way and found herself cowering against the far wall with the door impossibly far away while the closet door slowly opened and the doll's face, smiling, looked for her.

Miss Harper fled. Without stopping to look behind she

The Bus

flung herself across the room and through the door, down the hall and on down the wide lovely stairway. "Mommy," she screamed, "Mommy, Mommy."

Screaming, she fled out the door. "Mommy," she cried, and fell, going down and down into darkness, turning, trying to catch onto something solid and real, crying.

"Look, lady," the bus driver said. "I'm not an alarm clock. Wake up and get off the bus."

"You'll be sorry," Miss Harper said distinctly.

"Wake up," he said, "wake up and get off the bus."

"I intend to report you," Miss Harper said. Pocketbook, gloves, hat, suitcase.

"I'll certainly report you," she said, almost crying.

"This is as far as you go," the driver said.

The bus lurched, moved, and Miss Harper almost stumbled in the driving rain, her suitcase at her feet, under the sign reading RICKET'S LANDING.

THE STONE TAPE

(BBC, 1972)
Starring: Michael Bryant, Iain Cuthbertson &
Jane Asher
Directed by Peter Sasdy
Story 'The Trespassers' by Nigel Kneale

The Stone Tape was a screenplay intended originally for the cinema but instead ended up on television where it earned unstinted praise from viewers and critics alike and further enhanced the reputation of Nigel Kneale, one of the most original British writers of supernatural stories. Conceived as 'a ghost story for Christmas', the plot concerns a major electronics company who have taken over an old Victorian mansion for research purposes and found – surprise, surprise! – that it is built on even older foundations and is haunted. Ostensibly, a group of scientists would seem the ideal people to explain such a phenomenon – but events quickly prove otherwise. The producer Innes Lloyd, a veteran of *Doctor Who* and several other SF and fantasy programmes, made the film with painstaking attention to detail and some fine acting from the cast. The conflict between science and the supernatural made for excellent television, and the *Evening Standard* lead the applause. "This supernatural thriller by Nigel Kneale is one of the best plays of the genre that he has written," it said. No mean praise for a man who, since the mid-Fifties, has been one of the most influential names in the genre. Initially coming to attention with his trio of Quatermass stories

156

about an astronaut who returns to Earth with an infection that slowly turns him into a monster, Kneale has been in the news again recently through his association with the equally successful American horror series under the generic title *Halloween* produced by John Carpenter. And in between these milestones, Nigel has also produced a whole variety of scripts for mainstream pictures such as *Look Back in Anger* and *The Entertainer* as well as a number of highly controversial original screenplays including *The Year of the Sex Olympics* (1969) and the horror series, *Beasts* (1976), in which the beasts in question ranged from the psychological to the supernatural. Another of his ghostly stories *The Road* (1963), a tale set in the 18th Century in which two investigators in a haunted wood faced supernatural phenomena from the future, also earned high praise for its producer, John Elliot, and the leading actors, James Maxwell, Ann Bell and John Phillips. *The Daily Mirror* called it simply, "the best drama offered for many months".

Nigel Kneale actually began his working life by training to be an actor at the Royal Academy of Dramatic Art, but subsequently while filling in time between engagements started to write short stories. A collection of these, *Tomato Cain* (1949), won him the Somerset Maugham Literary Prize in 1950, and from there it was a short step into writing for the profession he had hoped to follow and has since so enriched with his imagination. *The Stone Tape* was, in fact, just one example of a theme that he has been exploring for much of his writing career: human investigations into haunted places and the terrifying events that can result. The concept actually first surfaced in a short story, 'The Trespassers', published as long ago as September 1958 in *Suspense* magazine, and it is reprinted here as a tribute to Kneale's major contribution to supernatural movies.

The estate agent kept an uncomfortable silence until we reached his car. "Frankly, I wish you hadn't got wind of that," he said. "Don't know how you did; I thought I had the whole thing carefully disposed of. Please get in."

He pulled his door shut and frowned. "It put me in a rather awkward spot. I suppose I'd better tell you all I know about that case, or you'd be suspecting me of heaven-knows-what kind of chicanery in your own deal."

As we set off to see the property I was interested in, he shifted the cigarette to the side of his mouth. "It's quite a distance, so I can tell you on the way there," he said. "We'll pass the very spot, as a matter of fact, and you can see it for yourself. Such as there is to see . . ."

It was way back before the war, the estate agent said. At the height of the building boom. You remember how it was: ribbon development in full blast everywhere; speculative builders sticking things up almost overnight. Though at least you could get a house when you wanted it in those days.

I've always been careful what I handle, I want you to understand that. Then one day I was handed a packet of coast-road bungalows, for letting. Put up by one of these gone-tomorrow firms, and bought by a local man. I can't say I exactly jumped for joy, but for once the things looked all right – and business is inclined to be business.

The desirable residence you heard about stood at the end of the row. Actually, it seemed to have the best site. On a sort of natural platform, as it were, raised above road level and looking straight out over the sea.

Like all the rest, it had a simple layout – two bedrooms, lounge, living-room, kitchen, bathroom. Red tiled roof, roughcast walls. Ornamental portico, garden strip all

round. Sufficiently far from town, but with all con-
veniences.

It was taken by a man named Pritchard. He was a
cinema projectionist, I think. Wife, a boy of ten or so,
and a rather younger daughter. Oh – and a dog, one of
those black, lop-eared animals. They christened the place
'Minuke,' M-I-N-U-K-E . . . My Nook. Yes, that's what
I thought too. And not even the miserable excuse of its
being phonetically correct.

Well, at the start everything seemed quite jolly. The
Pritchards settled in and busied themselves with rearing
a privet hedge and shoving flowers in. They'd paid the
first quarter in advance, and as far as I was concerned
were out of the picture for a bit.

Then about a fortnight after they'd moved in, I had a
telephone call from Mrs P. to say there was something odd
about the kitchen tap. Apparently the thing had happened
twice. The first time was when her sister was visiting
them, and tried to fill the kettle: no water would come
through for a long time, then suddenly it squirted violently
and almost soaked the woman. I gather the Pritchards
hadn't really believed this – thought she was trying to
find fault with their little nest. It had never happened
before, and she couldn't make it happen again.

Then about a week later it did. With Mrs Pritchard this
time. After her husband had examined the tap and could
find nothing wrong with it, he decided the water supply
must be faulty, so they got on to me.

I went round personally, as it was the first complaint
from any of these bungalows. The tap seemed normal
and I remember asking if the schoolboy son could have
been experimenting with their main stopcock, when Mrs
Pritchard, who had been fiddling with the tap, suddenly
said, "Quick, look at this! It's off now!" They were quite
cocky about its happening when I was there.

It really was odd. I turned the tap to the limit, but –
not a drop! Not even the sort of gasping gurgle you hear

when the supply is turned off at the main. After a couple of minutes, though, it came on. Water shot out with, I should say, about ten times normal force, as if it had been held under pressure. Then gradually it died down and ran steadily.

Both children were in the room with us until we all dodged out of the door to escape a soaking; so they couldn't have been up to any tricks. I promised the Pritchards to have the pipes checked. Before returning to town, I called at the next two bungalows in the row: neither of the tenants had had any trouble at all with the water. I thought that localized it, at least.

When I reached my office there was a telephone message waiting from Pritchard. I rang him back and he was obviously annoyed. "Look here," he said, "not ten minutes after you left, we've had something else happen! The wall of the large bedroom's cracked from top to bottom. Big pieces of plaster fell, and the bed's in a terrible mess." And then he said, "You wouldn't have got me in a jerry-built place like this if I'd known!"

I had plasterers on the job next morning, and the whole water supply to 'Minuke' under examination. For about three days there was peace. The tap behaved itself, and absolutely nothing was found to be wrong.

I was annoyed at what seemed to have been unnecessary expenditure. It looked as if the Pritchards were going to be difficult – and I've had my share of that type: fault-finding cranks occasionally carry eccentricity to the extent of a little private destruction, to prove their point. I was on the watch from now on.

*

Then it came again.

Pritchard rang me at my home, before nine in the morning. His voice sounded a bit shaky.

"For God's sake can you come round here right away?"

he said. "Tell you about it when you get here." And then he said, almost fiercely, but quietly and close to the mouthpiece, "There's something damned queer about this place!" Dramatizing is a typical feature of all cranks, I thought, but particularly the little mousy kind, like Pritchard.

I went to 'Minuke' and found that Mrs Pritchard was in bed, in a state of collapse. The doctor had given her a sleeping dose.

Pritchard told me a tale that was chiefly remarkable for the expression on his face as he told it.

I don't know if you're familiar with the layout of that type of bungalow. The living-room is in the front of the house, with the kitchen behind it. To get from one to the other you have to use the little hallway, through two doors. But for convenience at mealtimes there's a serving-hatch in the wall. A small wooden door slides up and down over the hatch-opening.

"The wife was just passing a big plate of bacon and eggs through from the kitchen," Pritchard told me, "when the hatch door came down on her wrists. I saw it and I heard her yell. I thought the cord must've snapped, so I said, 'All right, all right!' and went to pull it up, because it's only a light wooden frame." Pritchard was a funny colour, and as far as I could judge it was genuine.

"Do you know, it wouldn't come! I got my fingers under it and heaved, but it might have weighed two hundredweight. Once it gave an inch or so, and then pressed harder. That was it – it was pressing down! I heard the wife groan. I said, 'Hold on!' and nipped round through the hall. When I got into the kitchen she was on the floor, fainted.

"And the hatch door was hitched up as right as ninepence. That gave me a turn!" He sat down, quite deflated: it didn't appear to be put on. Still, ordinary neurotics can be almost as troublesome as out-and-out cranks.

I tested the hatch gingerly. The cords were sound and it ran easily.

"Possibly a bit stiff at times, being new," I said. "They're apt to jam if you're rough with them." And then, "By the way, just what were you hinting on the phone?"

He looked at me. It was warm sunlight outside, with a bus passing. Normal enough to take the mike out of Frankenstein's monster. "Never mind," he said, and gave a sheepish half-grin. "Bit of – well, funny construction in this house, though, eh?"

I'm afraid I was rather outspoken with him. Apart from any nonsense about a month-old bungalow being haunted, I was determined to clamp down on this "jerry-building" talk. Perhaps I was beginning to have doubts myself.

I wrote straight off to the building company when I'd managed to trace them – they were busy developing an arterial road three counties away. I dare say my letter was on the insinuating side: I think I asked if they had any record of difficulties in the construction of this bungalow.

At any rate, I got a sniffy reply by return, stating that the matter was out of their hands: in addition, their records were not available for discussion. Blind alley.

Meanwhile, things at 'Minuke' had worsened to a really frightening degree. I dreaded the phone ringing. One morning the two Pritchards senior awoke to find that nearly all the bedroom furniture had been moved around, including the bed they had been sleeping in. They had felt absolutely nothing. Food became suddenly and revoltingly decomposed. All the chimney pots had come down, not just into the garden, but on the far side of the high road, except one that appeared, pulverized, on the living-room floor.

I managed to find a local man who had been employed during the erection of the bungalows – he had worked only on the foundations of 'Minuke,' but what he had to say was interesting.

They had found the going slow because of striking a layer of enormous flat stones, apparently trimmed slate, but as the site was otherwise excellent they pressed on, using the stone as foundation where it fitted in with the plan, and laying down rubble where it didn't.

The concrete skin over the rubble – my ears burned when I heard about that, I can tell you – this wretched so-called concrete had cracked, or shattered, several times. Which wasn't entirely surprising, if it had been laid as he described. The flat stones, he said, had not been seriously disturbed. A workmate had referred to them as "a giant's grave," so it was possibly an old burial mound. Norse, perhaps – those are fairly common along this coast – or even very much older.

Apart from this – I'm no die-hard sceptic, I may as well confess – I was beginning to admit modest theories about a poltergeist. There were two young children in the house, and the lore has it that kids are often unconsciously connected with phenomena of that sort, though usually adolescents. Still, in the real-estate profession you have to be careful, and if I could see the Pritchards safely off the premises without airing these possibilities, it might be kindest to the bungalow's future.

I went to 'Minuke' the same afternoon.

It was certainly turning out an odd nook. I found a departing policeman on the doorstep. That morning the back door had been burst in by a hundredweight or so of soil, and Mrs Pritchard was trying to convince herself that a practical joker had it in for them. The policeman had taken some notes, and was giving vague advice about "civil action," which showed that he was out of his depth.

Pritchard looked very tired, almost ill. "I've got leave from my job to look after the children," he said, when we were alone. I thought he was wise. He had given his wife's illness as the reason, and I was glad of that.

"I don't believe in – unnatural happenings," he said.

I agreed with him, non-committally.

"But I'm afraid of what ideas the kids might get. They're both at impressionable ages, y'know."

I recognized the symptoms without disappointment. "You mean, you'd rather move elsewhere," I said.

He nodded. "I like the district, mind you. But what I—"

There was a report like a gun in the very room.

I found myself with both arms up to cover my face. There were tiny splinters everywhere, and a dust of fibre in the air. The door had exploded. Literally.

To hark back to constructional details, it was one of those light, hollow frame-and-plywood jobs. As you'll know, it takes considerable force to splinter plywood: and this was in tiny fragments. The oddest thing was that we had felt no blast effect.

In the next room I heard their dog howling. Pritchard was as stiff as a poker.

"I felt it!" he said. "I felt this lot coming. I've got to knowing when something's likely to happen. It's all around!"

Of course I began to imagine I'd sensed something too, but I doubt if I really had; my shock came with the crash. Mrs Pritchard was in the doorway by this time with the kids behind her. He motioned them out and grabbed my arm.

"The thing is," he whispered, "that I can still feel it, stronger than ever! Look, will you stay at home tonight, in case I need – well, in case things get worse? I can phone you."

On my way back I called at the town library and managed to get hold of a volume on supernatural possession and what-not. Yes, I was committed now. But the library didn't specialize in that line, and when I opened the book at home, I found it was very little help. "Vampires of South-Eastern Europe" kind of stuff.

I came across references to something called an 'elemental,' which I took to be a good deal more vicious and destructive than any poltergeist. A thoroughly nasty form of manifestation, if it existed. Those Norse gravestones were fitting into the picture uncomfortably well; it was fashionable in those days to be buried with all the trimmings, human sacrifices and even more unmentionable attractions.

But I read on. After half a chapter on zombies and Rumanian werewolves, the whole thing seemed so fantastic that I settled down with a whisky, and began to work out methods of exploding somebody's door as a practical joke. Even a totally certifiable joker would be likelier than vampires.

When the phone rang I was hardly prepared for it.

It was a confused, distant voice, gabbling desperately, but I recognized it as Pritchard. "For God's sake, don't lose a second! Get here – it's all hell on earth! Can't you hear it? My God, I'm going crazy!" And in the background I thought I was able to hear something. A sort of bubbling, shushing "wah-wah" noise. Indescribable. But you hear some odd sounds on telephones at any time.

"Yes," I said, "I'll come immediately. Why don't you all leave—" But the line had gone dead.

*

Probably I've never moved faster. I scrambled out to the car with untied shoes flopping, though I remembered to grab a heavy stick in the hall – whatever use it might be. I drove like fury, heart belting, straight to 'Minuke,' expecting to see heaven knows what.

But everything looked still and normal there. The moon was up and I could see the whole place clearly. Curtained lights in the windows. Not a sound.

I rang. After a moment Pritchard opened the door. He was quiet and seemed almost surprised to see me.

I pushed inside. "Well?" I said. "What's happened?"

"Not a thing, so far," he said. "That's why I didn't expect—"

I felt suddenly angry. "Look here," I said, "what are you playing at? Seems to me that any hoaxing round here begins a lot nearer home than you'd have me believe!" Then the penny dropped. I saw by the fright in his face that he knew something had gone wrong. That was the most horrible, sickening moment of the whole affair for me.

"Didn't you ring?" I said.

And he shook his head.

I've been in some tight spots. But there was always some concrete, actual business in hand to screw the mind safely down to. I suppose panic is when the sub-conscious breaks loose and everything in your head dashes screaming out. It was only just in time that I found a touch of the concrete and actual. A child's paintbox on the floor, very watery.

"The children," I said. "Where are they?"

"Wife's just putting the little 'un to bed. She's been restless tonight: just wouldn't go, crying and difficult. Arthur's in the bathroom. Look here, what's happened?"

I told him, making it as short and matter of fact as I could. He looked ghastly. "Better get them dressed and out of here right away," I said. "Make some excuse, not to alarm them."

He'd gone before I finished speaking.

I smoked hard, trying to build up the idea of a hoax in my mind. After all, it could have been. But I knew it wasn't.

Everything looked cosy and normal. Clock ticking. Fire red and mellow. Half-empty cocoa mug on the table. The sound of the sea from beyond the road.

I went through to the kitchen. The dog was there,

looking up from its sleeping-basket under the sink. "Good dog," I said, and it wagged its tail.

Pritchard came in from the hall. He jumped when he saw me.

"Getting nervy!" he said. "They won't be long. I don't know where we can go if we – well, if we have to – to leave tonight—"

"My car's outside," I told him. "I'll fix you up. Look here, did you ever hear things? Odd noises?" I hadn't told him that part of the telephone call.

He looked at me so oddly I thought he was going to collapse.

"I don't know," he said. "Can you? At this moment?"

I listened. "No," I said. "The clock on the shelf. The sea. Nothing else. No."

"The sea," he said, barely whispering. "But you can't hear the sea in this kitchen!"

He was close to me in an instant. Absolutely terrified. "Yes, I have heard this before! I think we all have. I said it was the sea, so as not to frighten them. But it isn't! And I recognized it when I came in here just now. That's what made me start. It's getting louder: it does that."

He was right. Like slow breathing. It seemed to emanate from inside the walls, not at a particular spot, but everywhere. We went into the hall, then the front room: it was the same there. Mixed with it now was a sort of thin crying.

"That's Nellie," Pritchard said. "The dog. She always whimpers when it's on – too scared to howl. My God, I've never heard it as loud as this before!"

"Hurry them up, will you!" I almost shouted. He went. The 'breathing' was ghastly. Slobbering. Stertorous, I think the term is. And faster. Oh, yes, I recognized it. The background music to the phone message. My skin was pure ice.

"Come along!" I yelled. I switched on the little radio to drown the noise. The old National Programme, as it was in those days, for late dance music. Believe it or not, what came through that loudspeaker was the same vile sighing noise, at double the volume. And when I tried to switch off, it stayed the same.

The whole bungalow was trembling. The Pritchards came running in, she carrying the little girl. "Get them into the car," I shouted. We heard glass smashing somewhere.

Above our heads there was an almighty thump. Plaster showered down.

Halfway out of the door the little girl screamed, "Nellie! Where's Nellie? Nellie, Nellie!"

"The dog!" Pritchard moaned. "Oh, curse it!" He dragged them outside.

I dived for the kitchen, where I'd seen the animal. Plaster was springing out of the walls in painful showers. In the kitchen I found water everywhere, one tap squirting like a fire-hose and the other missing, the water belching across the window from a torn end of pipe.

"Nellie!" I called.

Then I saw the dog. It was lying near the oven, quite stiff. Round its neck was twisted a piece of painted piping with the other tap on the end.

Sheer funk got me then.

The ground was moving under me. I bolted down the hall, nearly bumped into Pritchard. I yelled and shoved. I could actually feel the house at my back.

We got outside. The noise was like a dreadful snoring, with rumbles and crashes thrown in. One of the lights went out. "Nellie's run away," I said, and we all got into the car, the kids bawling. I started up. People were coming out of the other bungalows – they're pretty far apart and the din was just beginning to make itself felt.

Pritchard mumbled, "We can stop now. Think it'd be safe to go back and grab some of the furniture?" Just as if he was at a fire – but I don't think he knew what he was doing.

The Trespassers

"Daddy – look!" screeched the boy.

We saw it. The chimney of 'Minuke' was going up in a horrible way. In the moonlight it seemed to grow, quite slowly, to about sixty feet, like a giant crooked finger. And then it burst. I heard bricks thumping down. Somewhere somebody screamed.

There was a sudden glare like an ungodly great lightning flash.

Of course we were dazzled, but I thought I saw the whole of 'Minuke' fall suddenly and instantaneously flat, like a swatted fly. I probably did, because that's what happened, anyway.

There isn't much more to tell.

Nobody was really hurt, and we were able to put down the whole thing to a serious electrical fault. Main fuses had blown throughout the whole district, which helped this theory out.

There wasn't much recognizably left of 'Minuke'. But some of the bits were rather unusual. Knots in pipes, for instance – I buried what was left of the dog myself. Wood and brick cleanly sliced. Small quantities of completely powdered metal. The bath had been squashed flat, like tin foil. In fact Pritchard was lucky to land the insurance money for his furniture.

My professional problem, of course, remained. The plot where the wretched place had stood. I managed to persuade the owner it wasn't ideal for building on. Incidentally, lifting those stones might reveal something to somebody some day – but not to me, thank you!

I think my eventual solution showed a touch of wit: I let it very cheaply as a scrap-metal dump.

I know I've never been able to make any sense out of it. I hate telling you all this stuff, because it must make me seem either a simpleton or a charlatan. In so far as there's any circumstantial evidence in looking at the place, you can see it in a moment or two. Here's the coast road . . .

Nigel Kneale

*

The car pulled up at a bare spot beyond a sparse line of bungalows. The space was marked by a straggling, tufty square of privet bushes. Inside I could see a tangle of rusting iron: springs, a car chassis, oil drums.

"The hedge keeps it from being too unsightly," said the estate agent, as we crossed to it. "See – the remains of the gate."

A few half-rotten slats dangled from an upright. One still bore part of a chrome-plated name. "MI—" and, a little farther on, "K."

"Nothing worth seeing now," he said. I peered inside. "Not that there ever was much – Look out!"

I felt a violent push. In the same instant something zipped past my head and crashed against the car behind. "My God! Went right at you!" gasped the agent.

It had shattered a window of the car and gone through the open door opposite. We found it in the road beyond, sizzling on the tarmac.

A heavy steel nut, white-hot.

ASYLUM

(Amicus, 1972)
Starring: Peter Cushing, Charlotte Rampling &
Megs Jenkins
Directed by Roy Ward Baker
Based on 'Lucy Comes To Stay' by Robert Bloch

The Seventies proved a generally disappointing time for lovers of ghost movies – although cinemagoers after blood and gore had their tastes more than satiated by the flood of gruesome pictures from Hammer Films in the UK and Universal Pictures in America. However, the anthology supernatural film continued to appear from time to time and it was in these that ghost stories were most likely to be featured. A typical example of this was *Asylum*, made in 1972, which was one of a series of four-story movies produced by the partnership of Max J. Rosenberg and Milton Subotsky under their Amicus banner – the best of them utilising scripts and stories by the leading US horror writer, Robert Bloch (1917–1994). Bloch, who had become internationally famous as the author of Alfred Hitchcock's classic movie, *Psycho* (1959), had started his working relationship with Amicus in 1966 with his script for *The Psychopath*, directed by Freddie Francis and starring Margaret Johnston from *Night of the Eagle* and Patrick Wymark. The first anthology film of Bob's work was *Torture Garden* (1967) which Freddie Francis again directed with Jack Palance, Peter Cushing and Burgess Meredith; followed by *The House That Dripped Blood* which Peter Duffell

171

directed. The movie featured England's two premier horror stars, Peter Cushing and Christopher Lee, with co-star Denholm Elliott.

The linking framework of *Asylum* was the visit by a doctor (Robert Powell) to Dunsmoor Asylum where his interviews with patients gave rise to the four episodes. The sequence based on Robert Bloch's story 'Lucy Comes To Stay' (originally published in the legendary American horror pulp magazine, *Weird Tales*, in January 1952) was the one with the strongest supernatural connotations and certainly pleased many viewers. The picture itself was subsequently singled out as among the best of its kind when cinema historian Alan Frank delivered this verdict a few years ago: "Thanks to strong acting from Robert Powell, Peter Cushing and Patrick Magee, and uncomfortably good special effects by Ernie Sullivan, *Ayslum* made an effective Grand Guignol addition to the fantasy genre." Here is the story from *Weird Tales* that helped it earn that plaudit as well as further enhancing the reputation of Robert Bloch whose death last year was such a sad loss to fantasy fiction.

"You can't go on this way."

Lucy kept her voice down low, because she knew the nurse had her room just down the hall from mine, and I wasn't supposed to see any visitors.

"But George is doing everything he can – poor dear, I hate to think of what all those doctors and specialists are costing him, and the sanatorium bill, too. And now that nurse, that Miss Higgins, staying here every day."

"It won't do any good. You know it won't." Lucy didn't sound like she was arguing with me. She *knew*. That's because Lucy is smarter than I am. Lucy wouldn't have started the drinking and gotten into such a mess in the first place. So it was about time I listened to what she said.

"Look, Vi," she murmured. "I hate to tell you this. You aren't well, you know. But you're going to find out one of these days anyway, and you might as well hear it from me."

"What is it, Lucy?"

"About George, and the doctors. They don't think you're going to get well." She paused. "They don't want you to."

"Oh, Lucy!"

"Listen to me, you little fool. Why do you suppose they sent you to that sanatorium in the first place? They said it was to take the cure. So you took it. All right, you're cured, then. But you'll notice that you still have the doctor coming every day, and George makes you stay here in your room, and that Miss Higgins who's supposed to be a special nurse – you know what she is, don't you? She's a guard."

I couldn't say anything. I just sat there and blinked. I wanted to cry, but I couldn't, because deep down inside I knew that Lucy was right.

"Just try to get out of here," Lucy said. "You'll see how fast she locks the door on you. All that talk about special diets and rest doesn't fool me. Look at yourself – you're as well as I am! You ought to be getting out, seeing people, visiting your friends."

"But I have no friends," I reminded her. "Not after that party, not after what I did—"

"That's a lie." Lucy nodded. "That's what George wants you to think. Why, you have hundreds of friends, Vi. They still love you. They tried to see you at the hospital and George wouldn't let them in. They sent flowers to the sanatorium and George told the nurses to burn them."

"He did? He told the nurses to burn the flowers?"

"Of course. Look, Vi, it's about time you faced the truth. George wants them to think you're sick. George wants you to think you're sick. Why? Because then he

173

can put you away for good. Not in a private sanatorium, but in the—"

"No!" I began to shake. I couldn't stop shaking. It was ghastly. But it proved something. They told me at the sanatorium, the doctors told me, that if I took the cure I wouldn't get the shakes any more. Or the dreams, or any of the other things. Yet here it was – I was shaking again.

"Shall I tell you some more?" Lucy whispered. "Shall I tell you what they're putting in your food? Shall I tell you about George and Miss Higgins?"

"But she's older than he is, and besides he'd never—"

Lucy laughed.

"Stop it!" I yelled.

"All right. But don't yell, you little fool. Do you want Miss Higgins to come in?"

"She thinks I'm taking a nap. She gave me a sedative."

"Lucky I dumped it out." Lucy frowned. "Vi, I've got to get you away from here. And there isn't much time."

She was right. There wasn't much time. Seconds, minutes, hours, days, weeks – how long had it been since I'd had a drink?

"We'll sneak off," Lucy said. "We could take a room together where they wouldn't find us. I'll nurse you until you're well."

"But rooms cost money."

"You have that fifty dollars George gave you for a party dress."

"Why, Lucy," I said. "How did you know that?"

"You told me ages ago, dear. Poor thing, you don't remember things very well, do you? All the more reason for trusting me."

I nodded. I could trust Lucy. Even though she was responsible, in a way, for me starting to drink. She just had thought it would cheer me up when George brought all his high-class friends to the house and we went out to impress his clients. Lucy had tried to help. I could trust her. I must trust her—

"We can leave as soon as Miss Higgins goes tonight," Lucy was saying. "We'll wait until George is asleep, eh? Why not get dressed now, and I'll come back for you."

I got dressed. It isn't easy to dress when you have the shakes, but I did it. I even put on some make-up and trimmed my hair a little with the big scissors. Then I looked at myself in the mirror and said out loud, "Why, you can't tell, can you?"

"Of course not," said Lucy. "You look radiant. Positively radiant."

I stood there smiling, and the sun was going down, just shining through the window on the scissors in a way that hurt my eyes, and all at once I was so sleepy.

"George will be here soon, and Miss Higgins will leave," Lucy said. "I'd better go now. Why don't you rest until I come for you?"

"Yes," I said. "You'll be very careful, won't you?"

"Very careful," Lucy whispered, and tiptoed out quietly.

I lay down on the bed and then I was sleeping, really sleeping for the first time in weeks, sleeping so the scissors wouldn't hurt my eyes, the way George hurt me inside when he wanted to shut me up in the asylum so he and Miss Higgins could make love on my bed and laugh at me the way they all laughed except Lucy and she would take care of me she knew what to do now I could trust her when George came and I must sleep and sleep and nobody can blame you for what you think in your sleep or do in your sleep . . .

It was all right until I had the dreams, and even then I didn't really worry about them because a dream is only a dream, and when I was drunk I had a lot of dreams.

When I woke up I had the shakes again, but it was Lucy shaking me, standing there in the dark shaking me. I looked around and saw that the door to my room was open, but Lucy didn't bother to whisper.

She stood there with the scissors in her hand and called to me.

"Come on, let's hurry."

"What are you doing with the scissors?" I asked.

"Cutting the telephone wires, silly! I got into the kitchen after Miss Higgins left and dumped some of that sedative into George's coffee. Remember, I told you the plan."

I couldn't remember now, but I knew it was all right. Lucy and I went out through the hall, past George's room, and he never stirred. Then we went downstairs and out the front door and the streetlights hurt my eyes. Lucy made me hurry right along, though.

We took a streetcar around the corner. This was the difficult part, getting away. Once we were out of the neighborhood, there'd be no worry. The wires were cut.

The lady at the rooming house on the South Side didn't know about the wires being cut. She didn't know about me, either, because Lucy got the room.

Lucy marched in bold as brass and laid my fifty dollars down on the desk. The rent was $12.50 a week in advance, and Lucy didn't even ask to see the room. I guess that's why the landlady wasn't worried about baggage.

*

We got upstairs and locked the door, and then I had the shakes again.

Lucy said, "Vi – cut it out!"

"But I can't help it. What'll I do now, Lucy? Oh, what'll I do? Why did I ever—"

"Shut up!" Lucy opened my purse and pulled something out. I had been wondering why my purse felt so heavy but I never dreamed about the secret.

She held the secret up. It glittered under the light, like

the scissors, only this was a nice glittering. A golden glittering.

"A whole pint!" I gasped. "Where did you get it?"

"From the cupboard downstairs, naturally. You knew George still keeps the stuff around. I slipped it into your purse, just in case."

I had the shakes, but I got that bottle open in ten seconds. One of my fingernails broke, and then the stuff was burning and warming and softening—

"Pig!" said Lucy.

"You know I had to have it," I whispered. "That's why you brought it."

"I don't like to see you drink," Lucy answered. "I never drink and I don't like to see you hang one on, either."

"Please, Lucy. Just this once."

"Why can't you take a shot and then leave it alone? That's all I ask."

"Just this once, Lucy, I have to."

"I won't sit here and watch you make a spectacle of yourself. You know what always happens – another mess."

I took another gulp. The bottle was half-empty.

"I did all I could for you, Vi. But if you don't stop now, I'm going."

That made me pause. "You couldn't do that to me. I need you, Lucy. Until I'm straightened out, anyway."

Lucy laughed, the way I didn't like. "Straightened out! That's a hot one! Talking about straightening out with a bottle in your hand. It's no use, Vi. Here I do everything I can for you, I stop at nothing to get you away, and you're off on another."

"Please. You know I can't help it."

"Oh, yes, you can help it, Vi. But you don't want to. You've always had to make a choice, you know. George or the bottle. Me or the bottle. And the bottle always wins. I think deep down inside you hate George. You hate me."

"You're my best friend."

"Nuts!" Lucy talked vulgar sometimes, when she got really mad. And she was mad, now. It made me so nervous I had another drink.

"Oh, I'm good enough for you when you're in trouble, or have nobody else around to talk to. I'm good enough to lie for you, pull you out of your messes. But I've never been good enough for your friends, for George. And I can't even win over a bottle of rotgut whisky. It's no use, Vi. What I've done for you today you'll never know. And it isn't enough. Keep your lousy whisky. I'm going."

I know I started to cry. I tried to get up, but the room was turning round and round. Then Lucy was walking out the door and I dropped the bottle and the light kept shining the way it did on the scissors and I closed my eyes and dropped after the bottle to the floor . . .

*

When I woke up they were all pestering me, the landlady and the doctor and Miss Higgins and the man who said he was a policeman.

I wondered if Lucy had gone to them and betrayed me, but when I asked the doctor said no, they just discovered me through a routine checkup on hotels and rooming-houses after they found George's body in his bed with my scissors in his throat.

All at once I knew what Lucy had done, and why she ran out on me that way. She knew they'd find me and call it murder.

So I told them about her and how it must have happened. I even figured out how Lucy managed to get my fingerprints on the scissors.

But Miss Higgins said she'd never seen Lucy in my house, and the landlady told a lie and said I had registered for the room alone, and the man from the police just laughed when I kept begging him to find Lucy and make her tell the truth.

Only the doctor seemed to understand, and when we were alone together in the little room he asked me all about her and what she looked like, and I told him.

Then he brought over the mirror and held it up and asked me if I could see her. And sure enough—

She was standing right behind me, laughing. I could see her in the mirror and I told the doctor so, and he said yes, he thought he understood now.

So it was all right after all. Even when I got the shakes just then and dropped the mirror, so that the little jagged pieces hurt my eyes to look at, it was all right.

Lucy was back with me now, and she wouldn't ever go away any more. She'd stay with me forever. I knew that. I knew it, because even though the light hurt my eyes, Lucy began to laugh.

After a minute, I began to laugh, too. And then the two of us were laughing together, we couldn't stop even when the doctor went away. We just stood there against the bars, Lucy and I, laughing like crazy.

DON'T LOOK NOW

(British Lion, 1973)
Starring: Donald Sutherland, Julie Christie &
Hilary Mason
Directed by Nicolas Roeg
Based on 'Don't Look Now' by Daphne du Maurier

The same year that *Asylum* was released saw a remake of Henry James's ghostly classic novel, *The Turn of the Screw*, about the governess of two children under the supernatural 'control' of her predecessor and a gardener, which had originally been brought to the screen in 1961 entitled *The Innocents* with Deborah Kerr. It was the controversial film maker, Michael Winner, who produced this new Seventies version called *The Nightcomers* with Stephanie Beacham playing the governess and Marlon Brando as the evil gardener. Despite generally good reviews, it was another film of the supernatural, *Don't Look Now*, released just a few months later in 1973 that captured the public attention as well as the best reviews. Commenting on the movie, film historian Maurice Sellar has called it "Britain's best psychic thriller" and added, "Directed by Nicolas Roeg, who is perhaps the most enigmatic of British film makers, it is a stunning labyrinth of themes, reflections, neuroses and supernatural fears." The film is a story of precognition and second sight concerning a young couple who are suffering the trauma of the death by drowning of their daughter and are warned of impending danger by a pair of sisters – one of whom is a medium. The growing sense of unease which was devloped by the performances of Donald Sutherland and Julie Christie made the film something of a landmark and one that has stood the test of time extremely well.

Don't Look Now was adapted from a story of the same title by Daphne du Maurier (1907–1989) and retained much of its sense of the uncanny and the absurd. Although famous as a popular novelist for her books like *Jamaica Inn* (1936), *Rebecca* (1938) and *Frenchman's Creek* (1942) – all of which have been filmed – Daphne also wrote about the supernatural in a number of her other novels and short stories: in particular *My Cousin Rachel* (1951), *The House on the Strand* (1969), and the tales of 'The Blue Lens', 'The Apple Tree' and 'The Birds' which Alfred Hitchcock scarily filmed in 1963 with Tippi Hedren, the mother of Melanie Griffith. Nicolas Roeg's version of *Don't Look Now* was described at the time as a cautionary tale for the dissolute 1970s, then rapidly collapsing after the false optimism of the Swinging Sixties. Here is the equally disturbing story upon which it was based written just three years earlier in 1970.

"Don't look now," John said to his wife, "but there are a couple of old girls two tables away who are trying to hypnotise me."

Laura, quick on cue, made an elaborate pretence of yawning, then tilted her head as though searching the skies for a non-existent aeroplane.

"Right behind you," he added. "That's why you can't turn round at once – it would be much too obvious."

Laura played the oldest trick in the world and dropped her napkin, then bent to scrabble for it under her feet, sending a shooting glance over her left shoulder as she straightened once again. She sucked in her cheeks, the first tell-tale sign of suppressed hysteria, and lowered her head.

"They're not old girls at all," she said. "They're male twins in drag."

Her voice broke ominously, the prelude to uncontrolled laughter, and John quickly poured some more chianti into her glass.

"Pretend to choke," he said, "then they won't notice. You know what it is – they're criminals doing the sights of Europe, changing sex at each stop. Twin sisters here on Torcello. Twin brothers tomorrow in Venice, or even tonight, parading arm-in-arm across the Piazza San Marco. Just a matter of switching clothes and wigs."

"Jewel thieves or murderers?" asked Laura.

"Oh, murderers, definitely. But why, I ask myself, have they picked on me?"

The waiter made a diversion by bringing coffee and bearing away the fruit, which gave Laura time to banish hysteria and regain control.

"I can't think," she said, "why we didn't notice them when we arrived. They stand out to high heaven. One couldn't fail."

"That gang of Americans masked them," said John, "and the bearded man with a monocle who looked like a spy. It wasn't until they all went just now that I saw the twins. Oh God, the one with the shock of white hair has got her eye on me again."

Laura took the powder compact from her bag and held it in front of her face, the mirror acting as a reflector.

"I think it's me they're looking at, not you," she said. "Thank heaven I left my pearls with the manager at the hotel." She paused, dabbing the sides of her nose with powder. "The thing is," she said after a moment, "we've got them wrong. They're neither murderers nor thieves. They're a couple of pathetic old retired schoolmistresses on holiday, who've saved up all their lives to visit Venice. They come from some place with a name like Walabanga in Australia. And they're called Tilly and Tiny."

Her voice, for the first time since they had come away, took on the old bubbling quality he loved, and the worried frown between her brows had vanished. At last, he thought, at last she's beginning to get over it. If I can keep this going, if we can pick up the familiar routine of jokes shared on holiday and at home, the ridiculous fantasies about people at other tables, or staying in the hotel, or wandering in art galleries and churches, then everything will fall into place, life will become as it was before, the wound will heal, she will forget.

"You know," said Laura, "that really was a very good lunch. I did enjoy it."

Thank God, he thought, thank God . . . Then he leant forward, speaking low in a conspirator's whisper. "One of them is going to the loo," he said. "Do you suppose he, or she, is going to change her wig?"

"Don't say anything," Laura murmured. "I'll follow her and find out. She may have a suitcase tucked away there, and she's going to switch clothes."

She began to hum under her breath, the signal, to her husband, of content. The ghost was temporarily laid, and all because of the familiar holiday game, abandoned too long, and now, through mere chance, blissfully recaptured.

"Is she on her way?" asked Laura.

"About to pass our table now," he told her.

Seen on her own, the woman was not so remarkable. Tall, angular, aquiline features, with the close-cropped hair which was fashionably called an Eton crop, he seemed to remember, in his mother's day, and about her person the stamp of that particular generation. She would be in her middle sixties, he supposed, the masculine shirt with collar and tie, sports jacket, grey tweed skirt coming to mid-calf. Grey stockings and laced black shoes. He had seen the type on golf-courses and at dog-shows –

invariably showing not sporting breeds but pugs – and if you came across them at a party in somebody's house they were quicker on the draw with a cigarette-lighter than he was himself, a mere male, with pocket-matches. The general belief that they kept house with a more feminine, fluffy companion was not always true. Frequently they boasted, and adored, a golfing husband. No, the striking point about this particular individual was that there were two of them. Identical twins cast in the same mould. The only difference was that the other one had whiter hair.

"Supposing," murmured Laura, "when I find myself in the *toilette* beside her she starts to strip?"

"Depends on what is revealed," John answered. "If she's hermaphrodite, make a bolt for it. She might have a hypodermic syringe concealed and want to knock you out before you reached the door."

Laura sucked in her cheeks once more and began to shake. Then, squaring her shoulders, she rose to her feet. "I simply must not laugh," she said, "and whatever you do, don't look at me when I come back, especially if we come out together." She picked up her bag and strolled self-consciously away from the table in pursuit of her prey.

John poured the dregs of the chianti into his glass and lit a cigarette. The sun blazed down upon the little garden of the restaurant. The Americans had left, and the monocled man, and the family party at the far end. All was peace. The identical twin was sitting back in her chair with her eyes closed. Thank heaven, he thought, for this moment at any rate, when relaxation was possible, and Laura had been launched upon her foolish, harmless game. The holiday could yet turn into the cure she needed, blotting out, if only temporarily, the numb despair that had seized her since the child died.

"She'll get over it," the doctor said. "They all get over it, in time. And you have the boy."

"I know," John had said, "but the girl meant everything.

She always did, right from the start, I don't know why. I suppose it was the difference in age. A boy of school age, and a tough one at that, is someone in his own right. Not a baby of five. Laura literally adored her. Johnnie and I were nowhere."

"Give her time," repeated the doctor, "give her time. And anyway, you're both young still. There'll be others. Another daughter."

So easy to talk . . . How replace the life of a loved lost child with a dream? He knew Laura too well. Another child, another girl, would have her own qualities, a separate identity, she might even induce hostility because of this very fact. A usurper in the cradle, in the cot, that had been Christine's. A chubby, flaxen replica of Johnnie, not the little waxen dark-haired sprite that had gone.

He looked up, over his glass of wine, and the woman was staring at him again. It was not the casual, idle glance of someone at a nearby table, waiting for her companion to return, but something deeper, more intent, the prominent, light blue eyes oddly penetrating, giving him a sudden feeling of discomfort. Damn the woman! All right, bloody stare, if you must. Two can play at that game. He blew a cloud of cigarette smoke into the air and smiled at her, he hoped offensively. She did not register. The blue eyes continued to hold his, so that he was obliged to look away himself, extinguish his cigarette, glance over his shoulder for the waiter and call for the bill. Settling for this, and fumbling with the change, with a few casual remarks about the excellence of the meal, brought composure, but a prickly feeling on his scalp remained, and an odd sensation of unease. Then it went, as abruptly as it had started, and stealing a furtive glance at the other table he saw that her eyes were closed again, and she was sleeping, or dozing, as she had done before. The waiter disappeared. All was still.

Laura, he thought, glancing at his watch, is being a hell of a time. Ten minutes at least. Something to tease her about, anyway. He began to plan the form the joke would take. How the old dolly had stripped to her smalls, suggesting that Laura should do likewise. And then the manager had burst in upon them both, exclaiming in horror, the reputation of the restaurant damaged, the hint that unpleasant consequences might follow unless . . . The whole exercise turning out to be a plant, an exercise in blackmail. He and Laura and the twins taken in a police launch back to Venice for questioning. Quarter of an hour . . . Oh, come on, come on . . .

There was a crunch of feet on the gravel. Laura's twin walked slowly past, alone. She crossed over to her table and stood there a moment, her tall, angular figure interposing itself between John and her sister. She was saying something, but he couldn't catch the words. What was the accent, though – Scottish? Then she bent, offering an arm to the seated twin, and they moved away together across the garden to the break in the little hedge beyond, the twin who had stared at John leaning on her sister's arm. Here was the difference again. She was not quite so tall, and she stooped more – perhaps she was arthritic. They disappeared out of sight, and John, becoming impatient, got up and was about to walk back into the hotel when Laura emerged.

"Well, I must say, you took your time," he began, and then stopped, because of the expression on her face.

"What's the matter, what's happened?" he asked.

He could tell at once there was something wrong. Almost as if she were in a state of shock. She blundered towards the table he had just vacated and sat down. He drew up a chair beside her, taking her hand.

"Darling, what is it? Tell me – are you ill?"

She shook her head, and then turned and looked at him. The dazed expression he had noticed at first had given way to one of dawning confidence, almost of exaltation.

"It's quite wonderful," she said slowly, "the most wonderful thing that could possibly be. You see, she isn't

186

dead, she's still with us. That's why they kept staring at us, those two sisters. They could see Christine."

Oh God, he thought. It's what I've been dreading. She's going off her head. What do I do? How do I cope?

"Laura, sweet," he began, forcing a smile, "look, shall we go? I've paid the bill, we can go and look at the cathedral and stroll around, and then it will be time to take off in that launch again for Venice."

She wasn't listening, or at any rate the words didn't penetrate.

"John, love," she said, "I've got to tell you what happened. I followed her, as we planned, into the *toilette* place. She was combing her hair and I went into the loo, and then came out and washed my hands in the basin. She was washing hers in the next basin. Suddenly she turned and said to me, in a strong Scots accent, 'Don't be unhappy any more. My sister has seen your little girl. She was sitting between you and your husband, laughing.' Darling, I thought I was going to faint. I nearly did. Luckily, there was a chair, and I sat down, and the woman bent over me and patted my head. I'm not sure of her exact words, but she said something about the moment of truth and joy being as sharp as a sword, but not to be afraid, all was well, but the sister's vision had been so strong they knew I had to be told, and that Christine wanted it. Oh John, don't look like that. I swear I'm not making it up, this is what she told me, it's all true."

The desperate urgency in her voice made his heart sicken. He had to play along with her, agree, soothe, do anything to bring back some sense of calm.

"Laura, darling, of course I believe you," he said, "only it's a sort of shock, and I'm upset because you're upset . . ."

"But I'm not upset," she interrupted. "I'm happy, so happy that I can't put the feeling into words. You know what it's been like all these weeks, at home and everywhere we've been on holiday, though I tried to hide it from you. Now it's lifted, because I know, I just know, that the woman was right. Oh Lord, how awful of me, but I've forgotten their name – she did tell me. You see, the thing is that she's a retired doctor, they come from Edinburgh, and the one who saw Christine went blind a few years ago. Although she's studied the occult all her life and been very psychic, it's only since going blind that she has really seen things, like a medium. They've had the most wonderful experiences. But to describe Christine as the blind one did to her sister, even down to the little blue-and-white dress with the puff sleeves that she wore at her birthday party, and to say she was smiling happily . . . Oh darling, it's made me so happy I think I'm going to cry."

No hysteria. Nothing wild. She took a tissue from her bag and blew her nose, smiling at him. "I'm all right, you see, you don't have to worry. Neither of us need worry about anything any more. Give me a cigarette."

He took one from his packet and lighted it for her. She sounded normal, herself again. She wasn't trembling. And if this sudden belief was going to keep her happy he couldn't possibly begrudge it. But . . . but . . . he wished, all the same, it hadn't happened. There was something uncanny about thought-reading, about telepathy. Scientists couldn't account for it, nobody could, and this is what must have happened just now between Laura and the sisters. So the one who had been staring at him was blind. That accounted for the fixed gaze. Which somehow was unpleasant in itself, creepy. Oh hell, he thought, I wish we hadn't come here for lunch. Just chance, a flick of a coin between this, Torcello, and driving to Padua, and we had to choose Torcello.

"You didn't arrange to meet them again or anything, did you?" he asked, trying to sound casual.

"No, darling, why should I?" Laura answered. "I mean, there was nothing more they could tell me. The sister had had her wonderful vision, and that was that. Anyway, they're moving on. Funnily enough, it's rather like our original game. They *are* going round the world before returning to Scotland. Only I said Australia, didn't I? The old dears . . . Anything less like murderers and jewel thieves."

She had quite recovered. She stood up and looked about her. "Come on," she said. "Having come to Torcello we must see the cathedral."

They made their way from the restaurant across the open piazza, where the stalls had been set up with scarves and trinkets and postcards, and so along the path to the cathedral. One of the ferry-boats had just decanted a crowd of sightseers, many of whom had already found their way into Santa Maria Assunta. Laura, undaunted, asked her husband for the guidebook, and, as had always been her custom in happier days, started to walk slowly through the cathedral, studying mosaics, columns, panels from left to right, while John, less interested, because of his concern at what had just happened, followed close behind, keeping a weather eye alert for the twin sisters. There was no sign of them. Perhaps they had gone into the church of Santa Fosca close by. A sudden encounter would be embarrassing, quite apart from the effect it might have upon Laura. But the anonymous, shuffling tourists, intent upon culture, could not harm her, although from his own point of view they made artistic appreciation impossible. He could not concentrate, the cold clear beauty of what he saw left him untouched, and when Laura touched his sleeve, pointing to the mosaic of the Virgin and Child standing above the frieze of the Apostles, he nodded in sympathy yet saw nothing, the long, sad face of the Virgin infinitely remote, and turning on sudden impulse stared back over the heads of the tourists towards the door, where frescoes of the blessed and the damned gave themselves to judgement.

The twins were standing there, the blind one still holding on to her sister's arm, her sightless eyes fixed firmly upon him. He felt himself held, unable to move, and an impending sense of doom, of tragedy, came upon him. His whole being sagged, as it were, in apathy, and he thought, "This is the end, there is no escape, no future." Then both sisters turned and went out of the cathedral and the sensation vanished, leaving indignation in its wake, and rising anger. How dare those two old fools practise their mediumistic tricks on him? It was fraudulent, unhealthy; this was probably the way they lived, touring the world making everyone they met uncomfortable. Give them half a chance and they would have got money out of Laura – anything.

He felt her tugging at his sleeve again. "Isn't she beautiful? So happy, so serene."

"Who? What?" he asked.

"The Madonna," she answered. "She has a magic quality. It goes right through to one. Don't you feel it too?"

"I suppose so. I don't know. There are too many people around."

She looked up at him, astonished. "What's that got to do with it? How funny you are. Well, all right, let's get away from them. I want to buy some postcards anyway."

Disappointed, she sensed his lack of interest, and began to thread her way through the crowd of tourists to the door.

"Come on," he said abruptly, once they were outside, "there's plenty of time for postcards, let's explore a bit," and he struck off from the path, which would have taken them back to the centre where the little houses were, and the stalls, and the drifting crowd of people, to a narrow way amongst uncultivated ground, beyond which he could see a sort of cutting, or canal. The sight of water, limpid, pale, was a soothing contrast to the fierce sun above their heads.

"I don't think this leads anywhere much," said Laura.

"It's a bit muddy, too, one can't sit. Besides, there are more things the guidebook says we ought to see."

"Oh, forget the book," he said impatiently, and, pulling her down beside him on the bank above the cutting, put his arms round her.

"It's the wrong time of day for sightseeing. Look, there's a rat swimming there the other side."

He picked up a stone and threw it in the water, and the animal sank, or somehow disappeared, and nothing was left but bubbles.

"Don't," said Laura. "It's cruel, poor thing," and then suddenly, putting her hand on his knee, "Do you think Christine is sitting here beside us?"

He did not answer at once. What was there to say? Would it be like this forever?

"I expect so," he said slowly, "if you feel she is."

The point was, remembering Christine before the onset of the fatal meningitis, she would have been running along the bank excitedly, throwing off her shoes, wanting to paddle, giving Laura a fit of apprehension. "Sweetheart, take care, come back . . ."

"The woman said she was looking so happy, sitting beside us, smiling," said Laura. She got up, brushing her dress, her mood changed to restlessness. "Come on, let's go back," she said.

He followed her with a sinking heart. He knew she did not really want to buy postcards or see what remained to be seen; she wanted to go in search of the women again, not necessarily to talk, just to be near them. When they came to the open place by the stalls he noticed that the crowd of tourists had thinned, there were only a few stragglers left, and the sisters were not amongst them. They must have joined the main body who had come to Torcello by the ferry service. A wave of relief seized him.

"Look, there's a mass of postcards at the second stall," he said quickly, "and some eye-catching head scarves. Let me buy you a head scarf."

"Darling, I've so many!" she protested. "Don't waste your lire."

"It isn't a waste. I'm in a buying mood. What about a basket? You know we never have enough baskets. Or some lace. How about lace?"

She allowed herself, laughing, to be dragged to the stall. While he rumpled through the goods spread out before them, and chatted up the smiling woman who was selling her wares, his ferociously bad Italian making her smile the more, he knew it would give the body of tourists more time to walk to the landing stage and catch the ferry-service, and the twin sisters would be out of sight and out of their life.

"Never," said Laura, some twenty minutes later, "has so much junk been piled into so small a basket," her bubbling laugh reassuring him that all was well, he needn't worry any more, the evil hour had passed. The launch from the Cipriani that had brought them from Venice was waiting by the landing-stage. The passengers who had arrived with them, the Americans, the man with the monocle, were already assembled. Earlier, before setting out, he had thought the price for lunch and transport, there and back, decidedly steep. Now he grudged none of it, except that the outing to Torcello itself had been one of the major errors of this particular holiday in Venice. They stepped down into the launch, finding a place in the open, and the boat chugged away down the canal and into the lagoon. The ordinary ferry had gone before, steaming towards Murano, while their own craft headed past San Francesco del Deserto and so back direct to Venice.

He put his arm around her once more, holding her close, and this time she responded, smiling up at him, her head on his shoulder.

"It's been a lovely day," she said. "I shall never forget it, never. You know, darling, now at last I can begin to enjoy our holiday."

He wanted to shout with relief. It's going to be all

right, he decided, let her believe what she likes, it doesn't matter, it makes her happy. The beauty of Venice rose before them, sharply outlined against the glowing sky, and there was still so much to see, wandering there together, that might now be perfect because of her change of mood, the shadow having lifted, and aloud he began to discuss the evening to come, where they would dine – not the restaurant they usually went to, near the Fenice theatre, but somewhere different, somewhere new.

"Yes, but it must be cheap," she said, falling in with his mood, "because we've already spent so much today."

Their hotel by the Grand Canal had a welcoming, comforting air. The clerk smiled as he handed over their key. The bedroom was familiar, like home, with Laura's things arranged neatly on the dressing-table, but with it the little festive atmosphere of strangeness, of excitement, that only a holiday bedroom brings. This is ours for the moment, but no more. While we are in it we bring it life. When we have gone it no longer exists, it fades into anonymity. He turned on both taps in the bathroom, the water gushing into the bath, the steam rising. "Now," he thought afterwards, "now at last is the moment to make love," and he went back into the bedroom, and she understood, and opened her arms and smiled. Such blessed relief after all those weeks of restraint.

"The thing is," she said later, fixing her ear-rings before the looking-glass, "I'm not really terribly hungry. Shall we just be dull and eat in the dining-room here?"

"God, no!" he exclaimed. "With all those rather dreary couples at the other tables? I'm ravenous. I'm also gay. I want to get rather sloshed."

"Not bright lights and music, surely?"

"No, no . . . some small, dark, intimate cave, rather sinister, full of lovers with other people's wives."

"H'm," sniffed Laura, "we all know what *that* means. You'll spot some Italian lovely of sixteen and smirk at her through dinner, while I'm stuck high and dry with a beastly man's broad back."

They went out laughing into the warm soft night, and the magic was about them everywhere. "Let's walk," he said, "let's walk and work up an appetite for our gigantic meal," and inevitably they found themselves by the Molo and the lapping gondolas dancing upon the water, the lights everywhere blending with the darkness. There were other couples strolling for the same sake of aimless enjoyment, backwards, forwards, purposeless, and the inevitable sailors in groups, noisy, gesticulating, and dark-eyed girls whispering, clicking on high heels.

"The trouble is," said Laura, "walking in Venice becomes compulsive once you start. Just over the next bridge, you say, and then the next one beckons. I'm sure there are no restaurants down here, we're almost at those public gardens where they hold the Biennale. Let's turn back. I know there's a restaurant somewhere near the church of San Zaccaria, there's a little alleyway leading to it."

"Tell you what," said John, "if we go down here by the Arsenal, and cross that bridge at the end and head left, we'll come upon San Zaccaria from the other side. We did it the other morning."

"Yes, but it was daylight then. We may lose our way, it's not very well lit."

"Don't fuss. I have an instinct for these things."

They turned down the Fondamenta dell' Arsenale and crossed the little bridge short of the Arsenal itself, and so on past the church of San Martino. There were two canals ahead, one bearing right, the other left, with narrow streets beside them. John hesitated. Which one was it they had walked beside the day before?

"You see," protested Laura, "we shall be lost, just as I said."

"Nonsense," replied John firmly. "It's the left-hand one, I remember the little bridge."

Don't Look Now

The canal was narrow, the houses on either side seemed to close in upon it, and in the daytime, with the sun's reflection on the water and the windows of the houses open, bedding upon the balconies, a canary singing in a cage, there had been an impression of warmth, of secluded shelter. Now, ill-lit, almost in darkness, the windows of the houses shuttered, the water dank, the scene appeared altogether different, neglected, poor, and the long narrow boats moored to the slippery steps of cellar entrances looked like coffins.

"I swear I don't remember this bridge," said Laura, pausing, and holding on to the rail, "and I don't like the look of that alleyway beyond."

"There's a lamp halfway up," John told her. "I know exactly where we are, not far from the Greek quarter."

They crossed the bridge, and were about to plunge into the alleyway when they heard the cry. It came, surely, from one of the houses on the opposite side, but which one it was impossible to say. With the shutters closed each one of them seemed dead. They turned, and stared in the direction from which the sound had come.

"What was it?" whispered Laura.

"Some drunk or other," said John briefly. "Come on."

Less like a drunk than someone being strangled, and the choking cry suppressed as the grip held firm.

"We ought to call the police," said Laura.

"Oh, for heaven's sake," said John. Where did she think she was – Piccadilly?

"Well, I'm off, it's sinister," she replied, and began to hurry away up the twisting alleyway. John hesitated, his eye caught by a small figure which suddenly crept from a cellar entrance below one of the opposite houses, and then jumped into a narrow boat below. It was a child, a little girl – she couldn't have been more than five or six – wearing a short coat over her minute skirt, a pixie hood covering her head. There were four boats moored, line upon line, and she proceeded to jump from one to

195

the other with surprising agility, intent, it would seem, upon escape. Once her foot slipped and he caught his breath, for she was within a few feet of the water, losing balance; then she recovered, and hopped onto the furthest boat. Bending, she tugged at the rope, which had the effect of swinging the boat's after-end across the canal, almost touching the opposite side and another cellar entrance, about thirty feet from the spot where John stood watching her. Then the child jumped again, landing upon the cellar steps, and vanished into the house, the boat swinging back into mid-canal behind her. The whole episode could not have taken more than four minutes. Then he heard the quick patter of feet. Laura had returned. She had seen none of it, for which he felt unspeakably thankful. The sight of a child, a little girl, in what must have been near danger, her fear that the scene he had just witnessed was in some way a sequel to the alarming cry, might have had a disastrous effect on her overwrought nerves.

"What are you doing?" she called. "I daren't go on without you. The wretched alley branches in two directions."

"Sorry," he told her. "I'm coming."

He took her arm and they walked briskly along the alley, John with an apparent confidence he did not possess.

"There were no more cries, were there?" she asked.

"No," he said, "no, nothing. I tell you, it was some drunk."

The alley led to a deserted *campo* behind a church, not a church he knew, and he led the way across, along another street and over a further bridge.

"Wait a minute," he said. "I think we take this right-hand turning. It will lead us into the Greek quarter – the church of San Georgio is somewhere over there."

She did not answer. She was beginning to lose faith. The place was like a maze. They might circle round and round forever, and then find themselves back again, near the bridge where they had heard the cry. Doggedly he led her on, and then surprisingly, with relief, he saw people walking in the lighted street ahead, there was a spire of a church, the surroundings became familiar.

"There, I told you," he said. "That's San Zaccaria, we've found it all right. Your restaurant can't be far away."

And anyway, there would be other restaurants, somewhere to eat, at least here was the cheering glitter of lights, of movement, canals beside which people walked, the atmosphere of tourism. The letters 'Ristorante', in blue lights, shone like a beacon down a left-hand alley.

"Is this your place?" he asked.

"God knows," she said. "Who cares? Let's feed there anyway."

And so into the sudden blast of heated air and hum of voices, the smell of pasta, wine, waiters, jostling customers, laughter. "For two? This way, please." Why, he thought, was one's British nationality always so obvious? A cramped little table and an enormous menu scribbled in an indecipherable mauve biro, with the waiter hovering, expecting the order forthwith.

"Two very large camparis, with soda," John said. "*Then* we'll study the menu."

He was not going to be rushed. He handed the bill of fare to Laura and looked about him. Mostly Italians – that meant the food would be good. Then he saw them. At the opposite side of the room. The twin sisters. They must have come into the restaurant hard upon Laura's and his own arrival, for they were only now sitting down, shedding their coats, the waiter hovering beside the table. John was seized with the irrational thought that this was no coincidence. The sisters had noticed them both, in the street outside, and had followed them in. Why, in the name of hell, should they have picked on this particular spot, in the whole of Venice, unless . . . unless Laura herself, at Torcello, had suggested a further encounter, or

the sister had suggested it to her? A small restaurant near
the church of San Zaccaria, we go there sometimes for
dinner. It was Laura, before the walk, who had mentioned
San Zaccaria . . .

She was still intent upon the menu, she had not seen
the sisters, but any moment now she would have chosen
what she wanted to eat, and then she would raise her head
and look across the room. If only the drinks would come.
If only the waiter would bring the drinks, it would give
Laura something to do.

"You know, I was thinking," he said quickly, "we really
ought to go to the garage tomorrow and get the car, and
do that drive to Padua. We could lunch in Padua, see the
cathedral and touch St Antony's tomb and look at the
Giotto frescoes, and come back by way of those various
villas along the Brenta that the guidebook cracks up."

It was no use, though. She was looking up, across the
restaurant, and she gave a little gasp of surprise. It was
genuine. He could swear it was genuine.

"Look," she said, "how extraordinary! How really
amazing!"

"What?" he said sharply.

"Why, there they are. My wonderful old twins. They've
seen us, what's more. They're staring this way." She
waved her hand, radiant, delighted. The sister she had
spoken to at Torcello bowed and smiled. False old bitch,
he thought. I know they followed us.

"Oh, darling, I must go and speak to them," she said
impulsively, "just to tell them how happy I've been all
day, thanks to them."

"Oh, for heaven's sake!" he said. "Look, here are the
drinks. And we haven't ordered yet. Surely you can wait
until later, until we've eaten?"

"I won't be a moment," she said, "and anyway I want
scampi, nothing first. I told you I wasn't hungry."

She got up, and, brushing past the waiter with the
drinks, crossed the room. She might have been greeting

the loved friends of years. He watched her bend over the table and shake them both by the hand, and because there was a vacant chair at their table she drew it up and sat down, talking, smiling. Nor did the sisters seem surprised, at least not the one she knew, who nodded and talked back, while the blind sister remained impassive.

"All right," thought John savagely, "then I *will* get sloshed," and he proceeded to down his campari and soda and order another, while he pointed out something quite unintelligible on the menu as his own choice, but remembered scampi for Laura. "And a bottle of Soave," he added, "with ice."

The evening was ruined anyway. What was to have been an intimate, happy celebration would now be heavy-laden with spiritualistic visions, poor little dead Christine sharing the table with them, which was so damned stupid when in earthly life she would have been tucked up hours ago in bed. The bitter taste of the campari suited his mood of sudden self-pity, and all the while he watched the group at the table in the opposite corner, Laura apparently listening while the more active sister held forth and the blind one sat silent, her formidable sightless eyes turned in his direction.

"She's phoney," he thought, "she's not blind at all. They're both of them frauds, and they could be males in drag after all, just as we pretended at Torcello, and they're after Laura."

He began on his second campari and soda. The two drinks, taken on an empty stomach, had an instant effect. Vision became blurred. And still Laura went on sitting at the other table, putting in a question now and again, while the active sister talked. The waiter appeared with the scampi, and a companion beside him to serve John's own order, which was totally unrecognisable, heaped with a livid sauce.

"The signora does not come?" enquired the first waiter,

and John shook his head grimly, pointing an unsteady finger across the room.

"Tell the signora," he said carefully, "her scampi will get cold."

He stared down at the offering placed before him, and prodded it delicately with a fork. The pallid sauce dissolved, revealing two enormous slices, rounds, of what appeared to be boiled pork, bedecked with garlic. He forked a portion to his mouth and chewed, and yes, it was pork, steamy, rich, the spicy sauce having turned it curiously sweet. He laid down his fork, pushing the plate away, and became aware of Laura, returning across the room and sitting beside him. She did not say anything, which was just as well, he thought, because he was too near nausea to answer. It wasn't just the drink, but reaction from the whole nightmare day. She began to eat her scampi, still not uttering. She did not seem to notice he was not eating. The waiter, hovering at his elbow, anxious, seemed aware that John's choice was somehow an error, and discreetly removed the plate. "Bring me a green salad," murmured John, and even then Laura did not register surprise, or, as she might have done in more normal circumstances, accuse him of having had too much to drink. Finally, when she had finished her scampi and was sipping her wine, which John had waved away, to nibble at his salad in small mouthfuls like a sick rabbit, she began to speak.

"Darling," she said, "I know you won't believe it, and it's rather frightening in a way, but after they left the restaurant in Torcello the sisters went to the cathedral, as we did, although we didn't see them in that crowd, and the blind one had another vision. She said Christine was trying to tell her something about us, that we should be in danger if we stayed in Venice. Christine wanted us to go away as soon as possible."

So that's it, he thought. They think they can run our lives for us. This is to be our problem from henceforth.

Do we eat? Do we get up? Do we go to bed? We must get in touch with the twin sisters. They will direct us.

"Well?" she said. "Why don't you say something?"

"Because," he answered, "you are perfectly right, I don't believe it. Quite frankly, I judge your old sisters as being a couple of freaks, if nothing else. They're obviously unbalanced, and I'm sorry if this hurts you, but the fact is they've found a sucker in you."

"You're being unfair," said Laura. "They are genuine, I know it. I just know it. They were completely sincere in what they said."

"All right. Granted. They're sincere. But that doesn't make them well-balanced. Honestly, darling, you meet that old girl for ten minutes in a loo, she tells you she sees Christine sitting beside us – well, anyone with a gift for telepathy could read your unconscious mind in an instant – and then, pleased with her success, as any old psychic expert would be, she flings a further mood of ecstasy and wants to boot us out of Venice. Well, I'm sorry, but to hell with it."

The room was no longer reeling. Anger had sobered him. If it would not put Laura to shame he would get up and cross to their table, and tell the old fools where they got off.

"I knew you would take it like this," said Laura unhappily. "I told them you would. They said not to worry. As long as we left Venice tomorrow everything would come all right."

"Oh, for God's sake," said John. He changed his mind, and poured himself a glass of wine.

"After all," Laura went on, "we have really seen the cream of Venice. I don't mind going on somewhere else. And if we stayed – I know it sounds silly, but I should have a nasty nagging sort of feeling inside me, and I should keep thinking of darling Christine being unhappy and trying to tell us to go."

"Right," said John with ominous calm, "that settles

it. Go we will. I suggest we clear off to the hotel straight away and warn the reception we're leaving in the morning. Have you had enough to eat?"

"Oh, dear," sighed Laura, "don't take it like that. Look, why not come over and meet them, and then they can explain about the vision to you? Perhaps you would take it seriously then. Especially as you are the one it most concerns. Christine is more worried over you than me. And the extraordinary thing is that the blind sister says you're psychic and don't know it. You are somehow *en rapport* with the unknown, and I'm not."

"Well, that's final," said John. "I'm psychic, am I? Fine. My psychic intuition tells me to get out of this restaurant now, at once, and we can decide what we do about leaving Venice when we are back at the hotel."

He signalled to the waiter for the bill and they waited for it, not speaking to each other, Laura unhappy, fiddling with her bag, while John, glancing furtively at the twins' table, noticed that they were tucking into plates piled high with spaghetti, in very un-psychic fashion. The bill disposed of, John pushed back his chair.

"Right. Are you ready?" he asked.

"I'm going to say goodbye to them first," said Laura, her mouth set sulkily, reminding him instantly, with a pang, of their poor lost child.

"Just as you like," he replied, and walked ahead of her out of the restaurant, without a backward glance.

The soft humidity of the evening, so pleasant to walk about in earlier, had turned to rain. The strolling tourists had melted away. One or two people hurried by under umbrellas. This is what the inhabitants who live here see, he thought. This is the true life. Empty streets by night, and the dank stillness of a stagnant canal beneath shuttered houses. The rest is a bright façade put on for show, glittering by sunlight.

Laura joined him and they walked away together in silence, and emerging presently behind the ducal palace came out into the Piazza San Marco. The rain was heavy now, and they sought shelter with the few remaining stragglers under the colonnades. The orchestras had packed up for the evening. The tables were bare. Chairs had been turned upside down.

The experts are right, he thought. Venice is sinking. The whole city is slowly dying. One day the tourists will travel here by boat to peer down into the waters, and they will see pillars and columns and marble far, far beneath them, slime and mud uncovering for brief moments a lost underworld of stone. Their heels made a ringing sound on the pavement and the rain splashed from the gutterings above. A fine ending to an evening that had started with brave hope, with innocence.

When they came to their hotel Laura made straight for the lift, and John turned to the desk to ask the night-porter for the key. The man handed him a telegram at the same time. John stared at it a moment. Laura was already in the lift. Then he opened the envelope and read the message. It was from the headmaster of Johnnie's preparatory school.

Johnnie under observation suspected appendicitis in city hospital here. No cause for alarm but surgeon thought wise advise you.

Charles Hill

He read the message twice, then walked slowly towards the lift where Laura was waiting for him. He gave her the telegram. "This came when we were out," he said. "Not awfully good news." He pressed the lift button as she read the telegram. The lift stopped at the second floor, and they got out.

"Well, this decides it, doesn't it?" she said. "Here is the proof. We have to leave Venice because we're going home. It's Johnnie who's in danger, not us. This is what Christine was trying to tell the twins."

*

The first thing John did the following morning was to put a call through to the headmaster at the preparatory school. Then he gave notice of their departure to the reception manager, and they packed while they waited for the call. Neither of them referred to the events of the preceding day, it was not necessary. John knew the arrival of the telegram and the foreboding of danger from the sisters was coincidence, nothing more, but it was pointless to start an argument about it. Laura was convinced otherwise, but intuitively she knew it was best to keep her feelings to herself. During breakfast they discussed ways and means of getting home. It should be possible to get themselves, and the car, on to the special car train that ran from Milan through to Calais, since it was early in the season. In any event, the headmaster had said there was no urgency.

The call from England came while John was in the bathroom. Laura answered it. He came into the bedroom a few minutes later. She was still speaking, but he could tell from the expression in her eyes that she was anxious.

"It's Mrs Hill," she said. "Mr Hill is in class. She says they reported from the hospital that Johnnie had a restless night and the surgeon may have to operate, but he doesn't want to unless it's absolutely necessary. They've taken X-rays and the appendix is in a tricky position, it's not awfully straightforward."

"Here, give it to me," he said.

The soothing but slightly guarded voice of the head-master's wife came down the receiver. "I'm so sorry this may spoil your plans," she said, "but both Charles and I felt you ought to be told, and that you might feel rather easier if you were on the spot. Johnnie is very plucky, but of course he has some fever. That isn't unusual, the surgeon says, in the circumstances. Sometimes an appendix can get displaced, it appears, and this makes it more complicated. He's going to decide about operating this evening."

"Yes, of course, we quite understand," said John.

"Please do tell your wife not to worry too much," she went on. "The hospital is excellent, a very nice staff, and we have every confidence in the surgeon."

"Yes," said John, "yes," and then broke off because Laura was making gestures beside him.

"If we can't get the car on the train, I can fly," she said. "They're sure to be able to find me a seat on a 'plane. Then at least one of us would be there this evening."

He nodded agreement. "Thank you so much, Mrs Hill," he said, "we'll manage to get back all right. Yes, I'm sure Johnnie is in good hands. Thank your husband for us. Goodbye."

He replaced the receiver and looked round him at the tumbled beds, suitcases on the floor, tissue-paper strewn. Baskets, maps, books, coats, everything they had brought with them in the car. "Oh God," he said, "what a bloody mess. All this junk." The telephone rang again. It was the hall porter to say he had succeeded in booking a sleeper for them both, and a place for the car, on the following night.

"Look," said Laura, who had seized the telephone, "could you book one seat on the midday 'plane from Venice to London today, for me? It's imperative one of us gets home this evening. My husband could follow with the car tomorrow."

"Here, hang on," interrupted John. "No need for panic stations. Surely twenty-four hours wouldn't make all that difference?"

Anxiety had drained the colour from her face. She turned to him, distraught.

"It mightn't to you, but it does to me," she said. "I've lost one child, I'm not going to lose another."

"All right, darling, all right . . ." He put his hand out to her but she brushed it off, impatiently, and continued giving directions to the porter. He turned back to his packing. No use saying anything. Better for it to be as she wished. They could, of course, both go by air, and then when all was well, and Johnnie better, he could come back and fetch the car, driving home through France as they had come. Rather a sweat, though, and the hell of an expense. Bad enough Laura going by air and himself with the car on the train from Milan.

"We could, if you like, both fly," he began tentatively, explaining the sudden idea, but she would have none of it. "That really *would* be absurd," she said impatiently. "As long as I'm there this evening, and you follow by train, it's all that matters. Besides, we shall need the car, going backwards and forwards to the hospital. And our luggage. We couldn't go off and just leave all this here."

No, he saw her point. A silly idea. It was only – well, he was as worried about Johnnie as she was, though he wasn't going to say so.

"I'm going downstairs to stand over the porter," said Laura. "They always make more effort if one is actually on the spot. Everything I want tonight is packed. I shall only need my overnight case. You can bring everything else in the car." She hadn't been out of the bedroom five minutes before the telephone rang. It was Laura. "Darling," she said, "it couldn't have worked out better. The porter has got me on a charter flight that leaves Venice in less than an hour. A special motor-launch takes the party direct from San Marco in about ten minutes. Some passenger on the charter flight cancelled. I shall be at Gatwick in less than four hours."

"I'll be down right away," he told her.

He joined her by the reception desk. She no longer looked anxious and drawn, but full of purpose. She was on her way. He kept wishing they were going together. He couldn't bear to stay on in Venice after she had gone, but the thought of driving to Milan, spending a dreary night in a hotel there alone, the endless dragging day which would follow, and the long hours in the train the next night, filled him with intolerable depression, quite apart from the anxiety about Johnnie. They walked along to the San Marco landing-stage, the Molo bright and glittering after the rain, a little breeze blowing, the postcards and scarves and tourist souvenirs fluttering on the stalls, the tourists themselves out in force, strolling, contented, the happy day before them.

"I'll ring you tonight from Milan," he told her. "The Hills will give you a bed, I suppose. And if you're at the hospital they'll let me have the latest news. That must be your charter party. You're welcome to them!"

The passengers descending from the landing-stage down into the waiting launch were carrying hand-luggage with Union Jack tags upon them. They were mostly middle-aged, with what appeared to be two Methodist ministers in charge. One of them advanced towards Laura, holding out his hand, showing a gleaming row of dentures when he smiled. "You must be the lady joining us for the homeward flight," he said. "Welcome aboard, and to the Union of Fellowship. We are all delighted to make your acquaintance. Sorry we hadn't a seat for hubby too."

Laura turned swiftly and kissed John, a tremor at the corner of her mouth betraying inward laughter. "Do you think they'll break into hymns?" she whispered. "Take care of yourself, hubby. Call me tonight."

The pilot sounded a curious little toot upon his horn, and in a moment Laura had climbed down the steps into the launch and was standing amongst the crowd of passengers, waving her hand, her scarlet coat a gay patch of colour amongst the more sober suiting of her companions. The launch tooted again and moved away from the landing-stage, and he stood there watching it, a sense of immense loss filling his heart. Then he turned and walked away, back to the hotel, the bright day all about him desolate, unseen.

There was nothing, he thought, as he looked about

him presently in the hotel bedroom, so melancholy as a vacated room, especially when the recent signs of occupation were still visible about him. Laura's suitcases on the bed, a second coat she had left behind. Traces of powder on the dressing-table. A tissue, with a lipstick smear, thrown in the waste-paper basket. Even an old toothpaste tube squeezed dry, lying on the glass shelf above the washbasin. Sounds of the heedless traffic on the Grand Canal came as always from the open window, but Laura wasn't there any more to listen to it, or to watch from the small balcony. The pleasure had gone. Feeling had gone.

John finished packing, and leaving all the baggage ready to be collected he went downstairs to pay the bill. The reception clerk was welcoming new arrivals. People were sitting on the terrace overlooking the Grand Canal reading newspapers, the pleasant day waiting to be planned.

John decided to have an early lunch, here on the hotel terrace, on familiar ground, and then have the porter carry the baggage to one of the ferries that steamed direct between San Marco and the Porta Roma, where the car was garaged. The fiasco meal of the night before had left him empty, and he was ready for the trolley of hors d'oeuvres when they brought it to him, around midday. Even here, though, there was change. The head-waiter, their especial friend, was off-duty, and the table where they usually sat was occupied by new arrivals, a honeymoon couple, he told himself sourly, observing the gaiety, the smiles, while he had been shown to a small single table behind a tub of flowers.

"She's airborne now," John thought, "she's on her way," and he tried to picture Laura seated between the Methodist ministers, telling them, no doubt, about Johnnie ill in hospital, and heaven knows what else besides. Well, the twin sisters anyway could rest in psychic peace. Their wishes would have been fulfilled.

Lunch over, there was no point in lingering with a cup of coffee on the terrace. His desire was to get away as soon as possible, fetch the car, and be *en route* for Milan. He made his farewells at the reception desk, and, escorted by a porter who had piled his baggage onto a wheeled trolley, made his way once more to the landing-stage of San Marco. As he stepped onto the steam-ferry, his luggage heaped beside him, a crowd of jostling people all about him, he had one momentary pang to be leaving Venice. When, if ever, he wondered, would they come again? Next year . . . in three years . . . Glimpsed first on honeymoon, nearly ten years ago, and then a second visit, *en passant*, before a cruise, and now this last abortive ten days that had ended so abruptly.

The water glittered in the sunshine, buildings shone, tourists in dark glasses paraded up and down the rapidly receding Molo, already the terrace of their hotel was out of sight as the ferry churned its way up the Grand Canal. So many impressions to seize and hold, familiar loved façades, balconies, windows, water lapping the cellar steps of decaying palaces, the little red house where d'Annunzio lived, with its garden – our house, Laura called it, pretending it was theirs – and too soon the ferry would be turning left on the direct route to the Piazzale Roma, so missing the best of the Canal, the Rialto, the further palaces.

Another ferry was heading downstream to pass them, filled with passengers, and for a brief foolish moment he wished he could change places, be amongst the happy tourists bound for Venice and all he had left behind him. Then he saw her. Laura, in her scarlet coat, the twin sisters by her side, the active sister with her hand on Laura's arm, talking earnestly, and Laura herself, her hair blowing in the wind, gesticulating, on her face a look of distress. He stared, astounded, too astonished to shout, to wave, and anyway they would never have heard or seen him, for his own ferry had already passed and was heading in the opposite direction.

What the hell had happened? There must have been a hold-up with the charter flight and it had never taken off, but in that case why had Laura not telephoned him at the hotel? And what were those damned sisters doing? Had she run into them at the airport? Was it coincidence? And why did she look so anxious? He could think of no explanation. Perhaps the flight had been cancelled. Laura, of course, would go straight to the hotel, expecting to find him there, intending, doubtless, to drive with him after all to Milan and take the train the following night. What a blasted mix-up. The only thing to do was to telephone the hotel immediately his ferry reached the Piazzale Roma and tell her to wait – he would return and fetch her. As for the damned interfering sisters, they could get stuffed.

The usual stampede ensued when the ferry arrived at the landing-stage. He had to find a porter to collect his baggage, and then wait while he discovered a telephone. The fiddling with change, the hunt for the number, delayed him still more. He succeeded at last in getting through, and luckily the reception clerk he knew was still at the desk.

"Look, there's been some frightful muddle," he began, and explained how Laura was even now on her way back to the hotel – he had seen her with two friends on one of the ferry-services. Would the reception clerk explain and tell her to wait? He would be back by the next available service to collect her. "In any event, detain her," he said. "I'll be as quick as I can." The reception clerk understood perfectly, and John rang off.

Thank heaven Laura hadn't turned up before he had put through his call, or they would have told her he was on his way to Milan. The porter was still waiting with the baggage, and it seemed simplest to walk with him to the garage, hand everything over to the chap in charge of the office there and ask him to keep it for an hour, when he would be returning with his wife to pick up the car. Then he went back to the landing-station to await the next ferry to Venice. The minutes dragged, and he kept wondering all the time what had gone wrong at the airport and why in heaven's name Laura hadn't telephoned. No use conjecturing. She would tell him the whole story at the hotel. One thing was certain: he would not allow Laura and himself to be saddled with the sisters and become involved with their affairs. He could imagine Laura saying that they also had missed a flight, and could they have a lift to Milan?

Finally the ferry chugged alongside the landing-stage and he stepped aboard. What an anti-climax, thrashing back past the familiar sights to which he had bidden a nostalgic farewell such a short while ago! He didn't even look about him this time, he was so intent on reaching his destination. In San Marco there were more people than ever, the afternoon crowds walking shoulder to shoulder, every one of them on pleasure bent.

He came to the hotel and pushed his way through the swing door, expecting to see Laura, and possibly the sisters, waiting in the lounge to the left of the entrance. She was not there. He went to the desk. The reception clerk he had spoken to on the telephone was standing there, talking to the manager.

"Has my wife arrived?" John asked.

"No, sir, not yet."

"What an extraordinary thing. Are you sure?"

"Absolutely certain, sir. I have been here ever since you telephoned me at a quarter to two. I have not left the desk."

"I just don't understand it. She was on one of the vaporettos passing by the Accademia. She would have landed at San Marco about five minutes later and come on here."

The clerk seemed nonplussed. "I don't know what to say. The signora was with friends, did you say?"

"Yes. Well, acquaintances. Two ladies we had met at Torcello yesterday. I was astonished to see her with them on the vaporetto, and of course I assumed that the flight had been cancelled, and she had somehow met up with them at the airport and decided to return here with them, to catch me before I left."

Oh hell, what was Laura doing? It was after three. A matter of moments from San Marco landing-stage to the hotel.

"Perhaps the signora went with her friends to their hotel instead. Do you know where they are staying?"

"No," said John, "I haven't the slightest idea. What's more, I don't even know the names of the two ladies. They were sisters, twins, in fact – looked exactly alike. But anyway, why go to their hotel and not here?"

The swing-door opened but it wasn't Laura. Two people staying in the hotel.

The manager broke into the conversation. "I tell you what I will do," he said. "I will telephone the airport and check about the flight. Then at least we will get somewhere." He smiled apologetically. It was not usual for arrangements to go wrong.

"Yes, do that," said John. "We may as well know what happened there."

He lit a cigarette and began to pace up and down the entrance hall. What a bloody mix-up. And how unlike Laura, who knew he would be setting off for Milan directly after lunch – indeed, for all she knew he might have gone before. But surely, in that case, she would have telephoned at once, on arrival at the airport, had the flight been cancelled? The manager was ages telephoning, he had to be put through on some other line, and his Italian was too rapid for John to follow the conversation. Finally he replaced the receiver.

"It is more mysterious than ever, sir," he said. "The charter flight was not delayed, it took off on schedule with a full complement of passengers. As far as they could tell me, there was no hitch. The signora must simply have changed her mind." His smile was more apologetic than ever.

"Changed her mind," John repeated. "But why on earth should she do that? She was so anxious to be home tonight."

The manager shrugged. "You know how ladies can be, sir," he said. "Your wife may have thought that after all she would prefer to take the train to Milan with you. I do assure you, though, that the charter party was most respectable, and it was a Caravelle aircraft, perfectly safe."

"Yes, yes," said John impatiently, "I don't blame your arrangements in the slightest. I just can't understand what induced her to change her mind, unless it was meeting with these two ladies."

The manager was silent. He could not think of anything to say. The reception clerk was equally concerned. "Is it possible," he ventured, "that you made a mistake, and it was not the signora that you saw on the vaporetto?"

"Oh no," replied John, "it was my wife, I assure you. She was wearing her red coat, she was hatless, just as she left here. I saw her as plainly as I can see you. I would swear to it in a court of law."

"It is unfortunate," said the manager, "that we do not know the name of the two ladies, or the hotel where they were staying. You say you met these ladies at Torcello yesterday?"

"Yes . . . but only briefly. They weren't staying there. At least, I am certain they were not. We saw them at dinner in Venice later, as it happens."

"Excuse me . . ." Guests were arriving with luggage to check in, the clerk was obliged to attend to them. John turned in desperation to the manager. "Do you think it would be any good telephoning the hotel in Torcello in case the people there knew the name of the ladies, or where they were staying in Venice?"

"We can try," replied the manager. "It is a small hope, but we can try."

John resumed his anxious pacing, all the while watching the swing-door, hoping, praying, that he would catch sight of the red coat and Laura would enter. Once again there followed what seemed an interminable telephone conversation between the manager and someone at the hotel in Torcello.

"Tell them two sisters," said John, "two elderly ladies dressed in grey, both exactly alike. One lady was blind," he added. The manager nodded. He was obviously giving a detailed description. Yet when he hung up he shook his head. "The manager at Torcello says he remembers the two ladies well," he told John, "but they were only there for lunch. He never learnt their names."

"Well, that's that. There's nothing to do now but wait."

John lit his third cigarette and went out onto the terrace, to resume his pacing there. He stared out across the canal, searching the heads of the people on passing steamers, motor-boats, even drifting gondolas. The minutes ticked by on his watch, and there was no sign of Laura. A terrible foreboding nagged at him that somehow this was prearranged, that Laura had never intended to catch the aircraft, that last night in the restaurant she had made an assignation with the sisters. Oh God, he thought, that's impossible, I'm going paranoiac . . . Yet why, why? No, more likely the encounter at the airport was fortuitous, and for some incredible reason they had persuaded Laura not to board the aircraft, even prevented her from doing so, trotting out one of their psychic visions, that the aircraft would crash, that she must return with them to Venice. And Laura, in her sensitive state, felt they must be right, swallowed it all without question.

But granted all these possibilities, why had she not come to the hotel? What was she doing? Four o'clock, half-past four, the sun no longer dappling the water. He went back to the reception desk.

"I just can't hang around," he said. "Even if she does turn up, we shall never make Milan this evening. I might see her walking with these ladies, in the Piazza San Marco, anywhere. If she arrives while I'm out, will you explain?"

The clerk was full of concern. "Indeed, yes," he said. "It is very worrying for you, sir. Would it perhaps be prudent if we booked you in here tonight?"

John gestured, helplessly. "Perhaps, yes, I don't know. Maybe . . ."

He went out of the swing-door and began to walk towards the Piazza San Marco. He looked into every shop up and down the colonnades, crossed the piazza a dozen times, threaded his way between the tables in front of Florian's, in front of Quadri's, knowing that Laura's red coat and the distinctive appearance of the twin sisters could easily be spotted, even amongst this milling crowd, but there was no sign of them. He joined the crowd of shoppers in the Merceria, shoulder to shoulder with idlers, thrusters, window-gazers, knowing instinctively that it was useless, they wouldn't be here. Why should Laura have deliberately missed her flight to return to Venice for such a purpose? And even if she had done so, for some reason beyond his imagining, she would surely have come first to the hotel to find him.

The only thing left to him was to try to track down the sisters. Their hotel could be anywhere amongst the hundreds of hotels and pensions scattered through Venice, or even across the other side at the Zattere, or further again on the Giudecca. These last possibilities seemed remote. More likely they were staying in a small hotel or pension somewhere near San Zaccaria handy to the restaurant where they had dined last night. The blind one would surely not go far afield in the evening. He had been a fool not to have thought of this before, and he turned back and walked quickly away from the brightly lighted shopping district towards the narrower, more cramped quarter where they had dined last evening. He found the restaurant without difficulty, but they were not yet open for dinner, and the waiter preparing tables was not the one who had served them. John asked to see the *padrone*, and the waiter disappeared to the back regions, returning after a moment or two with the somewhat dishevelled-looking proprietor in shirtsleeves, caught in a slack moment, not in full tenue.

"I had dinner here last night," John explained. "There were two ladies sitting at that table there in the corner." He pointed to it.

"You wish to book that table for this evening?" asked the proprietor.

"No," said John. "No, there were two ladies there last night, two sisters, due sorelle, twins, gemelle" – what was the right word for twins? – "Do you remember? Two ladies, sorelle vecchie . . ."

"Ah," said the man, "si, si, signore, la povera signorina." He put his hands to his eyes to feign blindness. "Yes, I remember."

"Do you know their names?" asked John. "Where they were staying? I am very anxious to trace them."

The proprietor spread out his hands in a gesture of regret. "I am ver' sorry, signore, I do not know the names of the signorine, they have been here once, twice, perhaps for dinner, they do not say where they were staying. Perhaps if you come again tonight they might be here? Would you like to book a table?"

He pointed around him, suggesting a whole choice of tables that might appeal to a prospective diner, but John shook his head.

"Thank you, no. I may be dining elsewhere. I am sorry to have troubled you. If the signorine should come . . ." he paused, "possibly I may return later," he added. "I am not sure."

The proprietor bowed, and walked with him to the entrance. "In Venice the whole world meets," he said smiling. "It is possible the signore will find his friends tonight. Arrivederci, signore."

Friends? John walked out into the street. More likely kidnappers ... Anxiety had turned to fear, to panic. Something had gone terribly wrong. Those women had got hold of Laura, played upon her suggestibility, induced her to go with them, either to their hotel or elsewhere. Should he find the Consulate? Where was it? What would he say when he got there? He began walking without purpose, finding himself, as they had done the night before, in streets he did not know, and suddenly came upon a tall building with the word 'Questura' above it. This is it, he thought. I don't care, something has happened, I'm going inside. There were a number of police in uniform coming and going, the place at any rate was active, and, addressing himself to one of them behind a glass partition, he asked if there was anyone who spoke English. The man pointed to a flight of stairs and John went up, entering a door on the right where he saw that another couple were sitting, waiting, and with relief he recognised them as fellow-country-men, tourists, obviously a man and his wife, in some sort of predicament.

"Come and sit down," said the man. "We've waited half-an-hour but they can't be much longer. What a country! They wouldn't leave us like this at home."

John took the proffered cigarette and found a chair beside them.

"What's your trouble?" he asked.

"My wife had her handbag pinched in one of those shops in the Merceria," said the man. "She simply put it down one moment to look at something, and you'd hardly credit it, the next moment it had gone. I say it was a sneak thief, she insists it was the girl behind the counter. But who's to say? These Ities are all alike.

Anyway, I'm certain we shan't get it back. What have you lost?"

"Suitcase stolen," John lied rapidly. "Had some important papers in it."

How could he say he had lost his wife? He couldn't even begin . . .

The man nodded in sympathy. "As I said, these Ities are all alike. Old Musso knew how to deal with them. Too many Communists around these days. The trouble is, they're not going to bother with our troubles much, not with this murderer at large. They're all out looking for him."

"Murderer? What murderer?" asked John.

"Don't tell me you've not heard about it?" The man stared at him in surprise. "Venice has talked of nothing else. It's been in all the papers, on the radio, and even in the English papers. A grizzly business. One woman found with her throat slit last week – a tourist too – and some old chap discovered with the same sort of knife wound this morning. They seem to think it must be a maniac, because there doesn't seem to be any motive. Nasty thing to happen in Venice in the tourist season."

"My wife and I never bother with the newspapers when we're on holiday," said John. "And we're neither of us much given to gossip in the hotel."

"Very wise of you," laughed the man. "It might have spoilt your holiday, especially if your wife is nervous. Oh well, we're off tomorrow anyway. Can't say we mind, do we, dear?" He turned to his wife. "Venice has gone downhill since we were here last. And now this loss of the handbag really is the limit."

The door of the inner room opened, and a senior police officer asked John's companion and his wife to pass through.

"I bet we don't get any satisfaction," murmured the tourist, winking at John, and he and his wife went into the inner room. The door closed behind them. John stubbed out his cigarette and lighted another. A strange feeling of unreality possessed him. He asked himself what he was doing here, what was the use of it? Laura was no longer in Venice but had disappeared, perhaps forever, with those diabolical sisters. She would never be traced. And just as the two of them had made up a fantastic story about the twins, when they first spotted them in Torcello, so, with nightmare logic, the fiction would have basis in fact; the women were in reality disguised crooks, men with criminal intent who lured unsuspecting persons to some appalling fate. They might even be the murderers for whom the police sought. Who would ever suspect two elderly women of respectable appearance, living quietly in some second-rate pension or hotel? He stubbed out his cigarette, unfinished.

"This," he thought, "is really the start of paranoia. This is the way people go off their heads." He glanced at his watch. It was half-past six. Better pack this in, this futile quest here in police headquarters, and keep to the single link of sanity remaining. Return to the hotel, put a call through to the prep school in England, and ask about the latest news of Johnnie. He had not thought about poor Johnnie since sighting Laura on the vaporetto.

Too late, though. The inner door opened, the couple were ushered out.

"Usual clap-trap," said the husband sotto voce to John. "They'll do what they can. Not much hope. So many foreigners in Venice, all of 'em thieves! The locals all above reproach. Wouldn't pay 'em to steal from customers. Well, I wish you better luck."

He nodded, his wife smiled and bowed, and they had gone. John followed the police officer into the inner room.

Formalities began. Name, address, passport. Length of stay in Venice, etc., etc. Then the questions, and John, the sweat beginning to appear on his forehead, launched into his interminable story. The first encounter with the sisters, the meeting at the restaurant, Laura's state of suggestibility because of the death of their child, the telegram about Johnnie, the decision to take the chartered flight, her departure, and her sudden inexplicable return. When he had finished he felt as exhausted as if he had driven three hundred miles non-stop after a severe bout of 'flu. His interrogator spoke excellent English with a strong Italian accent.

"You say," he began, "that your wife was suffering the aftereffects of shock. This had been noticeable during your stay here in Venice?"

"Well, yes," John replied, "she had really been quite ill. The holiday didn't seem to be doing her much good. It was only when she met these two women at Torcello yesterday that her mood changed. The strain seemed to have gone. She was ready, I suppose, to snatch at every straw, and this belief that our little girl was watching over her had somehow restored her to what appeared normality."

"It would be natural," said the police officer, "in the circumstances. But no doubt the telegram last night was a further shock to you both?"

"Indeed, yes. That was the reason we decided to return home."

"No argument between you? No difference of opinion?"

"None. We were in complete agreement. My one regret was that I could not go with my wife on this charter flight."

The police officer nodded. "It could well be that your wife had a sudden attack of amnesia, and meeting the two ladies served as a link, she clung to them for support. You have described them with great accuracy, and I think they should not be too difficult to trace. Meanwhile, I suggest you should return to your hotel, and we will get in touch with you as soon as we have news."

At least, John thought, they believed his story. They

did not consider him a crank who had made the whole thing up and was merely wasting their time.

"You appreciate," he said, "I am extremely anxious. These women may have some criminal design upon my wife. One has heard of such things . . ."

The police officer smiled for the first time. "Please don't concern yourself," he said. "I am sure there will be some satisfactory explanation."

All very well, thought John, but in heaven's name, what?

"I'm sorry," he said, "to have taken up so much of your time. Especially as I gather the police have their hands full hunting down a murderer who is still at large."

He spoke deliberately. No harm in letting the fellow know that for all any of them could tell there might be some connection between Laura's disappearance and this other hideous affair.

"Ah, that," said the police officer, rising to his feet. "We hope to have the murderer under lock and key very soon."

His tone of confidence was reassuring. Murderers, missing wives, lost handbags were all under control. They shook hands, and John was ushered out of the door and so downstairs. Perhaps, he thought, as he walked slowly back to the hotel, the fellow was right. Laura had suffered a sudden attack of amnesia, and the sisters happened to be at the airport and had brought her back to Venice, to their own hotel, because Laura couldn't remember where she and John had been staying. Perhaps they were even now trying to track down his hotel. Anyway, he could do nothing more. The police had everything in hand, and, please God, would come up with the solution. All he wanted to do right now was to collapse upon a bed with a stiff whisky, and then put through a call to Johnnie's school.

The page took him up in the lift to a modest room on the fourth floor at the rear of the hotel. Bare, impersonal, the shutters closed, with a smell of cooking wafting up from a courtyard down below.

"Ask them to send me up a double whisky, will you?" he said to the boy. "And a ginger-ale," and when he was alone he plunged his face under the cold tap in the washbasin, relieved to find that the minute portion of visitor's soap afforded some measure of comfort. He flung off his shoes, hung his coat over the back of a chair and threw himself down on the bed. Somebody's radio was blasting forth an old popular song, now several seasons out-of-date, that had been one of Laura's favourites a couple of years ago. "I love you, Baby . . ." He reached for the telephone, and asked the exchange to put through the call to England. Then he closed his eyes, and all the while the insistent voice persisted, "I love you, Baby . . . I can't get you out of my mind."

Presently there was a tap at the door. It was the waiter with his drink. Too little ice, such meagre comfort, but what desperate need. He gulped it down without the ginger-ale, and in a few moments the ever-nagging pain was eased, numbed, bringing, if only momentarily, a sense of calm. The telephone rang, and now, he thought, bracing himself for ultimate disaster, the final shock, Johnnie probably dying, or already dead. In which case nothing remained. Let Venice be engulfed . . .

The exchange told him that the connection had been made, and in a moment he heard the voice of Mrs Hill at the other end of the line. They must have warned her that the call came from Venice, for she knew instantly who was speaking.

"Hullo?" she said. "Oh, I am so glad you rang. All is well. Johnnie has had his operation, the surgeon decided to do it at midday rather than wait, and it was completely successful. Johnnie is going to be all right. So you don't have to worry any more, and will have a peaceful night."

"Thank God," he answered.

222

"I know," she said, "we are all so relieved. Now I'll get off the line and you can speak to your wife."

John sat up on the bed, stunned. What the hell did she mean? Then he heard Laura's voice, cool and clear.

"Darling? Darling, are you there?"

He could not answer. He felt the hand holding the receiver go clammy cold with sweat. "I'm here," he whispered.

"It's not a very good line," she said, "but never mind. As Mrs Hill told you, all is well. Such a nice surgeon, and a very sweet Sister on Johnnie's floor, and I really am happy about the way it's turned out. I came straight down here after landing at Gatwick – the flight O.K., by the way, but such a funny crowd, it'll make you hysterical when I tell you about them – and I went to the hospital, and Johnnie was coming round. Very dopey, of course, but so pleased to see me. And the Hills are being wonderful, I've got their spare-room, and it's only a short taxi-drive into the town and the hospital. I shall go to bed as soon as we've had dinner, because I'm a bit fagged, what with the flight and the anxiety. How was the drive to Milan? And where are you staying?"

John did not recognise the voice that answered as his own. It was the automatic response of some computer.

"I'm not in Milan," he said. "I'm still in Venice."

"Still in Venice? What on earth for? Wouldn't the car start?"

"I can't explain," he said. "There was a stupid sort of mix-up . . ."

He felt suddenly so exhausted that he nearly dropped the receiver, and, shame upon shame, he could feel tears pricking behind his eyes.

"What sort of mix-up?" Her voice was suspicious, almost hostile. "You weren't in a crash?"

"No . . . no . . . nothing like that."

A moment's silence, and then she said, "Your voice

sounds very slurred. Don't tell me you went and got pissed."

Oh Christ . . . If she only knew! He was probably going to pass out any moment, but not from the whisky.

"I thought," he said slowly, "I thought I saw you, in a vaporetto, with those two sisters."

What was the point of going on? It was hopeless trying to explain.

"How could you have seen me with the sisters?" she said. "You knew I'd gone to the airport. Really, darling, you are an idiot. You seem to have got those two poor old dears on the brain. I hope you didn't say anything to Mrs Hill just now."

"No."

"Well, what are you going to do? You'll catch the train at Milan tomorrow, won't you?"

"Yes, of course," he told her.

"I still don't understand what kept you in Venice," she said. "It all sounds a bit odd to me. However . . . thank God Johnnie is going to be all right and I'm here."

"Yes," he said, "yes."

He could hear the distant boom-boom sound of a gong from the headmaster's hall.

"You had better go," he said. "My regards to the Hills, and my love to Johnnie."

"Well, take care of yourself, darling, and for goodness' sake don't miss the train tomorrow, and drive carefully."

The telephone clicked and she had gone. He poured the remaining drop of whisky into his empty glass, and sousing it with ginger-ale drank it down at a gulp. He got up, and crossing the room threw open the shutters and leant out of the window. He felt light-headed. His sense of relief, enormous, overwhelming, was somehow tempered with a curious feeling of unreality, almost as though the voice speaking from England had not been Laura's after all but a fake, and she was still in Venice, hidden in some furtive pension with the two sisters.

The point was, he *had* seen all three of them on the vaporetto. It was not another woman in a red coat. The women *had* been there, with Laura. So what was the explanation? That he was going off his head? Or something more sinister? The sisters, possessing psychic powers of formidable strength, had seen him as their two ferries had passed, and in some inexplicable fashion had made him believe Laura was with them. But why, and to what end? No, it didn't make sense. The only explanation was that he had been mistaken, the whole episode an hallucination. In which case he needed psychoanalysis, just as Johnnie had needed a surgeon.

And what did he do now? Go downstairs and tell the management he had been at fault and had just spoken to his wife, who had arrived in England safe and sound from her charter-flight? He put on his shoes and ran his fingers through his hair. He glanced at his watch. It was ten minutes to eight. If he nipped into the bar and had a quick drink it would be easier to face the manager and admit what had happened. Then, perhaps, they would get in touch with the police. Profuse apologies all round for putting everyone to enormous trouble.

He made his way to the ground floor and went straight to the bar, feeling self-conscious, a marked man, half-imagining everyone would look at him, thinking, "There's the fellow with the missing wife." Luckily the bar was full and there wasn't a face he knew. Even the chap behind the bar was an underling who hadn't served him before. He downed his whisky and glanced over his shoulder to the reception hall. The desk was momentarily empty. He could see the manager's back framed in the doorway of an inner room, talking to someone within. On impulse, coward-like, he crossed the hall and passed through the swing-door to the street outside.

"I'll have some dinner," he decided, "and then go back

and face them. I'll feel more like it once I've some food inside me."

He went to the restaurant nearby where he and Laura had dined once or twice. Nothing mattered any more, because she was safe. The nightmare lay behind him. He could enjoy his dinner, despite her absence, and think of her sitting down with the Hills to a dull, quiet evening, early to bed, and on the following morning going to the hospital to sit with Johnnie. Johnnie was safe, too. No more worries, only the awkward explanations and apologies to the manager at the hotel.

There was a pleasant anonymity sitting down at a corner table alone in the little restaurant, ordering vitello alla Marsala and half a bottle of Merlot. He took his time, enjoying his food but eating in a kind of haze, a sense of unreality still with him, while the conversation of his nearest neighbours had the same soothing effect as background music.

When they rose and left, he saw by the clock on the wall that it was nearly half-past nine. No use delaying matters any further. He drank his coffee, lighted a cigarette and paid his bill. After all, he thought, as he walked back to the hotel, the manager would be greatly relieved to know that all was well.

When he pushed through the swing-door, the first thing he noticed was a man in police uniform, standing talking to the manager at the desk. The reception clerk was there too. They turned as John approached, and the manager's face lighted up with relief.

"Eccolo!" he exclaimed. "I was certain the signore would not be far away. Things are moving, signore. The two ladies have been traced, and they very kindly agreed to accompany the police to the Questura. If you will go there at once, this agente di polizia will escort you."

John flushed. "I have given everyone a lot of trouble," he said. "I meant to tell you before going out to dinner, but you were not at the desk. The fact is that I have contacted my wife. She did make the flight to London after all, and I spoke to her on the telephone. It was all a great mistake."

The manager looked bewildered. "The signora is in London?" he repeated. He broke off, and exchanged a rapid conversation in Italian with the policeman. "It seems that the ladies maintain they did not go out for the day, except for a little shopping in the morning," he said, turning back to John. "Then who was it the signore saw on the vaporetto?"

John shook his head. "A very extraordinary mistake on my part which I still don't understand," he said. "Obviously, I did not see either my wife or the two ladies. I really am extremely sorry."

More rapid conversation in Italian. John noticed the clerk watching him with a curious expression in his eyes. The manager was obviously apologising on John's behalf to the policeman, who looked annoyed and gave tongue to this effect, his voice increasing in volume, to the manager's concern. The whole business had undoubtedly given enormous trouble to a great many people, not least the two unfortunate sisters.

"Look," said John, interrupting the flow, "will you tell the agente I will go with him to headquarters and apologise in person both to the police officer and to the ladies?"

The manager looked relieved. "If the signore would take the trouble," he said. "Naturally, the ladies were much distressed when a policeman interrogated them at their hotel, and they offered to accompany him to the Questura only because they were so distressed about the signora."

John felt more and more uncomfortable. Laura must never learn any of this. She would be outraged. He wondered if there were some penalty for giving the police misleading information involving a third party. His error began, in retrospect, to take on criminal proportions.

He crossed the Piazza San Marco, now thronged with after-dinner strollers and spectators at the cafés, all three orchestras going full blast in harmonious rivalry, while his companion kept a discreet two paces to his left and never uttered a word.

They arrived at the police station and mounted the stairs to the same inner room where he had been before. He saw immediately that it was not the officer he knew but another who sat behind the desk, a sallow-faced individual with a sour expression, while the two sisters, obviously upset – the active one in particular – were seated on chairs nearby, some underling in uniform standing behind them. John's escort went at once to the police-officer, speaking in rapid Italian, while John himself, after a moment's hesitation, advanced towards the sisters.

"There has been a terrible mistake," he said. "I don't know how to apologise to you both. It's all my fault, mine entirely, the police are not to blame."

The active sister made as though to rise, her mouth twitching nervously, but he restrained her.

"We don't understand," she said, the Scots inflection strong. "We said goodnight to your wife last night at dinner, and we have not seen her since. The police came to our pension more than an hour ago and told us your wife was missing and you had filed a complaint against us. My sister is not very strong. She was considerably disturbed."

"A mistake. A frightful mistake," he repeated.

He turned towards the desk. The police-officer was addressing him, his English very inferior to that of the previous interrogator. He had John's earlier statement on the desk in front of him, and tapped it with a pencil.

"So?" he queried. "This document all lies? You not speaka the truth?"

"I believed it to be true at the time," said John. "I could have sworn in a court of law that I saw my wife with these two ladies on a vaporetto in the

Grand Canal this afternoon. Now I realise I was mistaken."

"We have not been near the Grand Canal all day," protested the sister, "not even on foot. We made a few purchases in the Merceria this morning, and remained indoors all afternoon. My sister was a little unwell. I have told the police-officer this a dozen times, and the people at the pension would corroborate our story. He refused to listen."

"And the signora?" rapped the police-officer angrily. "What happen to the signora?"

"The signora, my wife, is safe in England," explained John patiently. "I talked to her on the telephone just after seven. She did join the charter flight from the airport, and is now staying with friends."

"Then who you see on the vaporetto in the red coat?" asked the furious police-officer. "And if not these signorine here, then what signorine?"

"My eyes deceived me," said John, aware that his English was likewise becoming strained. "I think I see my wife and these ladies but no, it was not so. My wife in aircraft, these ladies in pension all the time."

It was like talking stage Chinese. In a moment he would be bowing and putting his hands in his sleeves.

The police-officer raised his eyes to heaven and thumped the table. "So all this work for nothing," he said. "Hotels and pensiones searched for the signorine and a missing signora inglese, when here we have plenty, plenty other things to do. You maka a mistake. You have perhaps too much vino at mezzo giorno and you see hundred signore in red coats in hundred vaporetti." He stood up, rumpling the papers on his desk. "And you, signorine," he said, "you wish to make complaint against this person?" He was addressing the active sister.

"Oh no," she said, "no, indeed. I quite see it was all a mistake. Our only wish is to return at once to our pension."

The police-officer grunted. Then he pointed at John. "You very lucky man," he said. "These signorine could file complaint against you – very serious matter."

"I'm sure," began John, "I'll do anything in my power . . ."

"Please don't think of it," exclaimed the sister, horrified. "We would not hear of such a thing." It was her turn to apologise to the police-officer. "I hope we need not take up any more of your valuable time," she said.

He waved a hand of dismissal and spoke in Italian to the underling. "This man walk with you to the pension," he said. "Buona sera, signorine," and, ignoring John, he sat down again at his desk.

"I'll come with you," said John. "I want to explain exactly what happened."

They trooped down the stairs and out of the building, the blind sister leaning on her twin's arm, and once outside she turned her sightless eyes to John.

"You saw us," she said, "and your wife too. But not today. You saw us in the future."

Her voice was softer than her sister's, slower, she seemed to have some slight impediment in her speech.

"I don't follow," replied John, bewildered.

He turned to the active sister and she shook her head at him, frowning, and put her finger on her lips.

"Come along, dear," she said to her twin. "You know you're very tired, and I want to get you home." Then, sotto voce to John, "She's psychic. Your wife told you, I believe, but I don't want her to go into trance here in the street."

God forbid, thought John, and the little procession began to move slowly along the street, away from police headquarters, a canal to the left of them. Progress was slow, because of the blind sister, and there were two bridges. John was completely lost after the first turning, but it couldn't have mattered less. Their police escort was with them, and anyway, the sisters knew where they were going.

"I must explain," said John softly. "My wife would never forgive me if I didn't," and as they walked he went over the whole inexplicable story once again, beginning with the telegram received the night before and the conversation with Mrs Hill, the decision to return to England the following day, Laura by air, and John himself by car and train. It no longer sounded as dramatic as it had done when he had made his statement to the police-officer, when, possibly because of his conviction of something uncanny, the description of the two vaporettos passing one another in the middle of the Grand Canal had held a sinister quality, suggesting abduction on the part of the sisters, the pair of them holding a bewildered Laura captive. Now that neither of the women had any further menace for him he spoke more naturally, yet with great sincerity, feeling for the first time that they were somehow both in sympathy with him and would understand.

"You see," he explained, in a final endeavour to make amends for having gone to the police in the first place, "I truly believed I had seen you with Laura, and I thought . . ." he hesitated, because this had been the police-officer's suggestion and not his, "I thought that perhaps Laura had some sudden loss of memory, had met you at the airport, and you had brought her back to Venice to wherever you were staying."

They had crossed a large square and were approaching a house at one end of it, with a sign 'Pensione' above the door. Their escort paused at the entrance.

"Is this it?" asked John.

"Yes," said the sister. "I know it is nothing much from the outside, but it is clean and comfortable, and was recommended by friends." She turned to the escort. "Grazie," she said to him, "grazie tanto."

The man nodded briefly, wished them "Buona notte," and disappeared across the campo.

"Will you come in?" asked the sister. "I am sure we can find you some coffee, or perhaps you prefer tea?"

"No, really," John thanked her, "I must get back to the hotel. I'm making an early start in the morning. I just want to make quite sure you do understand what happened, and that you forgive me."

"There is nothing to forgive," she replied. "It is one of the many examples of second sight that my sister and I have experienced time and time again, and I should very much like to record it for our files, if you will permit it."

"Well, as to that, of course," he told her, "but I myself find it hard to understand. It has never happened to me before."

"Not consciously, perhaps," she said, "but so many things happen to us of which we are not aware. My sister felt you had psychic understanding. She told your wife. She also told your wife, last night in the restaurant, that you were to experience trouble, danger, that you should leave Venice. Well, don't you believe now that the telegram was proof of this? Your son was ill, possibly dangerously ill, and so it was necessary for you to return home immediately. Heaven be praised your wife flew home to be by his side."

"Yes, indeed," said John, "but why should I see her on the vaporetto with you and your sister when she was actually on her way to England?"

"Thought transference, perhaps," she answered. "Your wife may have been thinking about us. We gave her our address, should you wish to get in touch with us. We shall be here another ten days. And she knows that we would pass on any message that my sister might have from your little one in the spirit world."

"Yes," said John awkwardly, "yes, I see. It's very good of you." He had a sudden rather unkind picture of the two sisters putting on headphones in their bedroom, listening for a coded message from poor Christine. "Look, this is our address in London," he said. "I know Laura will be pleased to hear from you."

He scribbled their address on a sheet torn from his pocket-diary, even, as a bonus thrown in, the telephone number, and handed it to her. He could imagine the outcome. Laura springing it on him one evening that the "old dears" were passing through London on their way to Scotland, and the least they could do was to offer them hospitality, even the spare-room for the night. Then a seance in the living-room, tambourines appearing out of thin air.

"Well, I must be off," he said. "Goodnight, and apologies, once again, for all that has happened this evening." He shook hands with the first sister, then turned to her blind twin. "I hope," he said, "that you are not too tired."

The sightless eyes were disconcerting. She held his hand fast and would not let it go. "The child," she said, speaking in an odd staccato voice, "the child . . . I can see the child . . ." and then, to his dismay, a bead of froth appeared at the corner of her mouth, her head jerked back, and she half-collapsed in her sister's arms.

"We must get her inside," said the sister hurriedly. "It's all right, she's not ill, it's the beginning of a trance state."

Between them they helped the twin, who had gone rigid, into the house, and sat her down on the nearest chair, the sister supporting her. A woman came running from some inner room. There was a strong smell of spaghetti from the back regions. "Don't worry," said the sister, "the signorina and I can manage. I think you had better go. Sometimes she is sick after these turns."

"I'm most frightfully sorry . . ." John began, but the sister had already turned her back, and with the signorina was bending over her twin, from whom peculiar choking sounds were proceeding. He was obviously in the way, and after a final gesture of courtesy, "Is there anything I can do?", which received no reply, he turned on his heel and began walking across the square. He looked back once, and saw they had closed the door.

What a finale to the evening! And all his fault. Poor old girls, first dragged to police headquarters and put through an interrogation, and then a psychic fit on top of it all. More likely epilepsy. Not much of a life for the other sister, but she seemed to take it in her stride. An additional hazard, though, if it happened in a restaurant or in the street. And not particularly welcome under his and Laura's roof should the sisters ever find themselves beneath it, which he prayed would never happen.

Meanwhile, where the devil was he? The square, with the inevitable church at one end, was quite deserted. He could not remember which way they had come from police headquarters, there had seemed to be so many turnings.

Wait a minute, the church itself had a familiar appearance. He drew nearer to it, looking for the name which was sometimes on notices at the entrance. San Giovanni in Bragora, that rang a bell. He and Laura had gone inside one morning to look at a painting by Cima da Conegliano. Surely it was only a stone's throw from the Riva degli Schiavoni and the open wide waters of the San Marco lagoon, with all the bright lights of civilisation and the strolling tourists? He remembered taking a small turning from the Schiavoni and they had arrived at the church. Wasn't that the alleyway ahead? He plunged along it, but halfway down he hesitated. It didn't seem right, although it was familiar for some unknown reason.

Then he realised that it was not the alley they had taken the morning they visited the church, but the one they had walked along the previous evening, only he was approaching it from the opposite direction. Yes, that was it, in which case it would be quicker to go on and cross the little bridge over the narrow canal, and he would find the Arsenal on his left and the street leading down to the Riva degli Schiavoni to his right. Simpler than retracing his steps and getting lost once more in the maze of back streets.

He had almost reached the end of the alley, and the bridge was in sight, when he saw the child. It was the same little girl with the pixie-hood who had leapt between the tethered boats the preceding night and vanished up the cellar steps of one of the houses. This time she was running from the direction of the church the other side, making for the bridge. She was running as if her life depended on it, and in a moment he saw why. A man was in pursuit, who, when she glanced backwards for a moment, still running, flattened himself against a wall, believing himself unobserved. The child came on, scampering across the bridge, and John, fearful of alarming her further, backed into an open doorway that led into a small court.

He remembered the drunken yell of the night before which had come from one of the houses near where the man was hiding now. This is it, he thought, the fellow's after her again, and with a flash of intuition he connected the two events, the child's terror then and now, and the murders reported in the newspapers, supposedly the work of some madman. It could be coincidence, a child running from a drunken relative, and yet, and yet . . . His heart began thumping in his chest, instinct warning him to run himself, now, at once, back along the alley the way he had come – but what about the child? What was going to happen to the child?

Then he heard her running steps. She hurtled through the open doorway into the court in which he stood, not seeing him, making for the rear of the house that flanked it, where steps led presumably to a back entrance. She was sobbing as she ran, not the ordinary cry of a frightened child, but the panic-stricken intake of breath of a helpless being in despair. Were there parents in the house who would protect her, whom he could warn? He hesitated a moment, then followed her down the steps and through the door at the bottom, which had burst open at the touch of her hands as she hurled herself against it.

"It's all right," he called. "I won't let him hurt you, it's all right," cursing his lack of Italian, but possibly an English voice might reassure her. But it was no use – she ran sobbing up another flight of stairs, which were spiral, twisting, leading to the floor above, and already it was too late for him to retreat. He could hear sounds of the pursuer in the courtyard behind, someone shouting in Italian, a dog barking. This is it, he thought, we're in it together, the child and I. Unless we can bolt some inner door above he'll get us both.

He ran up the stairs after the child, who had darted into a room leading off a small landing, and followed her inside and slammed the door, and, merciful heaven, there was a bolt which he rammed into its socket. The child was crouching by the open window. If he shouted for help someone would surely hear, someone would surely come before the man in pursuit threw himself against the door and it gave, because there was no one but themselves, no parents, the room was bare except for a mattress on an old bed, and a heap of rags in one corner.

"It's all right," he panted, "it's all right," and held out his hand, trying to smile.

The child struggled to her feet and stood before him, the pixie-hood falling from her head onto the floor. He stared at her, incredulity turning to horror, to fear. It was not a child at all but a little thick-set woman dwarf, about three feet high, with a great square adult head too big for her body, grey locks hanging shoulder-length, and she wasn't sobbing any more, she was grinning at him, nodding her head up and down.

Then he heard the footsteps on the landing outside and the hammering on the door, and a barking dog, and not one voice but several voices, shouting, "Open up! Police!" The creature fumbled in her sleeve, drawing a knife, and as she threw it at him with hideous strength, piercing his throat, he stumbled and fell, the sticky mess covering his protecting hands.

And he saw the vaporetto with Laura and the two sisters steaming down the Grand Canal, not today, not tomorrow, but the day after that, and he knew why they were together and for what sad purpose they had come. The creature was gibbering in its corner. The hammering and the voices and the barking dog grew fainter, and, "Oh, God," he thought, "what a bloody silly way to die . . ."

HALLOWEEN

(Dino De Laurentis Corp., 1978)
Starring: Donald Pleasance, Nancy Loomis &
Jamie Lee Curtis
Directed by John Carpenter
Story 'Harlequin' by John Carpenter

The Seventies ended with the launching of the first
of the ground-breaking series of Halloween pictures
masterminded by John Carpenter (1951–) which produced two sequels in the Eighties and played a major
part in establishing him as a highly influential figure
in the ghost and horror story film genre. Carpenter
actually began shooting 8mm science fiction short
films at the age of eight, and while at the University
of Southern California gave an early indication of his
prodigious talent when another of his shorts, *The
Resurrection of Bronco Billy*, won an Oscar in 1970.
Four years later he made his feature-film debut with
Dark Star, a black comedy about some astronauts
high on drugs journeying through space. It was quite
clearly inspired by Stanley Kubrick's extravaganza
2001: A Space Odyssey – although *Dark Star* was
made on a budget of just $60,000 and Carpenter's
alien was a beachball with legs! The critical acclaim
which greeted this picture, and his next movie, a
police thriller, *Assault on Precinct 13*, made him a
name to watch – and in 1978 he fulfilled all his early
promise with *Halloween*. It had all the hallmarks
which have since become associated with Carpenter,
according to cinema historian Mark Adams, and

is a textbook example of how to manipulate an audience while retaining intelligence and humour. Mark adds, "*Halloween* – with its knowing *Psycho* references and Carpenter's Bernard Hermann-like theme – put all of the 'stalk-n-slash' imitators to shame as he cleverly used the darkened corners of an ordinary house to conceal the manic killer. It set a standard not often lived up to in this genre." Aside from the two hugely successful sequels in 1980 and 1983, with the late British master of terror Donald Pleasance starring in both with Jamie Lee Curtis, Carpenter has further enriched the horror genre with *The Thing* (1982), a re-make of the 1951 black-and-white classic, *The Thing From Another World* about a shape-changing alien in the Antarctic; *Christine* (1983) based on Stephen King's best-selling novel about a demonic car; and *Memoirs of an Invisible Man* (1992) an up-date of the H.G. Wells' SF masterpiece.

John Carpenter brings intelligence, humour and passion to all his pictures and has shown himself to be a fierce defender of the ghost and horror story genre against attacks over its excesses. Aside from directing, he has written the scripts for many of his films and often reveals his in-depth knowledge of the genre in some of the lines spoken by his characters. His delight in the printed word has, in fact, been around as long as his love affair with the camera – as the following spooky short story, written by him for *The Continent*, a student magazine of Bowling Green College, Kentucky, in 1969, demonstrates. It marks another landmark in the career of this incredibly versatile writer-director . . .

It was after midnight, and the sounds from the car radio had drifted into chorused murmurings. He had pulled off the road at about eleven and had been parked, watching the ocean, since.

The night air was cool; he didn't mind the darkness, and could hear the east wind stir the spruces along the beach. The ocean was beryl black and alive. It spoke to him in sibilant whispers as gull shapes whisked across a cloud-moon. He sat very still, listening, and found himself swallowing as the water rushed and bled into the sand. His fingers flicked at his collar, loosening his tie.

Too long, he thought, opening the door of the car. Ten years. He started walking, and the bushes and tree branches around the car willowed and softly pulled against him. Fingers of grass rippled on his socks. Ten years. His mouth was dry, and he swallowed, rubbing his lips with the back of his hand. Finally his feet touched the chalky sand; there were no trees around him, only the open air smell of the sea.

Ten years. He bent near the shore and scooped wet sand. His fist tightened, and it mushed between his fingers.

Suddenly there was no wind. He was standing at the edge of the shore, unbuttoning three buttons on his shirt, listening to the distant sound of carousel music. It was too late now, he thought as he put his tie in his pocket. Too late.

The music was drifting from a faint light across a dark field of grass. He squinted at the sound. It sounded like a harpsichord, with a black clown sitting at the keyboard, smearing colored grease on the keys. He turned back to the sea as the night wind picked up again, splashing against the inside of his coat.

He took off his coat and let it drop to the sand.

There was Karen. He smiled and touched the soft flesh of his neck. Tall, auburn-dust hair, eyes that always stayed on his face. In darkness, when his ears were ringing from the stillness, she would trace over the glassy smoothness of his neck and tell him his flesh was marble. She was warm and moist, but the sea was wet-cold.

When he turned, after he had taken the ring off his left hand, he couldn't see his car. It was just hidden by the trees above the beach, two hundred yards behind him, its chrome teeth faintly luminescent, its eyes dead.

The carousel music had increased, and the water at his feet screamed quietly. He leaned down and touched the liquid with his hands. Cold, splash-black, ice-green. He shivered.

Ten years. Too long. It couldn't wait.

With a twist he pulled off his coat. Buttons zipped through their holes; his pants fell to the sand, and he stepped out of them.

In a moment he was naked and soft white, and his mind was spinning with music.

He touched the top of his forehead, his fingers pushing into the flesh at his hairline. No pain. His fingers shook. He pulled the flesh forward, and the skin of his face lifted and pulled away. It shred off in rubbery layers as he stripped it down his neck. The black hair from the top of his head lifted and synthetic flesh flopped and crumbled on the sand.

Just slightly the music had become faster. He touched his face, along the high mound of his lips, in the deep craters around his eyes. The tips of his fingers brushed each scale as he caressed the gills of his neck.

Quickly he pulled off the rest of the flesh from his body, and instead of white there was silver-green. He stood naked in a moonburst as the clouds parted for a moment.

Then he heard a sound behind him, a rustle. He crouched. The music from the harpsichord-carousel was loud; it deafened him. It's been too long, he thought. Too long.

The trees moved. A wind. Then a clown stepped from behind a tree and stood watching him. His face was paste white, with a red slash of an insane grin around the lips.

"You," said the clown, laughing. "You," again, softly.

"No," he said. "I'm returning. I'm going back."

There was a movement. The clown was grinning. "You," he whispered.

"No. Please . . ."

The clown lifted a cluster of opal wind chimes on a string. The glittering pieces were making the sound of the harpsichord, colliding, driven together by the wind, smashing, clanging.

"I'm a fish."

The clown grinned. "You're a clown."

Ten years, thought the fish. It's been too long.

His hands moved to his forehead and began pulling away the strips of green, scaly flesh. They peeled off his face and hung down around his chest. Underneath the synthetic gills was a white, painted face, with a grease-slashed smile.

BEETLEJUICE

> (Warner Bros., 1988)
> Starring: Michael Keaton, Alec Baldwin &
> Geena Davis
> Directed by Tim Burton
> Story 'Halley's Passing' by Michael McDowell

The Eighties produced some of the best ghost movies seen for a long time and completely revitalised the genre at the box office. Leading the way in 1981 was *Ghost Story* from Universal, based on the multi-million selling novel by Peter Straub hailed as "the most popular spook story of the 1970s", which starred Douglas Fairbanks jnr and Fred Astaire as two ghost-story tellers who invoke the succubus of a wealthy young widow who they had murdered years before with horrific results. This was followed by Steven Spielberg's *Poltergeist* (MGM, 1982) directed by Tobe Hooper with Jo Beth Williams and Craig T. Nelson as haunted parents; and the even more successful *Ghostbusters* (Columbia Pictures, 1984) which Ivan Reitman produced and directed starring Bill Murray, Dan Aykroyd and Sigourney Weaver. This manic comedy about a trio of investigators trying to stem an avalanche of supernatural phenomena in New York, lead to several other films of spooky humour including *Scrooged* (1988) with Bill Murray as a hard-hearted television president who is made to change his ways in the same manner as Charles Dickens's Scrooge; and *Beetlejuice*, Warner Brothers' contribution to the genre that same year which sparked off a whole variety of spin-offs including masks, t-shirts and restaurants serving Beetlejuice-inspired menus. The story centred around an exorcist named Betelgeuse who comes to the aid of a young couple who have died in a car accident and return to haunt their own home. In the interim the house has been taken over by a trendy family with the most excruciating taste and the ghostly couple set about frightening them into leaving. Such was the success of the picture – which according to one review, "made an entire generation of American kids laugh in the face of death" – that Michael Keaton as Betelgeuse won himself the coveted role of Batman, while Alec Baldwin and Geena Davis also went on to become top-of-the-bill stars.

The script for *Beetlejuice* had been written by Michael McDowell (1950–) and its popularity was his reward for years of dedication to the supernatural genre. An author since his teens, he has published over 30 books – including *The Amulet, Cold Moon Over Babylon* and the serial novel, *Blackwater*, published in six volumes – as well as writing for a number of TV horror shows including the popular American series, *Tales From The Darkside*. Michael's inspiration for *Beetlejuice*, he says, came from his hobby: collecting Eighteenth and Nineteenth-Century death memorabilia and photographs of corpses, criminals and atrocities! Some of the ideas which made *Beetlejuice* such a success were already begining to surface in his books and short stories such as 'Halley's Passing' which he contributed to *Twilight Zone* magazine in June 1987. It needs no further introduction than the one given by the editor of *TZ* in which he described what follows as "one of the few stories we've read recently that brings new life (as it were) to an old legend . . ."

"Would you like to keep that on your credit card?" asked the woman on the desk. Her name was Donna and she was dressed like Show White because it was Halloween.

"No," said Mr Farley, "I think I'll pay cash." Mr Farley counted out twelve ten-dollar bills and laid them on the counter. Donna made sure there were twelve, then gave Mr Farley change of three dollars and twenty-six cents. He watched to make certain she tore up the charge slips he had filled out two days before. She ripped them into thirds. Original copy, Customer's Receipt, Bank Copy, two intervening carbons – all bearing the impress of Mr Farley's Visa card and his signature – they went into a trash basket that was invisible beneath the counter.

"Goodbye," said Mr Farley. He took up his one small suitcase and walked out the front door of the hotel. His suitcase was light blue Samsonite with an X of tape underneath the handle to make it recognizable at an airport baggage claim.

It was seven o'clock. Mr Farley took a taxi from the hotel to the airport. In the back of the taxi, he opened his case and took out a black loose-leaf notebook and wrote in it:

> 10385 *Double Tree Inn*
> *Dallas, Texas*
> *Checkout 1900/$116.74/*
> *Donna*

The taxi took Mr Farley to the airport and cost him $12.50 with a tip that was generous but not too generous.

Mr Farley went to the PSA counter and picked up an airline schedule and put it into the pocket of his jacket. Then he went to the Eastern counter and picked up another schedule. In a bar called the Range Room he sat at a small round table. He ordered a vodka martini from a waitress named Alyce. When she had brought it to him, and he had paid her and she had gone away, he opened his suitcase, pulled out his black loose-leaf notebook and added the notations:

Taxi $10.20 + 2.30/#1718
Drink at Airport Bar
$2.75 + .75/Alyce

He leafed backwards through the notebook and discovered that he had flown PSA three times in the past two months. Therefore he looked into the Eastern Schedule first. He looked on page 23 first because $2.30 had been the amount of the tip to the taxi driver. On page 23 of the Eastern airline schedule were flights from Dallas to Milwaukee, Wisconsin, and Mobile, Alabama. All of the flights to Milwaukee changed in Cincinnati or St Louis. A direct flight to Mobile left at 9:10 p.m. arriving 10:50 p.m. Mr Farley returned the black loose-leaf notebook to his case and got up from the table, spilling his drink in the process.

"I'm very sorry," he said to Alyce, and left another dollar bill for her inconvenience.

"That's all right," said Alyce.

Mr Farley went to the Eastern ticket counter and bought a coach ticket to Mobile, Alabama. He asked for an aisle seat in the non-smoking section. He paid in cash and after taking out his black loosleaf notebook, he checked his blue Samsonite bag. He went through security, momentarily surrendering a ringful of keys. The flight to Mobile departed Gate 15 but Mr Farley sat in the seats allotted to Gate 13, directly across the way. He read through a copy of *USA Today* and he gave a Snickers bar to a child in a pumpkin costume who trick-or-treated him. He smiled at the child, not because he liked costumes or Halloween or children, but because he was pleased with himself for having been foresightful enough to buy three Snickers bars just in case he ran into trick-or-treating children on Halloween night. He opened his black loose-leaf notebook and amended the notation of his most recent bar tab:

Drink at Airport Bar
$2.75 + 1.75/Alyce

The flight for Mobile began boarding at 8:55 p.m. as the announcement was made for the early accommodation of those with young children or other difficulties, Mr Farley went into the men's room.

A Latino man in his twenties with a blue shirt and a lock of hair dangling down his neck stood at a urinal, looking at the ceiling and softly farting. His urine splashed against the porcelain wall of the urinal. Mr Farley went past the urinals and stood in front of the two stalls and peered under them. He saw no legs or feet or shoes but he took the precaution of opening the doors. The stalls were empty, as he suspected, but Mr Farley did not like to leave such matters to chance. The Latino man, looking downwards, flushed the urinal, zipping his trousers and backing away at the same time. Mr Farley leaned down and took the Latino man by the waist. He swung the Latino man around so that he was facing the mirrors and the two sinks in the restroom and could see Mr Farley's face.

"Man—" protested the Latino man.

Mr Farley rolled his left arm around the Latino Man's belt and put his right hand on the Latino man's head. Mr Farley pushed forward very swiftly with his right hand. The Latino man's head went straight down towards the sink in such a way that the cold-water faucet, shaped like a Maltese Cross, shattered the bone above the Latino man's right eye. Mr Farley had gauged the strength of his attack so that the single blow served to press the Latino's head all the way down to the procelain. The chilled aluminum faucet was buried deeply in the Latino man's brain. Mr Farley took the Latino man's wallet from his back pocket, removed the cash and his Social Security card. He gently dropped the wallet into the sink beneath the Latino man's head and turned on the hot water. Mr Farley peered into the sink, and saw blood, blackish and brackish swirling into the rusting drain. Retrieving his black loose-leaf notebook from the edge of the left hand sink where he'd left it, Mr Farley walked out of the rest room. The Eastern flight to Mobile was boarding all seats and Mr Farley walked on directly behind a young woman with brown hair and a green scarf and directly in front of a young woman with slightly darker brown hair in a yellow sweater-dress. Mr Farley sat in Seat 4-C and next to him, in Seat 4-A, was a bearded man in a blue corduroy jacket who fell asleep before take-off. Mr Farley reached into his pocket and pulled out the bills he'd taken from the Latino man's wallet. There were five five-dollar bills and nine one-dollar bills. Mr Farley pulled out his own wallet and interleaved the Latino man's bills with his own, mixing them up. Mr Farley reached into his shirt pocket and pulled out the Latino man's Social Security card, cupping it from sight and slipping it into the Eastern Airlines In-Flight Magazine. He turned on the reading light and opened the magazine. The Social Security card read:

IGNAZIOS LAZO
424–70–4063

Mr Farley slipped the Social Security card back into his shirt pocket. He exchanged the in-flight magazine for the black loose-leaf notebook in the seat back pocket. He held the notebook in his lap for several minutes while he watched the man in the blue corduroy jacket next to him, timing his breaths by the sweep second hand on his watch. The man seemed genuinely to be asleep. Mr Farley declined a beverage from the stewardess, who did not wear a name tag, and put his finger to his lips with a smile to indicate that the man in the blue corduroy jacket was sleeping and probably wouldn't want to be disturbed. When the beverage cart was one row behind and conveniently blocking the aisle so that no one could look over his shoulder as he wrote, Mr Farley opened the black loose-leaf note book on his lap, and completed the entry for Halloween:

2155/Ignacios Lazo/c
27/Dallas Texas/ Airport/
RR/38/Head onto Faucet

RR meant Rest Room, and Mr Farley stared at the abbreviation for a few moments, wondering whether he shouldn't write out the words. There was a time when he had been a good deal given to abbreviations, but once, in looking over his book for a distant year, he had come across the notation CRB, and had had no idea what that stood for. Mr Farley since that time had been careful about his notations. It didn't do to forget things. If you forgot things, you might repeat them. And if you inadvertently fell into a repetitious pattern – well then, you just might get into trouble.

Mr Farley got up and went into the rest room at the forward end of the passenger cabin. He burned Ignacios Lazo's Social Security card, igniting it with a match torn from a book he had picked up at the casino at the MGM Grand Hotel in Las Vegas. He waited in the rest room till he could no longer smell the nitrate in the air from the burned match, then flushed the toilet, washed his hands, and returned to his seat.

The flight arrived in Mobile at three minutes past eleven. While waiting for his blue Samsonite bag, Mr Farley went to a Yellow Pages telephone directory for Mobile. His flight from Dallas had been Eastern Flight No. 71, but Mr Farley was not certain there would be that many hotels and motels in Mobile Alabama so he decided on number 36, which was half of 72 (the closest even number to 71). Mr Farley turned to the pages advertising hotels and counted down thirty-six to the Oasis Hotel. He telephoned and found a room was available for fifty-six dollars. He asked what the cab fare from the airport would be and discovered it would be about twelve dollars, with tip. The reservations clerk asked for Mr Farley's name, and Mr Farley, looking down at the credit card in his hand, said, "Mr T.L. Rachman." He spelled it for the clerk.

Mr Rachman claimed his bag, and went outside for a taxi. He was first in line, and by 11:30 p.m. he had arrived at the Oasis Hotel, downtown in Mobile. In the hotel's Shore Room Lounge, a band was playing in Halloween costume. The clerk on the hotel desk was made up to look like a mummy.

"You go to a lot of trouble here for holidays, I guess," said Mr Rachman pleasantly.

"Anything for a little change," said the clerk as he pressed Mr Rachman's MasterCard against three copies of a voucher. Mr Rachman signed his name on the topmost voucher and took back the card. Clerks never checked signatures at this point, and they never checked them later either, but Mr Rachman's had a practised hand, at least when it came to imitating a signature.

Mr Rachman's room was on the fifth and topmost floor, and enjoyed a view down to the street. Mr Rachman unpacked his small bag, carefully hanging his extra pair of trousers and his extra jacket. He set his extra pair of shoes, with trees inside, into the closet beneath the trousers and jacket. He placed his two laundered shirts inside the topmost bureau drawer, set his little carved box containing an extra watch and two pairs of cufflinks and a tie clip and extra pairs of brown and black shoe-laces on top of the bureau, and set his toiletries case next to the sink in the bathroom. He opened his black loose-leaf notebook and though it was not yet mid-night, he began the entry for 110185, beneath which he noted:

Halley's Passing

110185 Eastern 71 Dallas-Mobile
Taxi $9.80 + 1.70
Oasis Hotel/4th St
T.L. Rachman

In the bathroom, Mr Rachman took scissors and cut up the Visa card bearing the name Thomas Farley, and flushed away the pieces. He went down to the lobby and went into the Shore Room Lounge and sat at the bar. He ordered a vodka martini and listened to the band. When the bartender went away to the rest room, Mr Rachman poured his vodka martini into a basin of ice behind the bar. When the bartender returned, Mr Rachman ordered another vodka martini.

The cocktail lounge – and every other bar in Mobile – closed at 1 a.m. Mr Rachman returned to his room, and without ever turning on the light, he sat at his window and looked out into the street. After the laundry truck had arrived, unloaded, and driven off from the service entrance of the Hotel Oasis, Mr Rachman retreated from the window. It was 4:37 on the morning of the first of November, 1985. Mr Rachman pulled the shade and drew the curtains. Towards noon, when the maid came to make up the room, Mr Rachman called out from the bathroom, "I'm taking a bath."

"I'll come back later," the maid called back.

"That's all right," Mr Rachman said loudly. "Just leave a couple of fresh towels on the bed." He sat on the tile floor and ran his unsleeved arm up and down through the filled tub, making splashing noises.

*

Mr Rachman counted his money at sundown. He had four hundred fifty-eight dollars in cash. With all of it in his pocket, Mr Rachman walked around the block to get his bearings. He had been in Mobile before, but he didn't

251

remember exactly when. Mr Rachman had his shoes shined in the lobby of a hotel that wasn't the one he was staying in. When he was done, he paid the shoe-shine boy seventy-five cents and a quarter tip, and got into the elevator behind a businessman who was carrying a briefcase. The businessman with the briefcase got off on the fourth floor, and just as the doors of the elevator were closing Mr Rachman startled and said, "Oh this is my floor, too," and jumped off behind the businessman with the briefcase. Mr Rachman put his hand into his pocket, and jingled his loose change as if he were looking for his room key. The businessman with the briefcase put down his briefcase beside Room 419 and fumbled in his pocket for his own room key. Mr Rachman stopped and patted all the pockets of his jacket and trousers. "Did I leave it at the desk?" he murmured to himself. The businessman with the briefcase put the key into the lock of Room 419, and smiled a smile that said to Mr Rachman, *It happens to me all the time, too.* Mr Rachman smiled a small embarrassed smile, and said, "I sure hope I left it at the desk," and turned and started back down the hall past the businessman with the briefcase.

The businessman and his briefcase were already inside of Room 419 and the door was beginning to shut when Mr Rachman suddenly changed direction in the hallway and pushed the door open.

"Hey," said the businessman. He held his briefcase up protectively before him. Mr Rachman shut the door quietly behind him. Room 419 was a much nicer room than his own, though he didn't care for the painting above the bed. Mr Rachman smiled, though, for the businessman was alone and that was always easier. Mr Rachman pushed the businessman down on the bed and grabbed the briefcase away from him. The businessman reached for the telephone. The red light was blinking on the telephone telling the businessman he had a message at the desk. Mr Rachman held the briefcase high above his head and then brought it down hard, giving a little twist to his wrist just at the last so that a corner of the rugged leather case smashed against the bridge of the businessman's nose, breaking it. The businessman gaped, and fell sideways on the bed. Mr Rachman raised the case again and brought the side of it down against the businessman's cheek with such force that the handle of the case broke off in his hand and the businessman's cheekbones were splintered and shoved up into his right eye. Mr Rachman took the case in both hands and swung it hard along the length of the businessman's body and caught him square beneath his chin in the midst of a choking scream so that the businessman's lower jaw was shattered, detached, and then embedded in the roof of his mouth. In the businessman's remaining eye was one second more of conciousness and then he was dead. Mr Rachman turned over the businessman's corpse and took out his wallet, discovering that his name was Edward P. Maguire, and that he was from Sudbury, Massachusetts. He had one hundred and thirty-three dollars in cash, which Mr Rachman put into his pocket. Mr Richman glanced through the credit cards, but took only the New England Bell telephone credit card. Mr Maguire's briefcase, though battered and bloody, had remained locked, secured by an unknown combination. Mr Rachman would have taken the time to break it open and examine its contents but the telephone on the bedside table rang. The hotel desk might not have noticed Mr Maguire's entrance into the hotel, but Mr Rachman did not want to take a chance that Mr Maguire's failure to answer the telephone would lead to an investigation. Mr Rachman went quickly through the dead man's pockets, spilling his change onto the bedspread. He found the key of a Hertz rental car with the tag number indicated on a plastic ring. Mr Rachman pocketed it. He turned the dead man over once more and pried open his shattered mouth. A thick broth of clotting blood and broken teeth spilled out over the knot of Mr Maguire's tie. With the tips of two fingers, Mr Richman picked out a pointed fragment of incisor, and put it into his mouth, licking the blood from his fingers as he did so. As he peered out into the hallway, Mr Richman rolled the broken tooth around the roof of his mouth, and then pressed it there with his tongue till its jagged edge drew blood and he could taste it. No one was in the hall, and Mr Richman walked out of Room 419, drawing it closed behind him. He took the elevator down to the basement garage, and walked slowly about till he found Mr Maguire's rented car. He drove out of the hotel garage and slowly circled several streets till he found a stationery store that was still open. Inside he bought a detailed street map of Mobile. He studied it by the interior roof light of the rented car. For two hours he drove through the outlying suburbs of the city, stopping now and then before a likely house, and noting its number on the map with a black felt-tip marker. At half-past eleven he returned to the Oasis Hotel and parked the rental car so that it would be visible from his window. He went up to his room, and noted in his diary, under 110185:

> *1910/Edward P Maguire/c*
> *43/Mobile Alabama/Hotel*
> *Palafox 419/1133/Jaw and*
> *Briefcase*

On a separate page in the back of the loose-leaf notebook, he added:

> *Edward P Maguire*
> *(110185)/9 Farmer's*
> *Road/Sudbury MA 01776/*
> *617 392 3690*

That was just in case. Sometimes Mr Rachman liked to visit widows. It added to the complexity of the pattern, and so far as Mr Rachman was concerned, the one important thing was to maintain a pattern that couldn't be analyzed, that was arbitrary in every point. That was why he sometimes made use of the page of notations in the back of the book – because too much randomness was a pattern in itself. If he sometimes visited a widow after he had met her husband, he broke up the pattern of entirely unconnected deaths. Mr Rachman, who was methodical to the very core of his being, spent a great percentage of his waking time in devising methods to make each night's work seem entirely apart from the last's. Mr Rachman, when he was young, had lived in a great city and had simply thought that its very size would hide him. But even in a great city, his very pattern of randomness had become apparent, and he had very nearly been uncovered. Mr Rachman judged that he would have to do better, and he began to travel. In the time since then, he had merely refined his technique. He varied the length of his stays, he varied his acquaintance. That's what he called them, and it wasn't a euphemism – he simply had no other word for them, and really, they were the people he got to know best, if only for a short time. He varied his methods, he varied the time of the evening, and he even varied his variety. Sometimes he would arrange to meet three old woman in a row, three old women who lived in similar circumstances in a small geographical area, and then he would move on, and his next acquaintance would be a young man who exchanged his favors for cash. Mr Rachman imagined a perfect pursuer, and expended a great deal of energy in evading and tricking this imaginary hound. Increasingly, over the years Mr Rachman's greatest satisfaction lay in evading this non-existent, dogged detective. His only fear was that there was a pattern in the carpet he wove which was invisible to him, but perfectly apparent to anyone who looked at it from a certain angle.

*

No one took notice of Mr Maguire's rented car that night. Next morning Mr Rachman told the chambermaid he wasn't feeling well and would spend the day in bed, so she needn't make it up. But he let her clean the bathroom as she hadn't been able to do the day before. He lay with his arm over his eyes. "I hope you feel better," said the chambermaid. "Do you have any aspirin?"

"I've already taken some," said Mr Rachman, "but thank you. I think I'll just try to sleep."

That night, Mr Rachman got up and watched the rented car. It had two parking tickets on the windshield. At 11:30 p.m. he went downstairs, got into the car, and drove around three blocks slowly, just in case he was being followed. He was not, so far as he could tell. He opened his map of Mobile, and picked the house he'd marked that was nearest a crease. It was 117 Shadyglade Lane in a suburb called Spring Hill. Mr Rachman drove on, to the nearest of the other places he'd marked. He stopped in front of a house on Live Oak Street, about a mile away. No lights burned. He turned into the driveway and waited for fifteen minutes. He saw no movement in the house. He got out of his car, closing the door loudly, and walked around to the back door, not making any effort to be quiet.

There was no door bell so he pulled open the screen door and knocked loudly. He stood back and looked up at the back of the house. No lights came on that he could see. He knocked more loudly, then without waiting for a response he kicked at the base of the door, splintering it in its frame. He went into the kitchen, but did not turn on the light.

"Anybody home?" Mr Rachman called out as he went from the kitchen into the dining room. He picked up a round glass bowl from the sideboard and hurled it at a picture. The bowl shattered noisily. No one came. Mr Rachman looked in the other two rooms on the ground floor, then went upstairs, calling again, "It's Mr Rachman!"

He went into the first bedroom, and saw that it belonged

to a teenaged boy. He closed the door. He went into another bedroom and saw that it belonged to the parents of the teenaged boy. He went through the bureau drawers, but found no cash. The father's shirts, however, were in Mr Rachman size – 16 1/2 x 33 – and he took two that still bore the paper bands from the laundry. Mr Rachman checked the other rooms of the second floor just in case, but the house was empty. Mr Rachman went out the back door again, crossed the back yard of the house, and pressed through the dense ligustrum thicket there. He found himself in the back yard of a ranch house with a patio and a brick barbeque. Mr Rachman walked to the patio and picked up a pot of geraniums and hurled it through the sliding glass doors of the den. Then he walked quickly inside the house, searching for a light switch. A man in pajamas suddenly lurched through a doorway, and he too was reaching for the light switch. Mr Rachman put one hand on the man's shoulder, and with his other he grabbed the man's wrist. Then Mr Rachman gave a twist, and smashed the back of the man's elbow against the edge of a television set with such force that all the bones there shattered at once. Mr Rachman then took the man by the waist, lifted him up and carried him over to the broken glass door. He turned him sideways and then pushed him against the long line of broken glass, only making sure that the shattered glass was embedded deep into his face and neck. When Mr Rachman let the man go, he remained standing, so deep had the edge of broken door penetrated his head and chest. Just in case, Mr Rachman pressed harder. Blood poured out over Mr Rachman's hands. With a nod of satisfaction, Mr Rachman released the man in pajamas and walked quickly back across the patio and disappeared into the shrubbery again. On the other side, he looked back, and could see the lights going on in the house. He heard a woman scream. He took out a handkerchief to cover his bloody hands and picked up the shirts which he'd left on the back porch of the first house.

Then he got into his car and drove around till he came to a shopping mall. He parked near half a dozen other cars – probably belonging to night watchmen – and took off his blood-stained jacket. He tossed it out the window. He took off his shirt, and wiped off the blood that covered his hands. He threw that out of the window, too. He put on a fresh shirt and drove back to the Oasis Hotel. He parked the car around the block, threw the keys into an alleyway, and went back up to his room. In his black loose-leaf notebook he wrote, under 110285:

*1205/unk./mc 35/Spring
Hill (Mobile) Alabama/
$0/Broken glass*

Mr Rachman spent the rest of the night simply reading through his black loose-leaf notebook, not trying to remember what he could not easily bring to mind, but merely playing the part of the tireless investigator trying to discern a pattern. Mr Rachman did not think he was fooling himself when he decided that he could not.

When the chambermaid came the next day, Mr Rachman sat on a chair with the telephone cradled between his ear and his shoulder, now and then saying, "Yes" or "No, not at all" or "Once more and let me check those numbers", as he made notations on a pad of paper headed up with a silhouette cartouche of palm trees.

Mr Rachman checked out of the Oasis Hotel a few minutes after sundown, and smiled a polite smile when the young woman on the desk apologized for having to charge him for an extra day. The bill came to $131.70 and Mr Rachman paid in cash. As he watched the young woman on the desk tear up the credit card receipt, he remarked, "I don't like to get near my limit," and the young woman on the desk replied, "I won't even apply for one."

"But they sometimes come in handy, Marsha," said Mr Rachman, employing her name aloud as a reminder to note it later in his diary. Nametags were a great help to Mr Rachman in his travels, and he had been pleased to watch the rapid spread of their use. Before 1960 or thereabouts, hardly anyone had worn a nametag.

Mr Rachman drove around downtown Mobile for an hour or so, just in case something turned up. Once, driving slowly down an alleyway that was scarcely wider than his car, a prostitute on yellow heels lurched at him out of a recessed doorway, plunging a painted hand through his rolled-down window. Mr Rachman said, "Wrong sex," and drove on.

"Faggot!" the prostitute called after him.

Mr Rachman didn't employ prostitutes except in emergencies, that is to say, when it was nearly dawn and he had not managed to make anyone's acquaintance for the night. Then he resorted to prostitutes, but not otherwise. Too easy to make that sort of thing a habit.

And habits were what Mr Rachman had to avoid.

He drove to the airport, and took a ticket from a mechanized gate. He drove slowly around the parking lot, which was out of doors, and to one side of the airport buildings. He might have taken any of several spaces near the terminal, but Mr Rachman drove slowly about the farther lanes. He could not drive very long; for fear of drawing the attention of a guard.

A blue Buick Skylark pulled into a space directly beneath a burning sodium lamp. Mr Rachman made a sudden decision. He parked his car six vehicles down, and quickly climbed out with his blue Samsonite suitcase. He strode towards the terminal with purpose, coming abreast of the blue Buick Skylark. A woman, about thirty-five years old, was pulling a dark leather bag out of the backseat of the car. Mr Rachman stopped suddenly, put down his case and patted the pockets of his trousers in alarm.

"My keys . . ." he said aloud.

Then he checked the pockets of his suit jacket. He often

used the forgotten keys ploy. It didn't really constitute a habit, for it was an action that would never appear later as evidence.

The woman with the suitcase came between her car and the recreational vehicle that was parked next to it. She had a handbag over her shoulder. Mr Rachman suddenly wanted very badly to make this one work for him. For one thing, this was a woman, and he hadn't made the acquaintance of a female since he'd been in Mobile. That would disrupt the pattern a bit. She had a purse, which might contain money. He liked the shape and size of her luggage, too.

"Excuse me," she said politely, trying to squeeze by him. "I think I locked my keys in my car," said Mr Rachman, moving aside for her.

She smiled a smile which suggested that she was sorry but that there was nothing she could do about it.

She had taken a single step towards the terminal when Mr Rachman lifted his right leg and took a long stride forward. He caught the sole of his shoe against her right calf, and pushed her down to the pavement. The woman crashed to her knees on the pavement with such force that the bones of her knees shattered. She started to fall forward, but Mr Rachman spryly caught one arm around her waist and placed his other hand on the back of her head. In his clutching fingers, he could feel the scream building in her mouth. He swiftly turned her head and smashed her face into the high-beam headlight of the blue Buick Skylark. He jerked her head out again, and even before the broken glass had spilled down the front of her suit jacket, Mr Rachman plunged her head into the low-beam head-light. He jerked her head out, and awkwardly straddling her body, he pushed her between her Buick and the next car in the lane, a silver VW GTI. He pushed her head hard down against the pavement four times, though he was sure she was dead already. He let go her head, and peered at his fingers in the light of the sodium lamp. He smelled the splotches of blood on his third finger and his palm and his thumb. He tasted the blood, and then wiped it off on the back of the woman's bare leg. Another car turned down the lane, and Mr Rachman threw himself onto the pavement, reaching for the woman's suitcase before the automobile lights played over it. He pulled it into the darkness between the cars. The automobile drove past. Mr Rachman pulled the woman's handbag off her shoulder, and then rolled her beneath her car. Fishing inside the purse for her car keys, he opened the driver's door and unlocked the back door. He climbed onto the car and pulled in her bag with him. He emptied its contents onto the floor, then crawled across the back seat and opened the opposite door. He retrieved his blue Samsonite suitcase from beneath the recreational vehicle where he'd kicked it as he struck up his acquaintance with the woman. The occupants of the car that had passed a few moments before walked in front of the Buick. Mr Rachman ducked behind the back seat for a moment till he could no longer hear the voices – a man and a woman. He opened his Samsonite case and repacked all his belongings into the woman's black leather case. He reached into the woman's bag and pulled out her wallet. He took her Alabama driver's license and a Carte Blanche credit card that read A.B. Frost rather than Aileen Frost. He put the ticket in his pocket. Mr Rachman was mostly indifferent to the matter of fingerprints, but he had a superstition against carbon paper of any sort.

Mr Rachman surreptitiously checked the terminal display and found that a plane was leaving for Birmingham, Alabama in twenty minutes. It would probably begin to board in five minutes. Mr Rachman rushed to the Delta ticket counter, and said breathlessly, "Am I too late to get on the plane to Birmingham? I haven't bought my ticket yet."

Mark, the airline employee said, "You're in plenty of time – the plane's been delayed."

This was not pleasant news. Mr Rachman was anxious

to leave Mobile. Aileen Frost was hidden beneath her car, it was true, and might not be found for a day or so – but there was always a chance that someone would find her quickly. Mr Rachman didn't want to be around for any part of the investigation. Also, he couldn't now say, "Well, I think I'll go to Atlanta instead." That would draw dangerous attention to himself. Perhaps he should just return to Mr Maguire's car and drive away. The evening was still early. He could find a house in the country, make the acquaintance of anyone who lived there, sit out quietly the daylight hours, and leave early the following evening.

"How long a delay?" Mr Rachman asked Mark.

"Fifteen minutes," said Mark pleasantly, already making out the ticket. "What name?"

Not Frost, of course. And Rachman was already several days old.

"Como," he said, not knowing why.

"Perry?" asked Mark with a laugh.

"Peter," said Mr Como.

Mr Como sighed. He was already half enamoured of his alternative plan. But he couldn't leave now. Mark might remember a man who had rushed in, then rushed out again because he couldn't brook a fifteen-minute delay. The ticket from Mobile to Birmingham was $89, five dollars more than Mr Como had predicted in his mind. Putting his ticket into the inside pocket of his jacket that did not contain Aileen Frost's ticket to Wilmington, Mr Como went into the men's room and locked himself into a stall. Under the noise of the flushing toilet, he quickly tore up Aileen Frost's ticket, and stuffed the fragments into his jacket pocket. When he left the stall he washed his hands at the sink until the only other man in the rest room left. Then he wrapped the fragments in a paper towel and stuffed that deep into the waste paper basket. Aileen Frost's license and credit card he slipped into a knitting bag of a woman waiting for a plane to Houston.

Mr Como had been given a window seat near the front of the plane. The seat beside him was empty. After figuring his expenses for the day, Mr Como wrote in his black loose-leaf notebook:

0745/Aileen Frost/fc
35/Mobile Airport Parking
Lot/$212/Car headlights

Mr Como was angry with himself. Two airport killings within a week. That was laziness. Mr Como had fallen into the lazy, despicable habit of working as early in the evening as possible. This, even though Mr Como had *never* failed, not a single night, not even when only minutes had remained till dawn. But he tended to fret, and he didn't rest easy till he had got the evening's business out of the way. That was the problem of course. He had no other business. So if he worked early, he was left with a long stretch of hours till he could sleep with the dawn. If he put off till late, he only spent the long hours fretting, wondering if he'd be put to trouble. *Trouble* to Mr Como meant witnesses (whose acquaintance he had to make as well), or falling back on easy marks – prostitutes, nightwatchmen, hotel workers. Or, worst of all, pursuit and flight, and then some sudden, uncomfortable place to wait out the daylight hours.

On every plane trip, Mr Como made promises to himself: he'd use even more ingenuity, he'd rely on his expertise and work at late hours as well as early hours, he'd try to develop other interests. Yet he was at the extremity of his ingenuity, late hours fretted him beyond any pleasure he took in making a new acquaintance, and he had long since lost his interest in any pleasure but that moment he saw the blood of each night's new friend. And even that was only a febrile memory of what had once been a hot true necessity of desire.

Before the plane landed, Mr Como invariably decided

that he did too much thinking. For, finally, instinct had never failed him, though everything else – Mr Como, the world Mr Como inhabited, and Mr Como's tastes – everything else changed.

"Ladies and gentlemen," said the captain's voice, "we have a special treat for you tonight. If you'll look out the left side of the plane, and up – towards the Pleiades – you'll see Halley's Comet. You'll see it better from up here than from down below. And I'd advise you to look now, because it won't be back in our lifetimes."

Mr Como looked out of the window. Most of the other passengers didn't know which stars were the Pleiades, but Mr Como did. Halley's Comet was a small blur to the right of the small constellation. Mr Como gladly gave his seat to a young couple who wanted to see the comet. Mr Como remembered the 1910 visitation quite clearly, and that time the comet had been spectacular. He'd been living in Canada, he thought, somewhere near Halifax. It was high in the sky then, brighter than Venus, with a real tail, and no one had to point it out to you. He tried to remember the time before – 1834, he determined with a calculation of his fingernail on the glossy cover of the Delta In-flight magazine. But 1834 was beyond his power of recollection. The Comet was surely even brighter then, but where had he been at that time? Before airports, and hotels, and credit cards, and the convenience of nametags. He'd lived in one place then for long periods of time, and hadn't even kept proper records. There'd been a lust then, too, for the blood, and every night he'd done more than merely place an incrimsoned finger to his lips.

But everything had changed, evolved slowly and immeasurably, and he was not what once he'd been. Mr Como knew he'd change again. The brightness of comets deteriorated with every pass. Perhaps on its next journey around the sun, Mr Como wouldn't be able to see it at all.